One In
The HAND

Caitlin Drake

BELLA
BOOKS
2016

Bella Books, Inc.
P.O. Box 10543
Tallahassee, FL 32302

Printed in the United States of America on acid-free paper.

First Bella Books Edition 2016

Editor: KG MacGregor
Cover Designer: Linda Callaghan

ISBN: 978-1-59493-518-3

About the Author

Caitlin Drake grew up on a farm in rural Ohio and now lives in Portland, Oregon with her wife, cats and golden retriever. She teaches art and theatre and spends her summers writing, reading and traveling. Caitlin has been enamored with the Pacific Northwest since she was young and now enjoys exploring it one craft brewery at a time.

Dedication

For my little bird

Acknowledgments

Thank you, KG MacGregor for guiding me through this arduous, at times painful journey that is editing and whipping my book into shape. I have admired your work for many years so it is truly an honor to consider you a mentor.

To Bella Books, thank you for making this dream a reality.

Erica Boehnlein, I'm lucky to have you in my life and I'm even luckier that you majored in journalism. Thanks for reading my earliest manuscripts and providing gentle feedback.

Kim, you're my rock. In the time it took me to write this book we moved cross-country twice, raised a puppy, got engaged and then married and bought a house. Throughout it all you were my sounding board and my problem-solver. Thank you for your encouragement and love.

Also many thanks to The Arbor Lodge and its amazing staff for the daily iced vanilla lattes and allowing me to write the entirety of this book in your space.

CHAPTER ONE

"Birdy, you know your girlfriend—excuse me, *fiancée*—is totally borderline, right?"

Saul was apparently under the impression his status as her best friend entitled him to critique her life without the filter of social grace.

"She's not borderline, Saul. She's just...passionate."

"And she proposed to you in the most disgusting way possible."

"It wasn't *disgusting*. It was *romantic*!"

They were eating lunch at their favorite sandwich shop, Shmulsky & Stein, in Portland, Oregon. The small restaurant was quiet and her companion was anything but, so it was less than an ideal place to have this conversation.

"She put your ring in a baked potato," he continued, pointing at her hand with the thick, black-rimmed glasses he had just taken off to rub clean with the end of his tie.

Birdy self-consciously moved her hand from her water glass to her lap. She couldn't help but glance around to make sure no one was listening. Saul was on summer vacation from his work as a middle school guidance counselor, a job one would think would make him a little more sensitive about keeping her personal life confidential.

Straightening herself up and pushing a lock of nearly black, shoulder-length hair behind her ear, Birdy said, "She knows I love baked potatoes." She fiddled with the corner of her napkin, unable to meet his gaze as she continued her defense of her fiancée. "And that showed a surprising amount of planning. Think about how hard it would be to get a diamond ring into a baked potato at a fancy restaurant. And she never even left the table. I was impressed by her effort."

He replaced his glasses and leaned forward in his chair. "You chewed on your ring. You had to spit a giant glob of potato into your napkin." Using his own paper lunch napkin for effect, he pretended to spit out mashed-up potato much the same way a cat would work out a hairball. "She had to dig into the glob and wipe your masticated, saliva-filled potato from the diamond so she could present it to you again. I'm pretty sure there's still a chive in the setting. I swear every time I see the picture of you wearing that ring on Facebook, I can see a green glob in there." Finally, he sat back and refolded his napkin onto his knee, looking satisfied at his performance of, what should have been, the most romantic night of Birdy's life to date.

"First of all, it just happened last night. How many times could you have looked at the picture Brooke posted on Facebook? What was it? Thirteen hours ago?"

"You'd be surprised. My news feed is torturing me," he said dryly.

Rolling her eyes, she continued, "Secondly, as you can see, I'm chive-free." She wiggled her fingers for a moment before returning her hand, and the offending ring, to her lap. "Third, I'm sure it didn't go exactly as planned. She probably thought I would pull it out of my mouth and it would be perfectly clean and sparkling. I guess I just didn't handle it as gracefully as I should have." She trailed off as she fingered a potato chip on her plate.

Okay, so maybe it wasn't very romantic. It had been a disaster, which was why she had skimmed over the details when she called Saul to tell him Brooke had popped the question. He had, of course, weaseled the whole story out of her, ferreting out the truth, sniffing out her disappointment.

What a rat, she thought ruefully, nearly smiling at her own joke. But she was marrying the woman she loved, right? That was all that mattered. The baked potato would just be a funny story to tell at their twentieth anniversary celebration, which at this rate, Saul would not be invited to.

He wasn't ready to let it go, though. As Birdy's oldest friend, dating back to middle school he knew her better than anyone and had always been clear about his dislike for Brooke, which was mutual.

"The point, Birdy, is she manipulates you. She botched the big question and now suddenly it's *your* fault it didn't go smoothly. You go to sleep next to a ticking time bomb that resets each night, never knowing if it's going to be a good day or a bad day. For any reason, no matter how carefully you tread she could explode. You're constantly walking on eggshells with her."

Birdy had heard it all from him before. Their meet-ups came less often now because she knew he would harp on Brooke, as he'd done since they first started dating nearly five years ago. Yesterday's engagement only intensified his insistence that Brooke was not The One. Now, she glared at him sharply, with her jaw set to make clear she would no longer entertain his opinions.

Lighter than before, he continued. "I can tell from that look you're done listening to me now, and I know you're trying to think of a reason to go back to work early. I just have one last thing to say and then I'll let you go." He hesitated, apparently still wary of her annoyance. "Ever since you came out to me, you've always said you wanted to be the one who asks your girlfriend to marry you. You always had these huge, inventive schemes dreamed up, the type that would go viral on YouTube because they'd be so creative and full of love. You just hadn't found the right girl to ask. You told Brooke that, right? You told her you wanted to be the one to ask because that was important to you, right?"

Birdy shifted, uncomfortable as he lowered his head to make her meet his eyes. The truth was, she had told Brooke that. On their better days they would lie in bed and talk about getting married. What their wedding would look like, who would give each of them away, and how many they would have in their wedding parties. Birdy had said emphatically, "I want to be the one to propose to you when the perfect moment comes along. I've never dreamed of that day when someone would get down on their knee and ask me. I always saw myself on the other side."

Cupping her face, Brooke had said, "That would be wonderful."

Had Brooke forgotten her dream? Or was this yet another sign that the woman she'd fallen in love with had changed?

* * *

Birdy clomped back into work still fuming from Saul's words. *Why couldn't he just leave it alone*, she thought. *If he would just get to know her better, he'd like her. He doesn't see the side of her that I see.*

She flung herself into her desk chair, sending it rolling several feet from her desk. With a frustrated sigh, she kicked her feet like a paddling duck, scooting herself back up to her desk and then slumped deeper into her chair, brooding.

Furiously tapping a pen on her desk, she thought, why *had* Brooke asked her to marry? They had talked about marriage a lot, and Brooke knew it was important to her that she was the one to ask. Brooke also knew she'd been waiting until she had all of her ducks in a row—like a small chunk of her student loans paid off and a little nest egg in the bank rather than just her paltry checking account that was nearly depleted each month. She wanted her home too, which happened to be a boat floating just northwest of Portland off Sauvie Island, to be restored and functional. She had been saving up for a Tiffany ring for a year. It was the only money she could spare to put into her previously ignored savings account. Okay, so maybe she hadn't thought of a way to propose to Brooke yet but she sure as hell could have done better than a baked potato.

Birdy couldn't decide whom to be mad at. Damn Brooke for her poorly stitched plan and damn Saul for picking at the thread, trying to unravel her whole relationship. Deep down though, she knew it wasn't his fault. He was only holding up the mirror she damn well didn't want to look into.

Mare, Birdy's boss and friend, strode into the office appearing frazzled. Her face was red, and white ink smudged her wiry, auburn hair.

Mare owned PDX Ink, the screen printing shop that had been Birdy's second home for the past seven years. She had been hired as the company's graphic designer immediately after graduating from the University of Oregon. In her time working with Mare they had become close friends despite Mare's infuriating lack of insightfulness. The woman was completely unable to read people's emotions, making her the least perceptive person Birdy had ever met. She regularly hired the wrong people, going through more than a dozen screen printers since Birdy had started working for her.

Their most recent printer had been with them longer than any others, but after eight months had quit unexpectedly, leaving them in a lurch. Without a press operator, Mare had to step in and cover a full-time printing job as well as run the busy office. They weren't having any luck finding someone qualified, and she was wearing herself thin trying to make up for the loss. Despite her stress, she seemed in better spirits than she had in two weeks, but as usual, was oblivious to Birdy's sour mood.

"Hey lady, did you have a good lunch?"

Birdy continued to tap furiously with her pen.

Mare moved closer, sitting at her own desk, which faced Birdy's. "Hey, did you have a good lunch with Saul?"

"Yeah, wonderful," she replied, her voice dripping with sarcasm.

"Good!" Mare chirped, shuffling through the invoices on her desk, oblivious to her sarcasm as usual. "Oh, by the way, I hired a new printer while you were at lunch."

"You what?" Birdy sputtered. "What…how? What are you talking about?"

"Well, I got an email this morning from a girl—Sydney is her name, I think—and she sounded great. A bachelor's in fine arts…worked at a screen printing shop in Austin. Plus, she knows how to operate both the automatic and manual presses. She sounded perfect so I asked her to come in. And I hired her!"

"Mare, we both know your track record with new hires. I thought you were going to let me help with the hiring from now on?" Birdy tried to keep her voice light but the frustration that was once split between Brooke and Saul now converged on her boss.

"I know, I know, but I had a really good feeling about this one. I think you'll love her, and she seems to really know her stuff."

Birdy gaped at her disbelievingly. "You thought Steroid Steve knew his stuff too."

"How was I supposed to know he was as high as a kite on juice?"

"He came to the interview in a sleeveless muscle shirt. In January. He was so jacked up and sweaty, it looked like he'd just gotten out of a pool."

"Well, some people are just hotter than others. I can't not hire someone because they sweat too much."

"You're right. I think though, you would have gotten a clue when he literally had a heart attack during the interview."

"Okay, okay. So he was an addict. I don't see how I was supposed to know that, but I see your point. But no worries," Mare said with a wave of her hand as if dismissing any other negative comments Birdy might have for her, "Sydney is definitely not an addict. She gave five references and not a one of them, might I add, was her sponsor. Also, her previous address is not a rehab facility so she's already a step ahead of Steven."

"And Meth Mouth Michael," Birdy added with so much cynicism she thought even Mare couldn't miss it.

"Oh, Michael. He was a nice guy. Pretty cute too," she added, gazing dreamily out the window. *Yep, she missed it.*

"You mean besides the rotting teeth, right?"

"They weren't that bad. Anyway, her references are excellent. You're really going to like this one."

Mare's unerring good nature and naivety usually won Birdy over but this time she was too frustrated to go along with her boss's optimism.

She let out a long sigh, her anger turning to exasperation. "Mare, I love you but you've made a mistake. She's probably never screen printed in her life. Or she took one class in college and thinks she can run a shop now. At least you'll be training her so you'll see quickly enough that she can't cut it." Birdy straightened up in her seat and turned on her computer monitor, willing herself to get started on her mountain of work. "When does she start?"

"First thing tomorrow."

Birdy shook her head at the woman's impulsivity. And then she noticed her puckered lips and darting eyes, which gave the creeping impression another shoe was about to drop. She narrowed her eyes and raised her brow questioningly. "What?"

Mare took a deep breath, and speaking very quickly so Birdy wouldn't have a chance to interrupt, blurted out, "I actually won't be training her. I'll work with her tomorrow but my cousin's getting married next week in Vegas. I wasn't going to go because Jeff up and quit on us, but since Sydney is experienced I've decided to after all. So, actually, you'll be training her mostly…all next week. I fly out to Vegas Saturday."

CHAPTER TWO

Sydney Ramos stepped ashore onto the bank of an island in the Willamette River, setting firm foot in her new home of Portland, Oregon once again. She dragged her rented kayak up onto the gravel bank, tossed her lifejacket inside and found a shady spot on a washed up log to relax with her bottle of water. Across the slough she had just been paddling, wetlands and a wildlife refuge spread out before her. Long-necked and lanky, a bluish-gray bird swooped in, landing in the shallows. She thought it might be an egret. Or maybe a heron? Were egrets and herons the same thing? Sydney didn't know birds very well, especially in this new region, so she promised herself she would do some research before her next paddling trip.

The tapping of a woodpecker in the distance was calming until she lost the rhythm in the sloshing sounds of water nearby. Her friend Beth was wet docking her kayak next to the spot Sydney had just left hers.

"Thanks for leaving me in your dust back there," Beth called out while unbuckling her own lifejacket and dropping it on the bank.

"You used to be more competitive in college. I thought you could keep up, or at least die trying."

"We're old now."

"Twenty-nine isn't old."

"It feels old. I'm in bed by ten these days. Even on Saturdays. I can't have two glasses of wine without getting a hangover and I sure as hell can't paddle upstream like that." Beth collapsed tiredly on the log next to Sydney and guzzled her drink. "You're a beast. I'm glad you're in town now so you can whip my ass back in shape. It'll be like our old softball days."

"I'd be happy to. It's the least I can do to repay you for letting me stay on your couch the past two weeks."

"It's been fun. Staying up late, at least by my standards, catching up. I've liked sharing a space with you again. And it sure beats that shit hole we lived in our senior year. God, that house was nasty."

"Oh God, the roaches." Sydney shuddered at the memory.

"And the mold around the shower."

"I might be living on a couch with all my belongings in storage but I've definitely moved up in the world."

"And, as of today you're no longer unemployed. Cheers to that."

Sydney tipped her bottle to Beth as they toasted her new job. "I guess I'll start looking for an apartment this weekend."

"My one-room abode and itchy couch aren't good enough for you?" Beth made an exaggerated pouting face.

"That couch has given me a permanent rash on the left side of my body. Seriously though, thanks for helping me figure this all out. I thought I would just be passing through…I didn't expect to love it here. Seattle was supposed to be my next stop. Instead I was that weekend guest that just never left. Hope I haven't been a total imposition."

"It's been horrible, you freeloader." Beth jabbed Sydney with her elbow. "Just kidding. Glad I could help. When I moved from Texas, it was easy since I have family here. My uncle Al found me my apartment, bought me groceries, the whole shebang. I am *not* buying your groceries, but I'm glad I could support you in your time of need."

Their eyes drifted back over the water and Sydney was once again drawn in by the large gray bird, now grooming, its long neck buried under its extended wing.

"What is that? An egret?" Sydney asked.

"The gray one?"

"Yeah."

"It's a bird."

"And you're an ass."

CHAPTER THREE

Birdy returned home after work still in a crabby mood. She had spent all day crafting speeches in her head for Saul, Brooke and Mare, wishing she had the opportunity to unleash her fury on any of the three people who had made her day miserable. She would never have the guts to say any of it out loud, but she enjoyed her self-pity so much, she'd fueled the flame all afternoon.

Just over five years ago, a few months before meeting Brooke, Birdy had made real her lifelong dream of being a live-aboard. Swept up in the romanticism of living on a boat, she thought of live-aboards as preppy vagabonds, people with a sense of adventure and restlessness that only the constant lapping of waves against the boat hull could calm. The simplicity of the lifestyle—only the clothes that could fit in two large moisture-proof plastic tubs, virtually no furniture that wasn't bolted to the floor, and less clutter—both physically and emotionally appealed to her. She dreamed of spontaneous trips upriver, chugging past the scenery whenever inspiration struck, and languidly floating under the stars when she craved connection and introspection. Having saved every dime she could during her first two years at PDX Ink and with a sizable chunk loaned to her by her mom, she was able to buy the beautiful old boat. The only catch being that it didn't actually run.

She had bought it with the intention of fixing the engine and entirely overhauling both the interior and exterior. After several years spent learning her way around the boat, she'd logged many hours of her weekends and evenings sanding, sealing and painting. The perks of manual labor—a flat stomach and toned arms—were something she definitely enjoyed. She felt enormous pride whenever she saw her nearly completed project. All she needed now was to get the engine up and running. Unfortunately, two things stood in her way: money and expertise.

She really knew very little about the inner workings of a boat. Since moving aboard, she'd learned a lot about how to live on a boat and keep it shipshape, but she didn't have the slightest clue how to make it seaworthy.

Her parking spot was under a large oak tree that grew not far from the water's edge. This entire section of riverbank was thick and shady with trees. Following a path mulched with acorns and twigs through the small forest of vegetation, she relished the calm she always felt when the river broke out before her, the sun reflecting on its undulating surface. Standing on the dock always had a way of steadying her, despite the constant pitch and sway. Her boat hadn't always been a beauty but it was now. She slid her hand along the glossy black hull, enjoying the warmth of the sun that sat like a thick layer on the wood.

To say she had made improvements to the boat in the five years since she had bought it was an understatement. Crusty and peeling, it was no more than a weathered and dirty heap of wood when she had first laid eyes on it. The owners had it dry-docked, hoisted up on a rusty boat lift not far from where her car was now parked. It hadn't seen the river for a decade and, at first sight, she wasn't sure it would even float. Despite the disrepair and the patina of age, she had fallen in love with its sturdiness, its classic lines and most of all, its potential.

The entire hull had needed to be stripped, sanded and restored, tasks she did all by herself. Well, mostly by herself. John and Sylvie, the boat's former owners also owned the land she was now docked to. The couple lived in a beautiful old farmhouse about fifty yards from the dock. Though she'd bought the boat outright, she paid them a small monthly mooring fee, which came with a lot of perks that included the occasional freshly baked pie. At times, John lent a hand with the more grueling tasks, often doing more chatting than working. Unfortunately, his boating knowledge didn't stretch much farther than Birdy's, as he had only inherited the boat, never taking on the project of restoring it himself.

Gripping the glistening silver rails of the small stepladder, she pulled herself aboard. The teak decks were her favorite feature of the boat. They had been weathered with dark gray and black stains when she'd bought it, but with some help from John and a lot of elbow grease, she had managed to repair them, bringing them back to life. Now they gleamed in the sun, the richness of the wood shining through.

Unlocking the door to the cabin, she immediately heard raucous meowing from inside. Her cat Hoots, a large brown and white Snowshoe, was sitting on one of the built-in benches next to the galley. The elderly cat slid to the floor and trundled toward her, his large stomach swinging as he waddled. All the while he mewed loudly, as if he had been left alone for days rather than hours.

"Hello, Hoots." She bent over to scratch his head. "You'd get a lot more attention if you would stop yelling at me all the time."

Hoots had no intention of giving up his desperate pleas for affection so easily. He followed her around the small living room as she kicked off her shoes and hung up her bag.

The boat's cabin was sunken a few feet below deck. The same reddish-gold teak covered the floor and lower walls, while the upper portion was nearly encircled in large rectangular windows. Inviting and bright, the boat was now over fifty years old, and she loved the midcentury feel of the interior. She'd tried to keep as much of the original charm as possible, while updating where she could. Toward the back was the galley, where she had refinished the cabinets, installed new countertops and updated the small apartment-sized appliances.

Opposite the galley was a small set of stairs that dropped down into the bow of the boat. The stateroom, housing nothing more than her bed, had taken the most getting used to.

The first night aboard, Birdy feared she had made a mistake. Never one to suffer from claustrophobia, she was surprised when the small, dark space seemed to close in on her. Supine on her mattress, the boat swinging with the water, she stretched her arms wide and her fingertips grazed both the port and starboard walls.

In a bit of a panic that night, she had kneeled on her bed and reached up to slide open two of the long, high windows that dotted the hull just below the ceiling. The cool breeze that had been causing the boat to sway gently but steadily felt like silk against her clammy forehead. Allowing it to flow through the stateroom made the tight sleeping quarters feel twice as large.

Birdy was thankful she'd accepted the breeze as her ally that first night, as it led to much greater peace with the more aggressive winds she had since experienced. The stateroom was now her place of solace and she loved the cool wood that greeted her outstretched hands in the night.

When she plopped down on the end of her bed still in a huff about her afternoon, Hoots saw his opportunity. Lacking cat-like grace or agility, he shifted his weight from foot to foot preparing for the massive leap onto the bed. He made it halfway, digging his back claws into the mattress. With his nose peeking over the corner of the bed, his front legs pawed the sheet.

She took pity on the poor creature and hefted his considerable bulk onto the bed before laying back again, staring at the same woodgrain pattern on the ceiling her eyes usually sought out. One that looked eerily like John Travolta.

He immediately headed for her chest and settled down, legs splayed across her stomach and his wet nose inches from her cheek, not caring he was blocking her view of the Travolta ceiling which was luckily more reminiscent of John circa 1994's *Pulp Fiction* than his later role as Edna in *Hairspray*.

"You are the most annoying cat ever," she said, scratching his head lovingly. "What a shitty day, Hooters. Saul was a total bitch again about Brooke, which is ridiculous, since he hasn't kept a girlfriend for more than a year ever. He doesn't get it." She sat up, her legs folded in the middle of the bed, letting the cat slide to the mattress.

Hoots moaned his displeasure at the change of positions and peered at her with large blue eyes that were slightly crossed.

"He doesn't get that when you're in a relationship you have to make a lot of compromises. It's not all easy and you're going to have some bad days. But as long as you sacrifice and work at it, it'll all work out. Right, Hoots?" She picked him up by his armpits, his long body hanging between her elbows, and kissed his nose. He didn't appear amused to be dangling in the air, so she put him back down on the bed and smoothed his ruffled fur. "A place for everything and everything in its place. That's how you like it, huh Hoots? As long as your place is on top of me."

As if to agree, he settled on her hand before she had a chance to scoot off the bed. Carefully extricating her hand from under his soft belly, she began collecting clothes and toiletries for the night. She and Hoots would be spending the night at Brooke's apartment. Time away from her home, packing and unpacking almost daily, had become an unexpected chore. Given her growing collection of clothing at Brooke's, it was harder to find what she needed.

"I think you have it right, Hooters. Everything needs a place, which is exactly why it's okay that I'm selling the boat when we get married. At least everything will be in one place. Her place. This is the type of necessary sacrifice that Saul just doesn't understand."

* * *

"Hey babe," Birdy said as she entered Brooke's waterfront luxury condo.

Brooke greeted her at the front door with a quick kiss. Dressed in jeans and a loose-fitting button-up shirt that looked like she might have borrowed it from a boyfriend—if Birdy didn't know better—Brooke was the epitome of easy casualness. Her sexiest look by far. The heels she wore all day at work were kicked off into a corner by the door and the jacket of her usual power suit was draped over a dining room chair. Her long blond hair was pulled back in a thick, curling ponytail. With a cell phone wedged between her shoulder and her ear, she waved around a wooden spoon covered in red sauce. "I'm making spaghetti. Sound good?" At Birdy's excited nod, she spun back to the kitchen and resumed her phone conversation.

Birdy set Hoots's carrier on the ground and freed him into the foyer. Both surveyed the room cautiously, waiting for Pumpkin to bark his way into the room.

Neither she nor Hoots liked Brooke's Pomeranian rat-dog, who was five pounds of pure evil. The only thing saving Hoots from the dog's snapping and snarling was his size. At nearly three times Pumpkin's weight, Hoots usually could swat him hard enough to send him running to his mommy.

Tonight, however, the only sounds came from the kitchen—pots, pans, boiling water and Brooke's pleasant laugh. Birdy couldn't help thinking how nice the change was from Pumpkin's incessant barking.

She scooped up Hoots, since he was sitting on her foot anyway, and went into the kitchen.

"…And then I said…will you marry me? And she said yes! Can you believe it? I'm engaged to the love of my life." Brooke paused, listening to her friend. "Yes, we're both very happy. I'm so lucky to have her."

Birdy smiled. *Aha! Take that, Saul! Ticking time-bomb my ass!*

She pressed herself against Brooke's back and hugged her tightly, enjoying the way Brooke's butt wiggled against her suggestively. With a kiss to her cheek, she leaned in to inhale the simmering sauce.

As usual, it smelled delicious. Birdy's idea of spaghetti was dumping a jar of whatever was on sale at the grocery store over some boiled noodles. Brooke, on the other hand, was a fantastic cook, and this sauce was undoubtedly made from scratch. The smell of fresh basil was Birdy's undoing and she nabbed the wooden spoon to stir a moment before sneaking a taste. She was rewarded with a playful bump of Brooke's hip before the spoon was snatched away.

"Where's Pumpkin?" she mouthed during a pause in Brooke's conversation.

"Hold on, Emily." She put the phone against her chest. "I took him to get his teeth cleaned. They're keeping him overnight, so unfortunately it's just us and Hoots tonight." Brooke frowned and then turned her attention back to her phone.

"Poor guy," Birdy said, matching Brooke's solemn expression. She scooped up her cat and left the kitchen quickly. Once in the hallway, she celebrated with him, holding his paw in victory as she sang to him quietly.

"What are you doing?"

"Just…waiting for dinner." Birdy quickly dropped Hoots to the floor, where he scurried away, erasing any implication he'd been involved in the celebration.

"But you were dancing. And singing."

"That's just something Hoots and I do. I call it…cat dance time."

"You are so weird." Brooke rolled her eyes. "Dinner's ready."

* * *

Unable to take another bite, Birdy pushed her plate away. She swirled the last of the wine in her glass and moaned a sigh of contentment. "That was amazing. You make a mean plate of spaghetti, Miss Winters."

"Why, thank you," Brooke replied, straightening in her chair to add a haughtiness to her formal tone.

Birdy reached across the table, holding her hand open for Brooke and then squeezed when she felt the softness of her fiancée's palm against her own. "How was your first day as an engaged woman?"

The warmth that spread across Brooke's face seemed to travel through their hands and overtook Birdy as well. She felt a happy glow in her chest seeing the excitement and love she felt mirrored in Brooke.

Brooke kissed her knuckles and then said, "I had a fantastic day. I think being engaged suits me well. And it looks pretty good on you too."

This feeling of love and exhilaration was exactly how she should have felt all day, she realized. Instead she had allowed Saul's criticisms and Mare's decisions to shroud her joy. Stroking the back of her hand, she marveled in the amount of love she felt for this woman. Now that she was in Brooke's presence, surrounded by their love once again, she felt ready to shake off Saul's words. One little thought though niggled in the back of her mind. One last hesitation that she knew she needed to air.

"Why did you ask me to marry you?"

With no hint of uncertainty, Brooke responded, "Because you're the love of my life. I'm crazy about you, Birdy. You make me feel grounded, centered. And you make me feel loved. More than anyone else ever has. You're so devoted and attentive. I love you so much."

Even after five years of loving this woman, the sincerity of her words made Birdy's face warm and her stomach tingle. It wasn't the answer she was looking for though. She needed to know why Brooke had rushed the proposal rather than waiting for Birdy to ask.

"I love you too. What I meant though—"

"Hold on. My turn to ask. Why do you love me?"

The answer was easy for Birdy. "Because you make me feel. Love, happiness, anger, excitement—they all feel amped up with you. Like I'm experiencing everything at a higher voltage than before. You make me feel like I'm flying. You're exhilarating and addictive and it doesn't hurt that you're smoking hot."

Brooke laughed at the last comment. "I feel like we just wrote our vows."

"Well that's one thing we can mark off our list at least." Before she could get sidetracked Birdy asked her question again. "Why did you ask me to marry you instead of waiting for me to do it?"

Brooke scooted forward and took both of Birdy's hands in her own. "Oh, Birdy. I'm sorry if that's been bothering you. I knew you wanted to be the one to propose but I also knew that financially you weren't ready to buy a ring. I thought if I went ahead and did it, that would take some of the burden off of you. Maybe I was impatient but it's because I love you so much. I want to hurry up and marry you already. Did I totally ruin it by asking you first?"

"No, not at all." Birdy felt much better now that she had broached the subject. Her fear that she had forgotten, or worse, ignored her desire to be the one to propose had been laid to rest. She was merely trying to ease Birdy's burden, and Birdy felt ashamed for having given Saul's suspicions credence. Now that the time was here and they were engaged Birdy wanted to hurry up and marry her too, with one stipulation. "To make it up to me, you have to let me pick the music we walk down the aisle to."

"Deal." Brooke leaned back in her chair with a smile and drank the last of her wine.

"Let's see…I'm thinking maybe some AC/DC?"

"You're such a romantic. Take me to bed and you can shake me all night long."

"Now that's a deal."

CHAPTER FOUR

"Excuse me, is this fur-ball yours?"

Startled, Birdy looked up from the design she was working on and met a pair of light brown eyes that were decidedly amused. The woman smiled curiously and Birdy realized she was gawking slack-jawed. She quickly looked down only to find herself now staring at a pair of tanned, muscular legs that gave way to tiny pink running shorts that clung oh-so-wonderfully.

It was so inappropriate to ogle a customer like this.

Focus on the face, Birdy. Her eyes are up there.

The woman's long, dark hair was pulled back into a thick ponytail, accentuating her strong features. Everything about her expression felt open and warm, her smile inviting.

Whoever she was, she was gorgeous. Objectively, of course, as Birdy The Engaged had no opinion one way or the other. She herself had been described as delicate on more than one occasion, with her fair skin and small features. But there was nothing delicate about this woman before her—her athletic frame and wide smile exuded nothing but strength. Maybe focusing on her face wasn't such a good idea, as Birdy was having a very difficult time tearing her gaze away from those extraordinary and very kissable lips.

Kissable lips? Birdy shook herself.

Attempting to recover, she glanced down, away from that amazing mouth with even, white teeth, her eyes coming to rest on the woman's chest. She was positive this perfect woman would have a perfect rack, but her view was impeded by the cat hanging from her shoulder.

"Hoots! Oh my God, my cat is disgusting. I'm so sorry."

Hoots had draped himself over the woman's shoulder with his legs splayed, straddling her chest. She was petting his back while he purred loudly and lewdly, his tail swatting each of her chiseled biceps like a metronome.

"I am so sorry. He really has no sense of boundaries." She pried Hoots off the customer, who was grinning broadly at his unwillingness to part with her chest.

"I tried to hold him like a normal cat, but by the time I walked up here, he had shimmied himself up to what he obviously views as a more desirable location. Prime real estate, I guess," she said, brushing cat hair off her chest. One corner of her mouth twitched up in a very adorable crooked grin that highlighted a dimple in her right cheek.

"I'm sorry, he's usually too lazy to leave his bed by my desk. He almost never bothers customers. Thanks so much for bringing him over."

"Actually, I'm not a customer. I'm Sydney, the new printer."

Birdy felt her face grow warm, knowing she must be turning bright red. Now mortified, she put the pieces together. This was Sydney? The woman she was supposed to work with and train, and she just happened to be drool-worthy? *Oh, fuck. I hate you, Mare.*

She disentangled Hoots from her own cardigan and then stuck out her hand. "I'm Birdy, and this furry thing without manners or morals is Hoots. Was he in back? He doesn't usually leave the office. I didn't even realize he was gone."

"He spent about five minutes following me around. It was nice to have the company, but he got dangerously close to stepping in some white ink. After seeing how liberal he is with where he puts his paws, I can see I saved my shirt from damage." Sydney pulled her tight tank top away from her body and looked down at her chest where there was still a thick layer of cat hair. "Well, permanent damage anyway."

Birdy's eyes had also followed Sydney's attention to her breasts and her mouth went dry. She had been right—perfect woman, perfect rack.

With great effort, she stopped herself from licking her lips. She would not drool over this woman like a dog...or a man. When had she become such a boob hound?

Just as Sydney looked up from the cat catastrophe on her shirt, Birdy managed to study a very important and interesting Post-it note she had forgotten to throw away. Pulling herself together, she fumbled through the papers and files on her desk to find the lint roller she always kept handy.

"I'm so sorry he was bothering you. And molesting you." She stopped herself from copping a feel via the lint roller and reluctantly handed it over. "He's meticulous about not getting messy. He's very metro that way, so he's usually fine around the ink. But I appreciate you keeping an eye on him. I'll try to keep him in the office so he doesn't bother you anymore."

"Oh, don't worry about it. He's cute. I don't mind him being around."

"Well, he seems rather attached to you." Hoots was now perched on Sydney's foot, staring up at Birdy coolly as if this were the most natural place for him to sit. She couldn't help but laugh at him and shook her head. "What a dope." To Sydney, she asked, "Are you finding everything you need back there? Learning your way around the equipment?"

"Yeah, Mare's been walking me through everything. I should be good to start printing a small job later today on the manual press. I used to work at a sweatshop, busting out thousands of shirts a day. I'm thrilled to have a chance to focus on paper products and only do a few T-shirt orders here and there. It's nice to see an emphasis on design and quality rather than pure quantity."

"A sweatshop, huh?"

"Okay, maybe I'm using the term broadly. I don't want to take away from poor children in Bangladesh working their little fingers to the bone, but I was printing hundreds of shirts a day. In Texas, without air conditioning. So yeah, it was a literal sweatshop."

Birdy laughed, finding Sydney as charming as she was gorgeous.

Chill out. You're engaged!

"Well, I hope this is a better experience for you. If nothing else, at least it doesn't get as hot in Portland." She hesitated and then jumped in headfirst. "Listen, Mare gets busy with customers, so if you need help with anything, just ask me."

Why was she offering to help the new girl? It wasn't as if there wasn't already plenty of work to do in the office. Besides, this was what she always dreaded about new hires, showing them around and helping to train them. She usually tried to leave that to Mare. But the offer was already out there so she plowed on, "I've been working here a while so I know the basics, but I don't actually know the presses very well since I do graphic design rather than printing…but I can still try to help if you have any questions."

Well, okay, maybe she got herself out of that. It wasn't like she needed to spend more time around a woman so beautiful and charming who looked ridiculously good in a tank top and running shorts.

"Thanks for the offer. I'll let you know if I have any trouble. I'm sure when it's just you and me in here on Monday, I'll have some questions." Sydney reached down to rub Hoots's head. "See you around big guy." She flashed a smile up at Birdy and—

Was that a wink? Oh God, I'm hallucinating. There's no way she just winked at me.

Once she was sure Sydney was out of the office, Birdy sat down with a sigh and pulled Hoots into her lap. "You have good taste, sir…very good taste."

* * *

"I'll have an old-fashioned, please."

The tattooed bartender with suspenders and slicked-back hair nodded and set to work.

Sydney had used a lot of words to describe the bars she once frequented in Texas. A dive—dirty, homey, warm, welcoming—was her usual type of drinking establishment, but this bar was the complete opposite.

Beth had declared they were going out to celebrate her first day of work and had selected a two-week-old bar that had apparently gotten a lot of attention already. They were seated at the bar, where the bartender was put on display like a chef at a sushi restaurant.

Beth's champagne cocktail was delivered first, the bubbles cascading around the twist of lemon peel balanced on the lip.

"Oh God, this is delicious."

Sydney helped herself to a sip and agreed. "The lavender is a nice touch."

"See, *this* is why you come to a craft cocktail bar, not for a plain and boring old-fashioned," Beth reprimanded.

Before Sydney could respond, the bartender, or mixologist as the menu instructed he be called, placed a long tray of glasses in front of her, none of them resembling the drink she had asked for.

"Umm…I ordered an old-fashioned. I think you gave me the wrong thing."

"This is our version of the classic," the mixologist lectured in a bored tone. "It's a deconstructed old-fashioned. The glass on your right is water. Dissolve the sugar cube in it before you pour the concoction into the middle glass, which has your bitters, lemon peel and ice cube made from filtered and distilled water. The farthest left is two ounces of top-shelf, locally made rye whiskey."

"Interesting," Sydney said, waiting expectantly.

"Enjoy."

"Oh, wait, so you don't actually make the drink?"

"No, I deconstructed it for you." And the mixologist, sans mixing, walked away.

Sydney dropped her sugar cube into the water, stirring it with the small spoon supplied.

"Welcome to Portland," Beth said over the rim of her drink.

Dumping her sugar-water and jigger of whiskey into the glass of bitters, she stirred again.

"So, how was it," Beth prodded. "How was your first day?"

"It was good. I think I like my boss, Mare. She strikes me as a little spacey, but she's pretty easygoing. And it feels like I'll have some autonomy in the shop, which is exactly what I was hoping for. Everything is pretty straightforward. I've worked with all of the equipment so I don't think it will be a hard transition."

"Is it just you and Mare?" Beth asked suggestively. "Is she hot?"

"She's cute and she's straight. There's also a graphic designer that works there."

"Guy or girl?"

"Girl."

"And?"

"And what?"

"Surely you've picked up on my line of questioning by now. Is she hot?"

"Why do you care?"

"Aha! She is hot." Beth pumped her fist triumphantly.

"I didn't say that. I mean, she is. Like really hot but that's not the point."

"Is she gay?"

"To be determined."

"Oh, that sounds hot. The act of determining must be pretty sexy."

"You're very preoccupied with hot lesbians today."

Beth heaved a sigh. "Josh won't shave his stupid 'ironic' mustache and I hate kissing him when he has it. I think I'm living vicariously through your soft-lipped lesbian ways. So tell me about your co-worker. The hot one."

"She's really nice but I only talked to her for like two minutes. She has a cat."

"Lesbian sign number one. Go on."

"I don't know much else. I saw some of her designs today and they were amazing. I think she's really talented, which will be a nice change. In Austin we only printed cookie-cutter designs that the client put together online. Glorified clip-art."

"Talented and sexy. Are you going to hit that?"

"You realize part of the reason I left Texas was a girl. I don't know if immediately dating my coworker is the best idea."

"You and Carmen broke up a year ago. And you said it was amicable. You're ready to get back in it."

Sydney couldn't help but grin. "You might be right."

"I know I am. How's your drink?"

She had been stirring it absently, thinking more about her new, and yes, sexy co-worker than her deconstructed old-fashioned. The spoon clattered on the tray a little more loudly than she had meant it to and the mixologist gave her a sharp look. Sexy co-worker thoughts seemed to have her a bit flustered.

After taking a small sip, she set the glass back on the bar, this time careful not to draw the attention of the haughty bartender.

"It's good. It's actually…"

Interrupting, the mixologist brought a second spoon that matched the one already on her tray and stuck it in her drink. "Traditionally the spoon should be left in the glass," he said as if Sydney were the most unsophisticated creature he had ever been forced to serve.

"That was obnoxious," Beth admitted when he turned away, likely to lecture another patron.

"Do I have to tip him for *not* making my drink?"

"Yes. And they'll probably charge you extra for sullying two spoons. You barbarian."

CHAPTER FIVE

Birdy woke the next morning at Brooke's apartment to Pumpkin humping her foot, his tiny, evil teeth bared as he made small, grunting noises. "Ugh. Pumpkin! Get off. Why are you even in here?"

One of the concessions she had gotten out of Brooke was that Hoots would be allowed in the closed bedroom to protect him from being terrorized by the little rat now Velcroed to her foot. She shook her leg to remove the overzealous dog and reached for Brooke to call off her hound.

But before she even touched the cool sheets beside her she knew Brooke was already up and gone for the day.

Of course she was. Every Saturday, every Sunday, Brooke still got up by six to go to the gym.

Birdy missed those days in their early months when they would spend weekends rolling around in bed, making love until they were breathless and numb, tickling, kissing and holding each other. They used to lie in bed until two or three in the afternoon, getting up only because they couldn't go a minute longer without eating. But now, it was seven a.m. on a Saturday, and instead of waking up to her fiancée's gentle touch, she was jarred from sleep by Pumpkin's incessant humping.

At the commotion in the bedroom, Hoots started crying, his loud pathetic moans sounding clearly through the door.

She kicked the blankets back, sending Pumpkin to the floor in a tangled heap. Feeling bad for booting the dog off so aggressively, she searched the mound of fabric to extricate him. Once freed, he followed her to the door, snapping and growling at her ankles, making her wish she had left him to dig his own way out. "You're such a waste of fur, Humpkin."

She opened the door, allowing Hoots to rush in, his already large eyes widened more at the sight of the vengeful dog.

He scrambled to the bed and then made a heroic leap to a nearby windowsill, his fur, fat and skin spanning the space between his splayed legs like an overweight flying squirrel. His gallant, graceless flight left a barking Pumpkin on the floor snarling toward the window.

The situation under control, Birdy yawned the entire way to the kitchen to make some coffee. She nearly jumped when she turned the corner and saw Brooke standing at the counter already pouring two mugs. Her workout attire, black running tights and a matching pullover top with severe lines, gave her an elegant, sophisticated appearance. Dark and clean, Brooke's wardrobe was in sharp contrast with her own.

Birdy had slept in her favorite worn-in blue and white striped pajama pants and tight-fitting white tank top with a coffee stain in the middle. Knowing it was nowhere as chic and stylish as Brooke's ensemble, she pulled at her top self-consciously.

"Hey, babe," Brooke said with an amused grin. "I wondered how long it would take Pumpkin to get you up."

Still struggling to clear the fog of sleep from her brain, Birdy croaked, "What are you doing here? Why aren't you at the gym?"

Brooke's eyes flashed for a second, causing Birdy's heart to sink. "This is my apartment isn't it?" she replied hotly. "I'm allowed to be here when I want to be, aren't I?"

"Of course, baby. I didn't mean that. I was just asking why you aren't at the gym," Birdy said softly, trying to smooth out a situation she felt might escalate.

As quickly as it had come, the anger left Brooke's eyes. She approached Birdy like a lioness that wanted nothing more than to play with her food. As she slowly covered the space between them, she swung each hip seductively, eyeing Birdy through lashes that were heavily mascaraed, and biting her lower lip. She ran a finger from Birdy's chin to the coffee stain between her breasts and said, "You know I like to stay looking good for you, but I just didn't feel like going today." She gave her a lingering kiss before retrieving the second mug of coffee from the counter.

Birdy let out a sigh of relief. Okay, maybe they had made it past her remark without Brooke totally losing her head. *Walking on eggshells.* That was Saul's warning in her head, but she quickly pushed it aside. Brooke was a passionate woman. She worked hard, played hard, loved hard, and a consequence of that was a quick temper. There was no middle ground with Brooke, and Birdy had come to love and respect that about her. No walking on eggshells here, just a few carefully chosen words, which required at least one cup of coffee. Coffee was definitely needed.

Brooke extended the mug as an apparent peace offering. "Wait," she said in a snarky tone. "Is it okay for me to make coffee here, at my own house? Normally I wouldn't think to ask but since you seem so concerned about what I do and don't do this morning, maybe I should ask permission?"

The anger that Brooke so expertly disguised as passion was back.

Turning on her heel, Birdy stomped to the bedroom, grabbing her essential toiletries out of the bathroom on the way. *There is no way I'm putting up with this right now. I haven't even had my coffee yet.* She tugged on her jeans and began packing her overnight bag. Hoots hooted from the windowsill as if worried she would leave him behind with the crazy Pomeranian still snarling in his direction. As she turned to retrieve his carrier from the hall closet, she nearly ran into Brooke, who was leaning casually against the bedroom doorway with arms crossed, watching her.

"I don't understand why you're mad at me. You're the one who fucked up this morning and ruined our whole day. I stayed home so I could be with you."

Birdy was stung by her words. She knew this fight wasn't her fault and normally she would acquiesce, asking Brooke to forgive her, but not today. She could still hear Saul in her head. *Ticking time bomb.* "Wait, I fucked this up? I just wanted to know why you didn't go to the gym today. It was an innocent question, but instead of answering me like a normal human being, you went off into Crazyville on me."

"I am not crazy," Brooke spat, pushing away from the doorjamb and filling the exit with her body. "Don't *ever* call me crazy. You're the one who ruined today. Are you saying I'm not home enough with you? I work my ass off so I can take you to nice restaurants and buy you expensive things, like that ring on your finger. I had wedding venues lined up for us to see today, but that surprise is ruined now, thanks to you."

Birdy was jarred by the change in subject. "This is ridiculous. When did this become about money? Or our wedding?" She refused to be led down this path, allowing Brooke to pick fights over every topic along the way. "I'm not mad about your work schedule or the wedding. I'm mad about this morning."

She took a breath and her shoulders slumped. Feeling the fight drain out of her, she just wanted it to be over. Her arguments sounded petty when she said them aloud. She could, however, still feel the pain of the underlying issue, the problem that was actually bothering her.

In a small voice, she said, "We weren't always like this. We used to enjoy this time together." Birdy sat on the bed remembering, willing Brooke to remember. "We laughed here, held each other, made out. Jesus, the morning sex was incredible. We couldn't get enough of each other. We'd hit the snooze button ten times so we could cuddle longer. Remember that?" She smiled tentatively, watching Brooke's eyes soften a bit, the love creeping back into her expression.

Sitting beside her on the bed, her workout gear a sharp contrast to the wrinkled white sheets, Brooke slowly took her hand and held it in her own lap. "I remember."

Birdy relished the feel of Brooke's thumb tracing the contours of each of her fingers and knuckles. "Do you miss it as much as I do?"

"I do." Brooke squeezed her hand and met her eyes. "I'm sorry I lost my temper. I was...*am* really excited about today. Can we have a do-over?"

"Of course."

Brooke smiled and leaned in with a tender kiss that quickly rocketed into an intense make-out session.

Panting, Birdy asked, "What time do we have to be at the first venue?"

"Not for another couple of hours."

"Good. Time for that do-over." She scrambled to the top of the bed and quickly got back under the covers, pretending to be asleep. Opening one eye she added, "This time I want to wake up to you humping me rather than your dog."

CHAPTER SIX

Birdy dropped her keys with a clatter on the counter next to the back door and called into the kitchen. "Hey, Mom."

"Hi, baby girl. You're here early." Bea Cartwright finished setting the table and hugged Birdy tightly, kissing her on the cheek.

Bea's golden retriever, Cornflake, came barreling into the kitchen at the sound of Birdy's voice. The exuberant dog tried to stop running, but her paws couldn't get purchase on the linoleum, so she slid headfirst into Birdy.

Grunting from the impact, Birdy bent down and kissed the furry muzzle before turning her attention back to her mother.

She and her mom were physically opposite in almost every way, a point that surprised those who didn't know Birdy was adopted. Bea was round and stocky, her hair too short, curly, and gray to ever be considered chic, though her ruddy complexion, blue eyes and soft, rounded features were pleasant and inviting.

Birdy's birth mother Jo had been Bea's partner of ten years, and they'd dreamed of bucking society and raising a family together. She'd died of cancer before Birdy was out of diapers, but only after seeing to it that all the paperwork was in place for Bea to complete the adoption upon her death.

"I didn't expect you until after ten."

"I stayed on the boat last night, so I didn't have as far to drive."

Brunch and mimosas was their Sunday morning ritual. Her mother always cooked too much and today's breakfast was no exception—eggs, sausage, and waffles with strawberries and homemade whipped cream.

"So you two got in a fight, huh?"

Birdy hesitated, hating how quickly her mom could pinpoint the cracks in her relationship with Brooke. Knowing Bea wouldn't let it rest, she figured it best to just get it over with. "Yeah. We had a small fight."

"You two aren't splitting up, are you?" There was an unmistakable hint of hopefulness in her tone at the thought of them calling it quits.

"We had a fight yesterday morning but it was nothing. Everything is fine now, we made up, but I wanted to stay at the boat last night and have some time to myself. You don't have to sound so gleeful at the idea of us breaking up, you know."

"Oh, Birdy. I just want you to be happy. I know I've said all this before, but I don't think she's going to make you happy in the long run. I'm not sure she even makes you happy in the short run." As Bea talked, she gathered pots and pans with her usual efficiency. "I know she's charming and charismatic. And I know that *sometimes* she makes you very, very happy. But I just feel like you're stuck on this roller coaster with her. *Her* roller coaster. The ups are way up there. They're exciting and filled with passion. But then there's always the drop and she just pulls you right down with her. Are the highs really worth all the drama at the bottom?"

"You sound just like Saul, Mom. Ever since the two of you joined that bowling league together, I feel like I've been nagged from every direction. You guys must just sit around like a couple of old hens gossiping about me between frames." She picked up an apple and tossed it back and forth between her hands. "He's already warned me that she's borderline. He probably has a pamphlet about it in his office that he can't wait to 'accidentally' leave on my coffee table," she added, rolling her eyes and dropping the apple with a *thunk*. "Yes, she *is* a little dramatic, but that's because she's passionate, and I'd rather date someone like that with some drama and magnetism than some dead fish."

"I know, I know. I just wish you could see that there are plenty of people out there who are exciting without all of the ups and downs. Plenty more non-dramatic and non-dead fish in the sea. And don't be mean to Saul. He's trying to watch out for you. And he's a really good bowler so don't make fun of him for joining our team. We need him."

"Yeah, yeah, I know. The Golden Gutter Girls couldn't live without him," Birdy said with a smirk. "I know the two of you are just looking out for me, but I want you to be happy for me, for finding someone I love and who loves me back."

"Oh sweetie." Bea stopped gathering supplies for breakfast and gave her a tight hug. When she drew back, she continued to hold Birdy's shoulders tightly. "If you're happy, then I'm happy for you. Are you happy?"

"I love her, Mom." Birdy took a deep breath, mustering her courage. "And the thing is…she asked me to marry her."

Bea's eyes widened and her grip on Birdy's shoulders became tighter. "And?"

"And I said yes."

Bea seemed to hesitate a moment, as if needing to let the new information sink in before gathering her back into her arms. After a quiet "Congratulations, baby," she studied Birdy's eyes once more, as if searching for something, and turned back to the task of cooking breakfast.

"You don't have to sound so miserable about it," Birdy said as she drew the plates and glasses from the cabinet.

"Well, neither do you, honey."

"I'm not miserable," she replied defensively. Did she sound miserable? She wasn't an effusive person so why did people expect an engagement to change that? Marriages should be about the people involved and she was in this for Brooke. And how Brooke made her feel. Alive, vibrant, sexy, needed. That didn't mean she had to subscribe to the rainbows and butterflies, the commercialization of love. No rooftop screaming, just playing it cool. Zen.

"Maybe you're not miserable, but you're not happy either. This is the type of thing you should be screaming from the rooftops, not waiting half a week to tell your mother."

Birdy gulped and not for the first time wondered if Bea could read her mind. If she could, she hoped she was live streaming her new Joe Cool attitude.

They worked side by side for several minutes without speaking as each stewed on her own thoughts.

Finally, Birdy broke the silence, hoping she might get her mother excited about the upcoming wedding plans. "Brooke and I went to some wedding venues yesterday. She had some places lined up at fancy hotels and banquet halls."

Slowly, as if trying to be nonchalant, Bea said, "I thought you didn't want to get married at a hotel, or even have the reception at one. Haven't I heard you rant about soulless green carpet before? I thought you wanted a more intimate venue like a cute outdoor space or something." She stirred the batter a moment before raising her spatula in apparent triumph. "Your cousin Misty! Remember, she got married in that beautiful hotel. It was gorgeous and it had wall-to-wall green carpet. Oh, you hated it!"

"Well, I don't know. That was like a decade ago. I could be persuaded. Brooke has connections through work and can get us into some really fancy places. It's not really my scene, but it's not that big of a deal to me, I guess."

"Mm-hmm." Bea handed her the batter bowl and cracked some eggs into a pan on the oven. "So, when exactly did she ask you to marry her?"

She had been dreading this question, knowing her mother would be hurt by the answer. "Wednesday night."

Bea nodded, never looking up from the eggs.

Birdy poured the last of the batter in the waffle maker and finished setting the table, waiting and hoping silently for a sign of her mother's approval. It never came. When the food was ready, they sat down to the table.

As she reached for her knife and fork, Bea caught her hand and studied the diamond ring on her finger. Finally meeting Birdy's eyes, she said quietly, "Your mother and I always just wanted you to be happy. I think if she were still here and could see the way I've handled your relationship with Brooke, she would have put me in my place by now. She would have told you to follow your heart and to be happy, and if Brooke is where your heart leads you, then you have our blessing."

A thick bubble of emotion welled in Birdy's throat. She had been weighing hope against expectation, waiting for the missing piece. Her mother's sincerity, her acceptance was everything she had wanted, everything she had needed to move forward with her marriage to Brooke. Now that she had received it, she felt lighter in her own skin and more confident in her future.

Bea squeezed her fingers and then with a wave of her hand, she dismissed the serious mood that had fallen over the breakfast table. "Now," she said purposefully, with a slightly thicker voice, "poke your eggs and make sure they're runny enough."

Birdy laughed at the quick dismissal of "mushy stuff," as Bea would have put it, and poked her eggs. Perfect as usual. The smell of breakfast attracted the ever-hungry Cornflake, whose chin was now resting on her leg in hopes a piece of sausage might fall.

"So," Bea said, wiggling her eyebrows, "how did she ask you?"

"Oh, Jesus." Birdy shoved a large bite of waffle in her mouth to avoid the question. "Just ask Saul at your bowling league tomorrow night. I'm sure he would be beyond thrilled to give you every detail." She took her napkin off her knee and handed it to her mother. "Here, give him this. He'll need props."

CHAPTER SEVEN

When Birdy awakened on Monday before her alarm, she refused to acknowledge why she was getting up so early. When she spent more time than usual in the shower shaving her legs, she refused to think about why she was putting in the extra effort. When she styled her hair and applied her usual light makeup with extra care, she wouldn't meet her own eye in the mirror. In fact, she mused, she was doing a damn good job of not admitting any of this had to do with impressing her very attractive new co-worker. She just felt like looking her best today, that's all.

It was also a coincidence that she had worn her cutest outfit—her favorite pair of black skinny jeans that best matched her well-worn canvas slip-on shoes. And the new white, fitted T-shirt with a Morse code of black stripes, under her mustard yellow cardigan. She donned a long, stringy gold necklace she had bought months ago from a boutique close to work. The necklace had always seemed like too much, but today she felt good and wanted to accessorize her mood.

Arriving early, she had planned to busy herself with emails, coffee and putting the final touches on a new company's logo, as Sydney wasn't due at work for another half hour. When she unlocked the back door, she realized every light in the building was on and a low hum was coming from the shop. After dropping her bag at her desk, she walked into the shop wondering if Sydney had forgotten to close up on Friday.

Figures. Sydney might be beautiful but she was still hired by Mare, which meant she was most likely incompetent. If the dryer had been running all weekend, there would be hell to pay. The amount of electricity wasted and the wear on the machine would be astronomical.

When she turned the corner, though, all conjecture regarding her new co-worker's abilities was pushed from her mind as Sydney bent over to pick up a screen. *Note to self: Sydney's ass equals distraction of the century.*

Seemingly oblivious she was being watched, Sydney placed the screen in the washout tank and grabbed the hose to the pressure washer. The muscles in her biceps and shoulders rippled as she sprayed out the mesh to reveal the design that had been burned into the screen. Water misted from the tank and glistened on her skin. Her hair was pulled back in a messy ponytail that had Birdy wishing she had been the reason it was so unruly.

"Holy Texas," she murmured, staring transfixed. One, two, three screens Sydney sprayed out while she worshipfully watched her shimmering body.

Finally having finished her last screen, Sydney pulled her safety glasses off and wiped her damp forehead with the back of her forearm.

Birdy had never seen anything so sexy.

Sydney looked up and a lazy smile spread across her face.

Right then, Birdy decided she wanted to do whatever it took to make Sydney smile like that. As often as possible.

Walking toward her, Sydney said, "God, I'm glad you're here. Mare called me last night. Did she call you?"

"Umm...no. She didn't. Why? Why are you here so early?"

"Mare said she got a call from the event coordinator for that beer fest next weekend at the waterfront. She said it's your biggest moneymaker of the year."

"Yeah, Diane coordinates that. She and Mare are friends. We work with her a lot."

"Well, apparently Diane called her late last night and said there had been a mix-up. The thousand-shirt order that we thought was due on Friday now has to be done sooner. Like, today sooner. Or first thing tomorrow morning at the latest sooner. They need the shirts for a meeting tomorrow night so they can take inventory and then hand them out to beer fest volunteers before Friday. Four colors with front and back designs, so we have to run everything twice. That makes it pretty much a two-thousand-shirt job."

"What? They expect you to print two thousand shirts in one day? That's impossible for one person!"

"Well, that's the thing. And that's why I thought Mare would have called you. She said you'd be able to help me and that this needs to take priority, so the designs you're working on can be pushed back a day. I'm really surprised she didn't let you know."

Birdy snorted. "I'm not. She knew I'd be pissed at her so she made you do her dirty work. Even with two of us, this is going to take massive overtime," she grumbled. "I hate overtime." Her eyes rested just below the hem of Sydney's running shorts, which barely reached her thighs. Maybe several extra hours to check out those legs wouldn't be the worst thing in the world.

As if reading her mind, Sydney smirked. "I'm up for it if you are."

She nodded grimly.

"By the way, that outfit…it's really cute."

"Hunh." As her face warmed, she brushed imaginary lint from her shirt hem and scuffed her slip-on shoe with deliberate nonchalance. "Oh, thanks. It's no big deal. I just kind of threw on the first thing I saw."

* * *

By the time they were an hour in, Birdy was not feeling cute anymore. Gone was her cardigan and slinky gold necklace. Her jeans were rolled up as much as the skin-tight material would allow and her hair was pulled back into a small ponytail. She would have given anything for a pair of socks and sneakers.

"I'm completely miserable," she said for what had to be the hundredth time.

Her job was to pull the shirts off the boards that spun around the automatic press and put them on the dryer belt behind her, while Sydney, standing only inches away, would then position a new shirt on the board Birdy had just cleared. The machine spun the boards around, separately printing each color onto the blank shirts. Every four and a half seconds a fully printed shirt would swing to Birdy's station.

"Now you see why I wanted to get out of that sweatshop in Austin, right? It was just like this day in and day out, except I had to work next to a guy named Jorge who never spoke to me and smelled like B.O. and cigarettes. At least here I have much better company. Plus I only have to do this for a day or two at a time and then I can go back to paper prints."

"Give me another hour and I'll smell as bad as Jorge. Besides, what's the difference if you're doing paper prints? You'd still have to stand here and print poster after poster or sign after sign."

"Oh, it's way different. With big jobs like this you have to use the automatic press." Another empty board spun in front of her. With barely a pause in her explanation, she deftly placed a blank shirt on the board Birdy had just cleared. "So there's no artistry or soul left in the process. You're really just facilitating a machine. But when you're working with paper, it's usually limited editions. There's a craft to it."

Birdy noticed how quickly Sydney centered and smoothed each shirt. She even had time to prepare the next shirt before the boards spun again. All while carrying on a conversation with almost no hesitation.

Sydney went on, "It takes more skill because there are so many variables that go into making every print identical. This big, ugly machine takes almost all of the variables out of the equation. They make it so just about anybody can do a thousand shirts on it. You don't have to be an artist to do this. You just have to be willing to stand in one spot for countless hours and sweat. Or in your case, you have to be willing to turn around two thousand times. And sweat."

"In that case," Birdy paused, finding it difficult to talk and unload the shirts at the same time. "I don't think I meet the requirements for this position. I better quit. I'll call up Jorge and see if he needs a job. Maybe he'd be willing to relocate."

Sydney chuckled as she placed another shirt on the belt. "At least we have this time to get to know each other. I figure by the time we finish at…oh, two in the morning, you should know me better than anyone. Plus, the more we talk, the more you'll forget just how many times you've turned around on that same spot today."

"Oh, I see. So my options are either to get to know you or go insane? Is that it?"

"Pretty much."

"Well, you leave me no choice, Sydney… That's a good place to start this get-to-know-you-while-we-sweat experience. What's your last name?"

"Ramos."

"Latina?"

"Yep. Half."

"Explains the tan," Birdy said under her breath, while she admired for the three-hundred-and-forty-second time how Sydney's dark skin looked so bronzed and creamy against her white racer-back tank top.

"Speaking of tans," Sydney said with a smile, "Where'd you get your pasty skin?"

"Oh, funny. I'll have you know I tan quite well, thank you. But it *is* Portland and the weather has only been nice for a few weeks. The sun has probably been out every day since you got here, but you just wait. You're in for it."

It was late June and the weather had taken longer to turn around this year, but now that it had, she was excited to spend the summer sitting on the deck of her boat with a book and a beer. She had tossed around the idea of being more outdoorsy this summer. Saul had been bugging her to go camping with him for years. The only problem was she was probably the only person in Portland who didn't like hiking. She couldn't stand the idea of aimlessly walking through the woods with the only objective being to not trip on roots. *I'll stick with my book and beer.*

"I'll have to take your word for it. It's been gorgeous since the day I moved in. Not a cloud in the sky. Luckily I built up a pretty good base in Austin, or I might be as pale as you," Sydney said with a chuckle.

In the second she had between shirts, she playfully swatted Sydney's arm, hiding her grin long enough to give off a somewhat convincing "don't mess with me" face.

Sydney laughed harder as she loaded the next shirt. "Okay, okay. I'm just teasing you. I actually think you have really beautiful...I think you are really..." Sydney blushed.

Birdy turned away to hide her own warming cheeks. *Is she hitting on me?*

After clearing her throat, Sydney broke the uncomfortable silence, adding, "Anyway, I'm sure in several months after a Portland winter, I'll be just as pale as you."

"Then I'll enjoy your tan while I can." Birdy thought she sounded much braver than she felt.

Now who's flirting?

Sydney wiggled her eyebrows and winked.

Well, now we're even, Birdy thought. She flirted with me, I said something equally as embarrassing. Time to move on.

"Maybe you can show me around and we can work on our tans together. Do you like to hike? Or kayak?"

"Yes! Of course. You'd be hard pressed to find a Portlander who doesn't." *And apparently I've taken up lying along with my other new favorite hobbies.* "I mean, how else would I spend my summers? It's not like I just sit around all day...reading or something." She trailed off in a mumble.

"Awesome! We should go sometime then. You can show me your favorite trails. I've already found a few. Bonus points if it ends at a waterfall."

She's been here two weeks and she's probably hiked more than I have in my whole life.

It exhausted her just thinking about showing Sydney her favorite trails—mostly because she would have to find some first. "Sounds great. So why did you move here? Why give up sunny, warm Texas for rainy, cold, dreary Oregon?" She was anxious to move the topic from her trails-and-trees shortcomings.

"So I take it you love the weather here?"

"I've lived here my whole life. I love Portland more than anywhere else but yeah, the weather gets me down a little. By March, after four months of rain, I would kill to be in Texas and to see the sun."

"But by September in Austin, after four months of blistering heat, you would probably kill to cool off in Portland and enjoy the coziness of winter in the Pacific Northwest."

"Yeah, yeah. Aren't you just full of positive thoughts? I prefer to dwell in my self-pity. I see you're more of a glass-half-full sort of person."

Birdy knew she was laying the cynicism on a little thick. It seemed to humor Sydney, so she kept up the front, and once again her pessimism was rewarded with Sydney's warm laughter.

"Yeah, I guess you could say that. I like to find the good in things. And to address your previous question, I moved to Portland for a few different reasons."

"Like what?"

"Well, for starters there was Jorge and the sweatshop. I needed to get out and find a job I liked. Even an optimist like me could find no positive or redeeming qualities in that hellhole."

"Okay, so why else did you move here?"

"I've always wanted to. It's gorgeous here. In Texas everything feels baked. It's all brown and hot and dusty. Here it feels so alive and green and rich. The mountains are beautiful, the trees are amazing and it just smells perfect."

"You know that rain I was just complaining about? Wait until you smell that. The rain, the trees. It's...magical."

"You're not as cynical as you let on. No one can use the word 'magical' to describe the smell of rain and trees and be a dyed-in-the-wool killjoy."

"Don't tell anyone."

"I won't. Your curmudgeon status is safe with me. And I can honestly say I'm looking forward to the winter and the rain. I'm sure it will be just as beautiful as summer has been. So far everything about the Northwest has been exactly how I imagined it would be."

"Wait, so you're saying you've never even been here before?"

"Nope. I'd seen pictures in college from a friend's trip to Seattle. I knew immediately I wanted to live in the Northwest, but I never had a chance to visit till now."

"So what made you finally pack up and move here?"

"A girl."

Birdy's heart sank. *She has a goddamn girlfriend and here I am flirting with her.* Except she had a goddamn girlfriend too. A goddamn fiancée!

Hoping her disappointment didn't show, she asked, "So, you moved with your girlfriend?"

"Oh, God no, nothing like that. I stayed in Austin because of a girl...one who would never consider moving here. We broke up last year."

Birdy's pulse quickened. Was she relieved that Sydney was single? *Jesus, you need to shut down this silly little crush.* She realized that Sydney was still talking, and focused back in on her words.

"And suddenly my whole life opened up. I realized I could live anywhere and do anything. There wasn't much keeping me in Austin, just a shitty job and an ex. So I decided I'd move to the Northwest as soon as I could."

"What made you choose Portland?"

"I was headed for Seattle at first but I stopped in Portland to stay with a friend of mine from college. We hadn't seen each other in years, so I decided to spend a couple days seeing the city and I never left. I never made it to Seattle. I fell in love with this place. They really mean it when they say, 'Keep Portland Weird.' Everyone is really weird here and that makes it the perfect fit. Not too sure what that says about me."

Birdy had to laugh at that. Yes, everyone is weird here, and she had always loved it too. At times she fantasized about living in bigger cities, San Francisco or Chicago, but she never seriously considered moving. Portland was home and held on tight to her heart in a way that nowhere else ever could.

"It feels like home here," Sydney said with a wistful expression.

Birdy grinned and nodded her agreement before realizing just how much less disrupted her home would be if Sydney had stuck to her plan and settled her very distracting ass in Seattle.

* * *

The two of them worked steadily throughout the morning, occasionally sharing stories and laughing at each other as they slogged through the seemingly endless piles of shirts they had laid out. They fell into a steady rhythm, and as their hands worked, their conversation flowed easily.

Until today, Sydney had always hated this part of her job. The monotony was mind-numbing but being here, working so closely with Birdy was anything but boring. She marveled at the fact that she barely even cared that the shirt pile was still towering.

"I'd say we probably have about four hundred left for the fronts. And then we get to do it all over again on the backs."

"I'm never turning around again. From now on, if something is behind me, it is dead to me. I will only look forward."

"Good thing I'm a runner. I need to stay in front of you so you don't forget about me." She grinned and ran in place. "Look on the bright side. We have jobs and you like your co-worker."

"True. I see your point, but don't you ever get tired of being so cheerful? Wouldn't you rather just bitch with me about how much you hate this?"

"Okay, okay, I'll give it a try." Sydney thought for a moment, trying to come up with the most negative thing she could think of. All that came to mind though, was that she was having the best day possible here with Birdy. The thought put a smile on her face.

"You don't look like you're thinking negative thoughts."

"I'm trying but you make me laugh too much to get me down." Seeing the faux seriousness on Birdy's face, Sydney tried to buckle down and get serious about complaining. "Okay, how's this? My shoulders kinda hurt."

Birdy cocked her head and pasted on an incredulous expression.

With exaggerated grumpiness, Sydney amended her response, "Gosh, my shoulders hurt so bad from loading all of these GD T-shirts! If I ever see another T-shirt again, I'm going to rip it off the bastard who would dare to wear such an offensive rag. And I'll…I'll…throw it on the ground and…stomp on it!"

Holding a straight face, Birdy looked down at the cute striped T-shirt, which now clung to her with sweat. She glanced back up at Sydney, and in unison they both checked out her shirt again.

There was a deliberate pause, during which Sydney envisioned ripping off Birdy's shirt—though not to stomp it on the ground. For an instant, she thought she could see Birdy's pulse throbbing in her neck. Was the same image searing her thoughts?

A shiver of lust gave way to a sudden eruption of infectious giggles.

As Sydney doubled over with laughter, Birdy lunged to stop the press before it started printing on empty boards. "You," she managed between her own desperate gulps for air, "are the most optimistic person I have ever met. And that is *not* a good thing, Syd. You suck at bitching."

Sydney's laughter left her and she found herself trying to catch her breath for a totally different reason. Her heart beat faster and she felt flushed. They stood there, hands on knees, recovering from their outbreak of giggles, staring at each other through their lashes. It was impossible not to notice that Birdy's breathing was shallow as well, and her dark eyes were bright from the tears that had welled up while laughing.

"You just called me Syd."

"Yeah, I'm sorry. It felt right, but I won't—"

"No, I liked it. I liked it a lot, Bird."

They held each other's gaze for a long moment, and Sydney felt surprisingly unselfconscious, completely lost in Birdy, aware only of her slowed breathing and the ache of laugh-tired muscles in her cheeks.

A singsong voice drifted through the shop causing Birdy to stiffen. "Birdy! Birdy where are you?"

The contentment that had settled on Sydney as heavily and comfortably as a worn blanket was yanked away as she registered the discomfort on Birdy's face. The loss was not unlike waking from a pleasant dream cold, the covers having fallen from her body. She shook off the feeling as Birdy yelled out, "I'm in the back!" Her voice seemed sharper, more forced than before, as if she had just woken up.

A woman rounded the corner carrying a paper sack in one hand and a very expensive purse in the other.

"Hey, baby. What are you doing back here? You look horrible!" Hand on hip, she took in Birdy's disheveled appearance. She touched Birdy's shoulder but withdrew in disgust. "Eww, why are you so sweaty?" Not waiting for a response, her eyes fell on Sydney, studying her up and down, from shoes to ponytail.

The inspection had probably lasted only a second but Sydney felt as if she had been entirely exposed. It was all she could do not to cross her arms over her chest. Apparently the woman liked what she saw because she turned her full attention to Sydney, leaving Birdy forgotten beside her.

"Well, hi there," she said, extending her hand. "Brooke Winters. I'm Birdy's fiancée. Are you the new hire?"

Suddenly, Sydney's heart felt just as exposed to Brooke Winters as the rest of her. *How did I not know Birdy was in a relationship? Engaged, for Christ's sake?*

But now was not the time to let the disappointment show on her face. "Yep, that's me." She lifted her chin and politely shook the offered hand. "Sydney Ramos. And fiancée…Wow, congratulations, you two."

"She hadn't mentioned that she's engaged?" Brooke asked pointedly, looking at Birdy.

"It didn't come up."

"It was only last week. Honestly, Birdy, I would think you'd want to tell everyone. I mean, look at this rock I—" Brooke snatched Birdy's hand from her pocket, presumably to show off the ring, but stopped mid-gloat at finding a completely unadorned finger. "Where's your ring?"

"I…I took it off. It was getting tight since I'm sweating so much. It felt…constricting. It's in my desk drawer. I'll go put it back on now."

Sydney not only felt caught in the middle of a lover's quarrel about to boil over, but also embarrassed for how aggressively Brooke was steamrolling over Birdy with just a look.

Before Birdy could walk away, she explained awkwardly to Brooke, "Printing can get really messy. It would be a shame if something happened to the ring. Getting ink out of the setting would be tough."

No wonder I hadn't known she was engaged. A clue—like a goddamn ring—would have been nice. "I'm sure it's beautiful."

Apparently placated, Brooke pulled Birdy back to her side. "Just as long as you don't forget to put it back on, baby." Her nuzzling caused Birdy to redden.

At this onslaught of overly gooey affection, Sydney used the excuse of checking the controls on the press to extricate herself. Leaning against one of the boards she crossed her arms over her chest, hoping her heart would feel less exposed. Brooke obviously wanted to mark her territory, and she'd gotten the message loud and clear. With forced enthusiasm, she cleared her throat and asked, "Have you set a date?"

"No," Birdy stated without flair, though it was drowned out by Brooke's affirmative reply. She dropped her jaw in dismay. "What do you mean, yes?"

"Well, you see, sweetie," Brooke said carefully, as if breaking news of a lost toy to a child, "that's why I'm here." She took

Birdy's shoulders, her designer purse hanging between them. "I have great news. I was able to get us into the Heathman Hotel in January. The sixth. Isn't that great?" She squealed with excitement and hugged an obviously stunned Birdy.

"But that's only six months away! I thought you wanted to get married in the summer? How are we supposed to plan an entire wedding in six months?"

"Well, we'll just have a lot of work to do. They had a cancellation, and since Bradley"—she turned to Sydney to explain—"Bradley's a co-worker of mine at the convention center. He's currently sleeping with Michael, who's in charge of bookings for the hotel, so he was able to get us in." To Birdy, she continued, "I jumped on it and already paid our deposit. Normally you'd have to wait ages to get into the Heathman. So, we have tons to do. And I'm putting you in charge of the invitations, which have to go out in a couple of months."

The woman seemed oblivious to the agitated expression on her fiancée's face. Sydney however was not.

"Oh, and while you do that, I'll work on securing a caterer, photographer and florist. We need to come up with a guest list and decide on our colors. I was thinking emerald and ebony, which would contrast nicely with the cream wedding dress I picked out. I really want to try it on this week. And we have to figure out what you're going to wear. Pants seem too stereotypically butch and femme, and you're not even butch really, but two dresses are harder to coordinate in color and style. I'm just so excited! We have so much to do." Her voice had escalated to a squeal. "Anyway, enough wedding talk. I don't want to bore Sydney."

She flashed a smile so charming, Sydney almost thought it was sincere.

Birdy looked shell-shocked. She probably would have preferred for this conversation to have taken place elsewhere, not at work or in front of her new co-worker. The bomb Brooke had dropped seemed to have her vacillating between humiliation and fury.

"So, Sydney," Brooke began. "What brought you to work here?"

She pulled her eyes from Birdy, whose jaw was tightening rhythmically, making her high cheekbones more prominent. "I just moved here from Texas," she said distractedly. Those cheekbones seemed to distract her easily.

"Oh, really? Whereabouts in Portland are you living?"

Forcing herself to focus, she replied, "I'm staying with a friend in Southeast temporarily until I find an apartment." She desperately wanted this conversation over. Something about Brooke set her on edge. The revelation of Birdy's very un-single status had her head reeling, while the couple's interaction had her stomach just as unsettled. She wished Brooke would drop the small talk and just leave for lunch. Or better yet, drop the sandwiches and leave Birdy to eat them with Sydney. The thought put a small smile on her lips. She realized she had let the moment stretch on too long and that Brooke was watching her expectantly to continue. She searched her thoughts trying to pick up their previous thread of conversation. "Where...uh, where do you live? I'm trying to figure out what neighborhoods I want to look in." With luck, that sounded genuine.

"Well, *I* live on the Southwest waterfront, in a beautiful high-rise condo with a view of Mt. Hood to kill for. As soon as we get married, I'm going to make Birdy sell that ugly old boat she lives on and move in with me." She put her arm around Birdy's waist and pulled her possessively to her side again.

The entire day had been a roller coaster for Sydney. Starting a new job, learning her way around the shop while handling a massive order. Getting to know Birdy, becoming conscious of the massive crush, finding out Birdy was engaged—*to an asshole troll*. And then seeing her get railroaded by said troll, *who totally checked me out in front of Birdy*.

Sydney wanted to know why she hadn't mentioned she was engaged, why she hadn't mentioned she was taken when Sydney was so blatantly flirting with her. Had she been flirting back like she'd originally thought? Asking her directly was out of the question. This called for the subtle approach, but with a pointed expression that made her meaning clear. "So how come you didn't tell me such an important detail in your life—that you live on a boat?"

"I guess it just never came up...that I live on a boat." Birdy shifted uncomfortably under Brooke's controlling glare. "My boat doesn't actually run very well...and...and I don't know how to fix it."

She wasn't sure if Birdy was talking about more than just the boat, but she was very aware of Brooke glancing back and forth between them.

The morning had gone so smoothly. They had worked together acting like old friends, not strangers who had met only a few days ago. She was worried the ease she felt with Birdy was apparent to Brooke, so she tried to steer the conversation to safer ground instead of thinly-veiled boat-speak. "My friend, Beth, the one I'm staying with, said her uncle works at a marina. I'm not sure if he's a mechanic or not but I could check?"

Birdy's eyes seemed to light up for the first time since Brooke had interrupted their work. "Really? Wow, that would be amazing! Thank you."

The soft sincerity in her voice and the way the left corner of her mouth pulled gently back into a small, private smile caught Sydney off guard. She took a quick breath, trying to regain her equilibrium. Suddenly the safer ground she had searched for felt more like quicksand.

She tried to compose herself and glanced at Brooke, who, fortunately, was busy adjusting the strap of her purse, pushing it farther up her shoulder.

"I guess if you get it up and running it would be a lot easier to sell," Brooke said. She kissed Birdy roughly on the cheek and then turned to Sydney. "Thanks for the offer. Now, if you'll excuse us, I'm going to steal my fiancée away for lunch." She grabbed Birdy's hand and pulled her along.

As Sydney watched them round the corner, the sinking feeling continued to grow. Yep, this was definitely a quicksand situation.

CHAPTER EIGHT

Birdy arrived to work early again on Tuesday, feeling none of the excitement she had felt the morning before. She was exhausted and sore from the previous night. They had slaved away until after midnight, deciding to leave the folding and boxing for the morning. As she dragged herself inside, she found Sydney already working through piles of shirts. Three boxes had been filled and stacked. Only eleven more to go, Birdy thought mournfully.

She and Sydney had not exactly picked up where they left off after lunch. Birdy had felt a wall between them that hadn't been there that morning, despite Sydney's constant smile and good-natured conversation. Selfishly she was hoping today would be different.

"Hi," she said sheepishly.

"Good morning," Sydney said, barely looking up from the shirts she was counting.

"Listen, about yesterday. I'm sorry things got weird after lunch." She absently picked at a loose thread on one of the shirts laid out on the folding table. "I don't even know why it got weird."

"It's okay." Sydney turned back to the shirts she was stacking. When the stack reached ten, she folded them together into a bundle.

Birdy picked up more and began separating them by size. Despite Sydney's apparent sincerity, she didn't feel like anything had been resolved. Empty words had merely been tossed around.

Nervously she continued, "I think it got weird because I didn't tell you that I'm engaged. I don't know why but I didn't and then things felt different."

The only response was more counting, stacking and folding.

"Were you flirting with me?" she finally blurted out. "I mean, before. Before Brooke came in, before the engagement ring thing. Before things got weird." She blundered through the question, alarmed by the hopefulness in her tone.

Stopping at six, Sydney marked her place in the shirts with her finger.

"I'm sorry," Birdy quickly added. "I don't just normally assume every lesbian I meet is flirting with me. I actually assume that *no* lesbian I meet is flirting with me, so I don't know why I would assume that *you* were. Were you?" She hesitated as Sydney opened her mouth to respond, but then rushed forward. "Of course you weren't. This is really embarrassing. I'm imagining things and I've just made everything way weirder than it was. I'll shut up now."

And she did, re-counting the stack of medium shirts she had already counted twice before. She could feel her face flaming and couldn't bring herself to look at Sydney to gauge her reaction.

Resting her elbows on the table, Sydney leaned toward her. "I was flirting with you."

Birdy's jaw dropped. She risked a quick glance at Sydney. The intensity with which Sydney was staring at her caused her to avert her eyes just as quickly, and she began counting the stack of shirts again.

Stretching across the table, Sydney rested her hand in the middle of Birdy's stack of shirts. "There's still ten there, just like the last two times you counted it."

Birdy gave up on the pile and reluctantly made eye contact, surprised to find Sydney smiling. "Was I flirting back?"

"I had hoped so, but I think that was just wishful thinking on my part."

Even though Birdy disagreed, she wasn't in a position to counter the opinion. After several false starts, she settled on, "I don't know what to say." The banality of her statement left her feeling frustrated.

Sydney withdrew and started moving the bundles of shirts into boxes. "That's the beauty of it. You don't have to say anything. I thought about it a lot last night and I decided I shouldn't let this silly little crush I have on you get in the way. I really like you, and I'd like to get to know you better and be your friend. And"—she broke into an unexpected smile—"I'll try not to hold it against you that you have a fiancée."

Birdy was still speechless. Sydney had a crush on her? Why was that information making her feel so good? "Wow."

"So, do you think you can forgive my sullen mood yesterday and we can go back to being friends?"

"You were hardly sullen, but yes, I'd like that."

"Good. Because Mare called me again late last night."

"Oh, no! No way. I am not printing another two thousand shirts. Get another sucker to do it, because now that I know how horrible it is, I am never helping you print anything again."

After holding a straight face long enough to make Birdy really worry, Sydney then broke out into a loud, beautiful laugh and Birdy joined in despite herself.

"Actually, what Mare called about was to say Diane apologized again for their mistake. Because we got the order done…well, almost done…she thought we should get a little extra something to make up for our troubles. So, she offered up a couple tickets to the beer fest on Saturday."

"Well, that's nice and all but that's like, what? Thirty bucks. Someone should have made Diane print those shirts for seventeen hours. Get it together, Diane!"

"That's what I told Mare you'd say. After your thorough demonstration yesterday of how much you hate overtime I knew you wouldn't settle for such measly reparations. But don't worry, Diane also threw in two tickets to the sold-out show at the waterfront that night."

"Wait, wait, wait. The Semis show?"

"You know them?"

"Oh, my God, I love them." Giddy at the news, she elaborated, "They're this amazingly weird, electronic indie girl band from Spokane. They broke up a few years ago but they're reuniting for this show. I've wanted to see them for years but then they stopped touring, and I thought I'd never get a chance...which is apparently what everyone else thought because this show sold out in, like, a day." Almost jumping with excitement, her words tumbled out. "This makes yesterday totally worth it. God, I love Diane. Diane's got her shit together. That's what I've always said."

"We each only get one ticket. You should take mine since I've never even heard of them before. It would be wasted on me."

"No, I couldn't do that. You worked your ass off. You can't turn down your reparation!"

"Take Brooke. You guys can enjoy it together."

"That's really sweet of you but I insist you keep it. You earned it. Or you could sell it if you really don't want to go."

"And turn down my only chance to see an amazingly weird indie girl band? You make it sound like something I would be stupid to miss."

"The stupidest," Birdy chided.

"All right. I'm in."

"Do you want to meet up there? Maybe go to the beer fest first and then the show?"

"A friend date?" Sydney asked, making it sound like something their parents had arranged.

"Yeah. Get to know each other better, hang out, you not hold it against me that I have a fiancée? That kind of friend date."

"I'd like that."

"Holy crap, we're seeing the Semis! I'm so excited." Birdy threw her arms around Sydney's neck. "This is awesome."

Sydney slowly, as if reluctantly, reached up and hugged her back.

The warmth of her hands, the feel of their bodies pressed up against each other only elevated Birdy's excitement. Except this particular kind of excitement made her dizzy enthusiasm about the concert feel childlike. Nothing about this new exhilaration felt innocent.

* * *

Diane, you're the best. Sydney mentally high-fived the mythical event coordinator. She was blissfully aware of the way Birdy leaned ever so slightly into her embrace, pulling her closer. She knew it meant nothing, that it was probably done innocently, but it felt too good. She had to give herself space, so she stepped back, giving Birdy's shoulder a small squeeze. The entire encounter couldn't have lasted more than a few seconds but the contact had a lasting and profound effect on Sydney. She moved to the other side of the table, hoping to put a safe distance between them, but the warmth of Birdy's body against her own still lingered. The physical separation apparently wasn't enough to get back to safe footing so she cleared her throat and said, "Also last night, I was thinking about your wedding and…" Her words were like the emotional equivalent of taking a cold shower.

"Oh, God. Really, I am so, so sorry about that." Birdy covered her face in embarrassment. With her hands still pulling on her cheeks, she made her wide brown eyes seem even bigger. *And more adorable.* "I'm sorry that conversation was so awkward with Brooke yesterday. I was just so mad at her for booking a venue and date without consulting me and she wants to get everything done in six months. I'm sorry you had to witness that. Brooke is great. Really. She just comes off a little strong at times."

Sydney forced herself not to roll her eyes at Birdy's carefully crafted statement. *In other words,* Sydney thought, *she's a bully.*

But instead of voicing her inner monologue, she picked a more diplomatic approach. "It's fine. I hardly noticed." She mentally congratulated herself for keeping the sarcasm out of her voice. "I think I might be able to help you with your time crunch. What I was thinking is that I could print the invitations here. You could design something and then we could make them together. It would save a lot of time and a ton of money."

"That would be amazing. Are you sure you wouldn't mind?"

"No, of course not. It would be fun." It would also be torture.

Birdy seemed to hesitate.

"I'm sorry. If it's a stupid idea you can say no. I was just trying to think of a way to help you."

"No, I love the idea. They would be so personal and intimate. Syd, thank you. That is really sweet of you. You're a lifesaver."

She felt a small touch on her elbow before Birdy quickly drew her hand away. Refusing to think about her motives for offering her services, she instead focused on the soft glow of heat emanating from her skin where Birdy had touched her.

CHAPTER NINE

The rest of the week flew by as Birdy scrambled to catch up on the work she had neglected on Monday and Tuesday. There were deadlines to meet and consultations with new clients to arrange so she hadn't had much of a chance to talk to Sydney since they finished boxing the last of the rush order. Every time she thought of Sydney there was a twinge in her stomach that she refused to acknowledge. It was a bad habit, she knew, but she had taken to staring through the window that separated the office and the shop area, hoping to catch a glimpse of Sydney working. Convincing herself it was nothing but a totally normal way to feel about a new platonic friend had been easy, as she had no interest in examining the flipping or the flopping of her abdominal region.

Sydney walked into the office, stopping just inside the doorway. She was wearing a loose, vintage Nike tank top and tight, fraying jean shorts that hugged her thighs perfectly and stopped just above her knees. A T-shirt was draped around her neck and she lightly grasped each end of the shirt, rolling her head as if working out the tension in her neck.

Birdy's heart quickened with excitement. Her eyes locked onto Sydney's chest, exposed as she leaned back to stretch. Suddenly, she was excruciatingly aware of the pulsing between her legs. She should not be looking at another woman like this and she certainly shouldn't be *feeling* things. Hot, throbbing things.

With a final roll of her head, Sydney strolled toward her desk. "Hey, Bird. I've barely gotten to see you the past three days. We're still on for tomorrow, right?"

She swooned at the nickname, hardly managing a nod.

"Oh, what did Brooke think of the idea to print the invitations ourselves?"

"I actually think I'm going to surprise her."

"As soon as the shop slows down a little bit, we'll print them. Maybe in a couple weeks if your design is ready." At Birdy's nod, she continued, "So, tomorrow, I'll meet you by the front gate at three for the beer fest." With a wink, she sauntered away, leaving Birdy to wonder if her torturous displays of sensuality were intentional or just something she couldn't help.

Totally platonic. Keep telling yourself that, Birdy.

* * *

Birdy stood in the middle of the dusty grounds, searching for Sydney. Surrounding her were dozens of white tents sheltering a huge crowd of beer drinkers from the hot summer sun. She had invited Brooke to the beer fest but wasn't surprised by her casual dismissal. She had been spending her weekends training for a triathlon, a hobby the two of them certainly did not share.

Despite her confidence and swagger, Brooke had a streak of possessiveness in her, and if there was ever a woman who could incite jealousy, it would have been Sydney. But when she nonchalantly mentioned she was attending the beer fest with her new co-worker, Brooke's reaction shocked her. Instead of the possessiveness Birdy had feared, she had seemed thrilled. It was actually in keeping with her encouragement for Birdy to be more social, to make more friends, probably hoping one of them would dethrone Saul as her best friend.

Brooke's flippant reaction had set off a battle of emotions inside Birdy. In one corner was relief, almost as if she'd been given permission to spend more time with Sydney. In the other corner was guilt over the butterflies she felt in her stomach every time she saw Sydney. Was butterfly repellent a thing? If so, she would invest in gallons.

She saw Sydney at the gate and as if on cue, the butterflies took flight.

Birdy called out to her. "I don't know how you can stand it."

"What?"

"Seeing all of these goddamn shirts we printed." Birdy gestured at the hordes of people at the beer fest, most of whom were wearing the yellow shirts that she still saw spinning in front of her every four and a half seconds when she closed her eyes.

"I don't know. It kind of makes me proud that we made all of these."

"I used to feel that way. When I would create a design and then see someone wearing it on the street I would always think, 'Hey, I designed that!' But now, after slaving away over these shirts for seventeen straight hours, not counting the time to design them and box them up, I've decided I never want to see this horrible shirt again. I may never even wear yellow again."

Sydney's amused grin was contagious.

"I actually feel exactly the same way, Bird. I kind of hate these horrible yellow shirts. I mean, I've touched every single one of these shirts at least four times," Sydney said, spreading out her hands to show the calluses on her palms. Gritting her teeth, she continued, "I missed dinner for these shirts. I lost sleep over these shirts. I think I might actually hate these stupid shirts."

"Wow."

"Yeah. I had no idea I felt that passionately about it," Sydney said, laughing at herself.

"Your thinly-veiled T-shirt rage is actually pretty hot." The moment the words left her lips, Birdy felt her color rise. *Why did I just say that?*

"You think I'm hot, huh?" Sydney said with a devilish grin.

Birdy stammered, "I… uh…" She saw Sydney's mischievous grin and punched her in the arm. "Oh, shut up and go get me a beer, woman."

Sydney wiggled her eyebrows suggestively. "Let's go together. I'll let you off the hook for that comment. It must just be the heat because you look pretty hot too." Sydney winked and then turned away, making Birdy follow her. "Okay, so tell me how this works. I've never been to a beer fest before."

"Not much of a craft beer scene in Austin?"

"Oh, I'm sure there is. I just never explored it. For me, trying something new meant Bud Light Lime instead of my usual Bud Light. I have a lot to learn. I doubt I've tried any of these beers."

"Okay, novice. Here's how it works. You take your cup around to the different booths and you can buy a taste of their beer for a token or a whole glass for four tokens. I suggest only getting tastes. All the taps are run by volunteers and most will give you a generous pour, so you'll get more beer for your money with tastes usually."

"Got it. Tastes, not pints."

"Next, you have to plan your day properly. We didn't get here first thing this morning, so the really popular beers might already be running out. This would be a good time to consult our programs and make notes about what we definitely want to try. We have twenty tokens each to start with so we can potentially try twenty different beers, forty if we share them." Birdy handed her a pink highlighter. "Here, take this."

Sydney smirked. "You brought highlighters to a beer fest?"

"It's the optimal way to efficiently experience the festival. Personally, I have two categories. Beers I absolutely must try and beers I would like to try if I have time, tokens and sufficient sobriety. My bar is set pretty low on that third one."

"This seems like it could get sloppy."

"That's the marker of a good beer fest. I'll use this yellow highlighter for my must-haves and your pink one for the others and then we can switch. I also brought a pen so we can make notes in the programs about which ones we liked and why."

Sydney quickly flipped through several pages of the exhaustive program. "You're serious about all of this?"

"Is it too much?"

"No," Sydney said seriously. "It's perfect."

* * *

Two hours later they were standing in the longest line yet as it slowly snaked toward the kegs.

"Okay," Sydney said, studying Birdy's creased and marked program. "So this is a yellow highlighter beer which makes it a must-have. Why do you want to try this one?"

"Well, actually I've had this one before. A brewery just on the other side of the river makes it," Birdy said, pointing across the Willamette. "It's possibly my favorite brewery and this is possibly my all-time favorite beer."

"So if you've had it before why are we waiting in this massive line?"

"We're waiting because I want you to try it. We've established that you like fruit beers and this one is an apricot beer brewed with Scotch bonnet peppers. I think you're really going to like it. The pepper gives it a real kick when you get it on tap like this. That should appeal to you, Tex. If you get it bottled, it tends to mellow out, so this is the best way to have it."

Sydney liked that Birdy was thinking about her, leading her from booth to booth all day to find beers she thought she would like. They had focused their efforts on fruit beers, since Sydney had loved the first, an organic blueberry beer from the Oregon coast. The ambers and pale ales were good but she was having trouble appreciating the bitterness of India pale ales, which were Birdy's favorites.

"You get used to them," Birdy had said. "They're definitely an acquired taste, but now that you're on the West Coast, you're going to have access to some of the best and most bitter IPAs in the country."

"I thought bitterness in beer was a bad thing. You know those commercials where the hot guy drinks a bitter beer and his face contorts until his lower lip is up to his nose and all the hot chicks run away from him? I don't want that to happen to me. I'd prefer you not run away when my face does this." Sydney tried to simulate the commercial's bitter beer-faced man.

"That wouldn't make anyone run away. You look way too cute." Birdy continued on quickly as if trying to draw attention away from her comment. "Anyway, bitterness in beer is more like a point of pride now with craft brewers. They've redefined what 'real men' drink. They've made it very uncool to drink fizzy, yellow beer, so now you're a real 'man' if you drink beer loaded with hops, flavor and huge alcohol levels. That's why we're buzzed already. Almost all these beers are well over five percent alcohol."

As they slowly progressed through the line, Sydney realized she indeed was feeling buzzed, which only made her want to continue their casual flirting. A friendship, however, was the only thing on the table currently and she knew it was that or nothing. Time to get this friendship rolling, she decided.

The alcohol gave her the courage to broach the subject she was most scared to talk about, but one she knew they needed to get out in the open.

"Tell me about Brooke."

"We don't need to talk about her. I'm sure that's the last thing you want to do."

"Why would you think that? We've already acknowledged this pesky little crush I have on you and we've decided to be friends, right? Friends talk about their relationships. So I decided if we're going to be friends, I need to man up, drink an IPA and talk to you about what's important in your life."

Birdy nodded, albeit with obvious hesitation.

"Good. Start at the beginning. How did you meet?"

"We met where all the great, timeless couples must have met—a queer dance party called Blow Pony," she deadpanned.

Sydney paused, not sure she had heard right. "There's a gay dance called Blow Pony?"

"Yep. It happens once a month at a bar in Southeast Portland."

"So Fred and Ginger met at Blow Pony?"

"Yep," Birdy replied, nodding authoritatively.

"And Johnny and June?"

"Blow Pony."

"Ellen and Portia?"

"Do I even have to answer that?"

Sydney laughed, enjoying Birdy's sense of humor. "Okay, so you and Brooke met at Blow Pony. Who picked up who?"

"She picked me up. I was dancing with some friends and she just walked right up to me and asked me to dance."

"And you said yes and here we are today, huh? Happily ever after?"

"Not exactly. I turned her down. I just wasn't that interested. I thought she was extremely hot, but I found her to be rather arrogant and pushy."

No kidding. Sydney was always one to give credit where credit was due, and she could attest to how attractive and charming Brooke was, engaging even. But something about her set Sydney on edge. Arrogance, pushiness. It appeared she and Birdy had the same first impression.

"She kept buying me drinks and asking me to dance. By one a.m. I was drunk enough to join her on the dance floor. She was sexy and we actually had a lot of physical chemistry, but I wanted to take it slow. I wanted to actually date around, you know?"

"That's understandable," she said, nodding. Though she wasn't actually interested in being understanding when it came to Brooke.

"Back when I was in college, I was a stereotypical U-Haul lesbian. I moved in with the first girl I dated. After that, I just kind of wanted to play the field. But with Brooke, there's really no taking it slow. She's persistent and persuasive. Next thing I knew we were five dates in and sleeping in the same bed every night. I have, however, held onto my own home. I refused to be a U-Haul lesbian again, giving up my life and home for someone else."

"So what's changed? Why sell your boat now?"

"We're getting married. If there's ever a time to rent a U-Haul, I think it's now."

"But it's a boat. It's not like you're keeping a bachelor pad downtown. You can still have it without it being your home." Sydney didn't dare express her inner monologue, which was currently in full-on snarky mode. It was frustrating that Birdy didn't seem to stand up to Brooke. Aware that she didn't know the intricacies of their relationship, her frustration was on Birdy's behalf, and admittedly with Birdy herself. She had a feeling Birdy's unwillingness to assert herself to Brooke would be an ongoing cause of friction in their friendship if they continued to grow closer.

"I've thought about it but Brooke just doesn't like it. Boats take a ton of time and money. I spend most of my weekends working on it and that's not something she's interested in. Plus, she just doesn't appreciate it like I do."

Sydney expected some bitterness in Birdy's tone but was instead surprised to detect what sounded more like resignation.

"She's incapable of sitting on the deck, watching the sun move across the sky. She'd rather go to a movie or go shopping. To her there's no point of having a boat unless it's fast enough to pull someone on skis. She wants me to get rid of it so we can live a polished, perfect life in the high-rise condo."

Aha! A hint of bitterness detected. "Not a fan of your future home, huh?"

"It's just so…beige and…*clean.*" Birdy laughed sardonically. "I know that sounds ridiculous. It's just that it's too soulless. Don't get me wrong. I love the amenities. I would kill for a washer and dryer on the boat, and a gourmet kitchen. But while I enjoy those things, I need a place with character, something original and different. Something that feels like it's alive and has lived and seen and heard enough for a lifetime, well before I ever came along."

They had finally reached the front of the long line and Sydney took Birdy's cup. The white plastic tables stretched in front of dozens of taps that were built into the sides of refrigerated semitrailers. She handed their cups to the volunteer behind the table and started counting out their tokens. "I know exactly what you mean. I think this calls for a full pour rather than a taste."

Expertly, she cradled both of their cups in one hand and led Birdy away from the line with a light touch on the small of her back.

* * *

The contact gave Birdy chills, despite the sweltering heat.

"I have a lot more questions about Brooke you know," Sydney said when she had steered them away from the worst of the crowd.

Birdy made a face to show her discomfort.

Undeterred, Sydney chuckled softly and said, "Trust me, this topic is much more uncomfortable for me than it is for you."

"You're right. What do you want to know?"

"Where is she? I thought she might come along. She doesn't like beer fests?"

"She does, though she's more of a wine drinker. She's training for a triathlon right now with a friend from the gym. I think they're doing thirty miles on the bike today. Probably running too."

Sydney let out a low whistle. "Wow, that's really impressive. Do you run?"

Birdy couldn't hold back her derisive snort. "God, no."

"Bike?"

"Not really."

"So what do you do? I know you like to hike. And obviously you like beer."

"Well, beer can take up a surprising amount of your time if you devote yourself to the hobby appropriately. I like to read. I read most evenings when I get home from work. I work on my boat. What about you?"

"I run."

In response, Birdy stuck a finger in her mouth and made a gagging sound.

Sydney chucked her shoulder playfully. "And I like to build things, fix things. I have a tool belt."

"Those are magic words to a girl with a broken boat."

After a moment of hesitation Sydney asked, "Seriously, Brooke doesn't mind that you're here with me?"

"Why should she? We're just friends," she said, wagging her finger between the two of them. "Let's not talk about her anymore."

"All right. Let's sit over there under that tree in companionable silence and just enjoy our day without any more talk of fiancées or crushes. How's that sound?"

Birdy held her drink up, toasting Sydney. "It sounds like blissful avoidance and I can definitely drink to that."

* * *

Several hours and twenty beer samples later, the sun was setting behind the city's tallest buildings, which cast long shadows that didn't quite reach the opposite bank of the river. Sydney was very much drunk and having the most fun she'd had since arriving in Portland. From a bench on the edge of the festival grounds, she watched Birdy walk toward her, holding something behind her back.

"You look a little smashed," she said as Birdy clumsily sat next to her.

"You seem pretty tossed yourself."

"Yes, yes I believe I am. What are you hiding there?"

"I got you something."

"Really? What is it?" Birdy lobbed something at her that she caught without her usual deftness just before it hit her face. Holding it out, she let the fabric unfurl. The bright yellow T-shirt said, "Portland Beer Fest."

"This is the ugliest thing I have ever seen."

"That's why I got one for myself too. A couple of ugly shirts to remember a really wonderful day."

Tugging the shirt over her head, Sydney silently agreed that it had been a perfect day.

"Hey, Syd. I really hate your shirt."

* * *

Sydney was positive she had never seen a weirder or more spectacular sight. "Is she wearing a dress made out of tampons?"

"Yes! Isn't it amazing?" Birdy was staring up at the Semis adoringly, jumping and dancing to their music.

The lead singer indeed was wearing a white dress with tampons sewn and draped from shoulder to hem. Only in Portland, Sydney thought, and she too danced along to the energetic beat.

As Birdy sang along, they both swayed with the music, with Sydney acutely aware of their arms brushing together. She stilled, feeling the contact more firmly. Not wanting to push this electric current between them too far—which might cause Birdy to break away from it—she settled instead for the occasional bump of shoulders or knock of elbows, wishing so badly she could hold Birdy against her, to feel the length of their bodies mold together.

As if Sydney's thoughts had scared her, Birdy stepped away, leaving a rift between them that felt enormous.

Her drunk and desperate heart dropped. She knew she couldn't have Birdy, but God, she wanted her. Just as she felt the elation of the day start to slip away, leaving her empty, she rejoiced at the touch of Birdy's hand on her elbow guiding her back again. With a sudden swell the crowd pushed and pulled, rushing the stage, shoving them together forcefully. Her hand fell to Birdy's hip and gripped tightly to keep them from being separated by the dancing, thrashing crowd.

She distantly registered that the song had changed. The audience was going crazy for it but she couldn't even begin to listen to the music. Instead, everything sounded like it was at the other end of a long tunnel. She heard the band, but all she felt was Birdy's hips pressed hard against her own. While she sensed the crowd shifting against their backs, she could only think about the motion of her hands as they slid along Birdy's waist. The energy of the audience filled her, but only because it throbbed in her neck where Birdy's face was pressed against her pulse. Though lost, she had never felt more alive.

Birdy looked up and caught her staring. Both were breathing hard and not even pretending to dance or sway with the music. Sydney's gaze dropped to her lips and she thought she heard Birdy moan. She wanted those lips, she needed those lips against her own. Any thoughts of Brooke, of Birdy's engagement had been swept away by the crowd, the lights, the energy and the alcohol.

She saw the passion smoldering in Birdy's eyes and she was sure they were mirroring her own intense desire. The pressure of the crowd relaxed a bit, no longer pushing them from every direction.

Surely Birdy had noticed too, but instead of stepping away, she slid her hand up Sydney's arm, brushing along her shoulder and neck, her fingers entwining with Sydney's hair as she cupped the back of her head.

Sydney's hold on her hips tightened, pressing their stomachs and thighs more tightly together. Their breasts touched, nipples straining against their shirts. Her lips parted and she ducked her head, searching for Birdy's mouth.

Birdy grunted and her eyes widened. She was shoved roughly into Sydney as a body crashed into her from behind.

Sydney instinctively wrapped her in a bear hug and spun her away from the crowd, which had transformed into a mosh pit. Bodies threw themselves into each other as the music gained momentum. Pushing through with her elbows out, she hoped to form a buffer around them.

Everything that had once seemed at the end of a very long tunnel came rushing back. The lights, music and movement all suddenly felt very close and overwhelming. She scanned the crowd, hoping to find a path away from the aggressive, intoxicated fans. As she searched for an exit, a blinding white light flashed and her cheek felt like it had been split open. A tall, wasted teenager was flailing to the music, all elbows as he slammed into the people around him.

"Oh shit." Cupping Sydney's jaw gently, Birdy leaned into Sydney's ear and yelled, "Follow me."

Birdy grabbed her hand, entwining their fingers as she pushed through the crowd. Without speaking, they walked away from the waterfront until the music was only a distant *thump-thump*. Under a streetlamp, she tilted Sydney's chin again and frowned.

"That bad, huh?" Sydney asked.

"You're definitely going to have a shiner." She gently touched the inflamed skin. "Does that hurt?"

Sydney reached up to hold her hand in place. Her breath hitched to see Birdy's flicker of passion, which dissipated when she seemed to regain her composure. "You sure pack a mean punch, Bird."

"That's what you get when you look at an engaged woman like you're going to kiss her."

"I don't think I was the only one doing the looking." She stared at Birdy intensely, lightly rubbing the back of her hand as she held it against her face.

Clearing her throat, Birdy freed her hand and shoved it in her pocket. "Yeah, well we're both drunk," she said, suddenly sounding very sober.

CHAPTER TEN

It wasn't their usual table at Shmulsky & Stein, but Birdy and Saul had managed to claim a spot at the end of a communal picnic table. The sandwich shop was lacking its relaxed workday vibe, reminding Birdy why she didn't usually come here on the weekend. Saul had already given the stink eye to the fanny-packed tourists who were occupying their regular table.

"I thought maybe this time you really wouldn't forgive me."

Birdy sighed. "I'll always forgive you, Saul. You're my oldest friend. You and Mare are pretty much all I've got."

"Mare, who you *still* haven't set me up with, you know," Saul whined.

Birdy rolled her eyes and continued, "Need I remind you that she's my boss?"

"So?"

"So if my two best friends date, where does that leave me?"

"I get it. You're worried you're going to be a third wheel?"

"Exactly. I'll be on the outside looking in on you two lovebirds."

"Are you saying you want to watch? I don't know, Birdy. That could get weird."

She kicked him under the table as he giggled gleefully at his own joke.

"You're a complete jackass but it turns out you're my favorite jackass." She smiled despite herself at his goofy grin, before he grew serious again.

"I thought maybe I had crossed the line with the engagement stuff. You know, harping on the way she asked you…even though she did do a shitty job of it."

Birdy didn't hide her sigh of exasperation.

"Okay, anyway, that's not the point, that she totally fucked up the proposal, which she did totally fuck up, mind you. The point is that when you didn't call me for a couple weeks, I thought maybe I had gone too far, said some of that stuff one too many times. And while I still totally stand behind it, I realized it's not worth pushing you away just because of her and my complete and pure hatred of her."

She raised her eyebrows pointedly to remind him who his audience was.

Taking the hint, Saul continued, "So, yeah, I'm sorry, and I'm really glad you texted me. What's going on? You seem to have something else on your mind."

She had typed out a message to Saul this morning asking to meet for lunch, something she had never done on a Sunday before. That had meant skipping out on brunch with Bea, since she was worried the guilt over her near-kiss last night would be all too obvious to her perceptive mother. A lunch date on a weekend was highly unusual and had obviously piqued Saul's interest. She had hesitated only a moment that morning before hitting send on the text after reliving, again, the events of the night before with Sydney. While he was certainly not an unbiased observer of her life—he had plenty of biases and they all were directed against Brooke—he was without rival her biggest supporter and confidante. He knew about every misdeed and sexual conquest, failed or otherwise. While she would rather deny the building heat between her and Sydney, she knew she had to confess her sins to someone, and who better than her best friend?

"I think I cheated on Brooke last night," she finally blurted, burying her face to cover her misery.

Saul slowly returned his soda to the table. "Say that again."

"I think I cheated on Brooke last night."

"That's what I thought I heard." After a slight pause he continued, "I never imagined I would hear you say that, but if I had imagined it, I think I would have also imagined standing and cheering, maybe marching around the table to my high school's fight song while banging an imaginary bass drum in beat to my high step, but something is stopping me, keeping my ass firmly in this horribly uncomfortable metal chair, and I *think* that something is the fact that you *think* you cheated on Brooke. I mean either someone was in your vagina or they weren't, or I suppose you could have been in theirs, but either way, how do you only *think* you cheated on Brooke?"

"I was not in someone's vagina!" she huffed. And at his triumphant expression, she added, "And no one was in mine. Jesus, Saul."

"Then you didn't cheat."

"That's a limited view."

"Okay, so maybe a tad oversimplified. Tell me what happened."

"There's this girl…"

"I assumed."

"Shut up. There's this girl and she almost kissed me."

"Well, that sounds like a fun night out. What'd you do?"

"I almost kissed her back."

He sat back in his chair, a bit more smugly than she would have liked. "What's her name?"

"Sydney." She couldn't help the way her chest tightened when she said it. Nor the goose bumps on her legs, which she hoped he didn't notice.

"Do you have a crush on her?"

"I'm getting married, Saul! Of course I don't have a crush on her. But I have to work with her and see her a lot, and I think she might have a crush on me."

"But it's totally one-sided, right? You feel absolutely nothing for her?"

"Absolutely nothing."

"Then you didn't cheat. Personally, I wish you had." Saul batted away the napkin she threw, smiling as he continued, "She's not the first one to have a crush on you, Birdy. It will take a while but she'll get over you, just like the rest of us."

"That was middle school, Saul."

"And I thought my eighth grade heart would never recover, but it did and we even managed to maintain a friendship throughout. I see no reason why you and Sydney can't do the same. And it will be especially easy since you feel absolutely nothing for her."

She gave a quick nod. "Right, we can be friends. There's no reason I can't still see her. You know, from time to time. Hang out."

"Nope, no reason at all. Friends."

There was no reason to question Saul's motives, nor her own. After all, she felt absolutely nothing for Sydney. Nothing at all. Easy.

CHAPTER ELEVEN

Sydney arrived at work on Monday and found Mare in the office chatting with Birdy.

"Hey, Sydney! I was just telling Birdy about my Vegas trip and now she's trying to set me up on a date."

She gave Birdy a small smile, feeling the pain in her cheek that hadn't subsided much since Saturday night. "Hey," she said quietly.

"Hey, you," Birdy said back, just above a whisper.

Mare smiled at them, oblivious to the intimacy in their voices.

"How's your eye?"

Mare studied Sydney's face. "Oh, my God! What happened?"

"Birdy decked me."

"What? Why on earth would you hit her?"

"I didn't hit her, Mare. She was joking. We went to the Semis show you got us tickets for. Thank you by the way, and we got caught in a mosh pit. Sydney protected me," Birdy said, uncharacteristically gushing at Sydney who felt the part of her face that wasn't already black and blue turn red. Finishing dryly, Birdy added, "And then she got elbowed in the face."

"By the way," Sydney interjected, "I talked to my friend Beth last night and her uncle is a mechanic at the marina. She called him and he said he could come take a look at your boat on Saturday. Do you want me to set it up?"

Mare squealed and clapped excitedly. "You're finally fixing your boat! Thank God. I can't wait till we can take it out. Maybe watch the Fourth of July fireworks while drifting on the Willamette River."

"I'm fixing it so I can sell it, Mare. I'm not going to need it when Brooke and I are married."

"Oh, Birdy, don't sell it! You love that boat. First you tell me you're engaged via a text message while I'm in Vegas and now you're going to sell your home? I don't know. I don't feel good about this."

Seemingly ignoring Mare's pleas, Birdy addressed Sydney. "Thank you for checking with your friend. Saturday would be great." Then she turned back to Mare, whose pale cheeks were flushed, matching her wild auburn hair. "Thank you for your concern but you sound exactly like Saul, which brings me back to our initial conversation. This weekend. I think you two should go out."

"On a date?"

"On a date."

"You guys would be adorable together."

"I don't know, Birdy. I know this isn't exactly a blind date but I'm scared it's going to be awkward. What if we don't have anything to talk about?"

"Saul has been begging me to set you up with him over a year. Do it for me?"

"Okay, fine. I'll do it for you but only if you promise to do something for me." Mare paused to make sure she had Birdy's full attention. "Promise me you will at least consider keeping your boat even though Brooke wants you to get rid of it. It doesn't have to be one or the other. You can have both."

"Yeah, I'll think about it," she said though she didn't actually sound like she would. Turning her attention to her computer screen, Birdy put on her headphones and went back to work on a design.

"Or she could just keep the boat," Sydney said quietly to Mare with an innocent shrug.

Mare nodded. "I like that idea even better."

* * *

Saturday morning, Sydney drove her old green Jeep out to Sauvie Island where Birdy lived. She wasn't due for another hour but she wanted time to drive around the small island. The late July day was beautiful and hot so she pulled onto the gravel shoulder to roll down the soft top of the Wrangler. The road followed the riverbank mostly, occasionally curling inland past farms, orchards and berry patches that populated the rural area. Stopping at a farmers' market, she picked up organic strawberries and marionberries to share with Birdy for lunch and then slowly looped her way back toward Birdy's place, enjoying the beautiful summer day.

When she reached the address, she was surprised to find a cute and tidy farmhouse tucked behind a row of pine trees. She had expected Birdy to live at a marina but instead of pavement and parking lots, she found a shaded gravel driveway that she slowly followed as it curved behind the house. The woods opened up and Sydney suddenly had a breathtaking view of the Multnomah Channel. The drive led to the shore, where she parked next to Birdy's car before walking the long L-shaped dock that hugged the riverbank and then jutted out into the river. It was secluded, as the tree line blocked the boat from the house. And peaceful. No road noise, no people. Just the birds cawing and the water lapping against the side of the boat.

The dock swayed lightly under her weight and she stood still, taking a moment to appreciate the feel of the current pushing against the rough wood under her feet. With her eyes closed and her face upturned to the hot sun, she reveled in the sensation of the breeze across the back of her neck until a gentle, familiar voice broke her meditation.

"Hey."

Birdy was on the boat deck, leaning against the rail, appearing more relaxed than Sydney had ever seen her.

"Wow. This is beautiful, Bird! I had no idea. I think I envisioned a pontoon boat with green outdoor carpet on the deck or something. Your boat is amazing,"

Birdy grinned at the compliment. "Thank you. Fifty-seven Chris-Craft Constellation. Thirty-eight feet."

Sydney took a moment to admire the boat. The hull was a glossy black that perfectly accented the beautifully finished red teak deck. The sleek, two-tiered cabin that sheltered the living quarters and pilothouse was a brilliant white. Everything about this boat was warm and inviting. Sydney had been landlocked her entire life, she had never set foot on a boat larger than a kayak, but she knew looking at this beauty that it was magnificent. "Birdy, I'm stunned."

Birdy grinned shyly, clearly basking in the praise.

Walking the length of the boat, Sydney took it all in, rubbing her hand along the smooth, black surface. "This isn't fiberglass is it?"

"No, wood."

"You're kidding? I don't know much about boats but aren't wooden boats a ton of work?"

"Well, yes. They can be. I was lucky with this one. It mostly just needed cosmetic work...other than the engine, of course. I've always loved wooden boats but I was prepared to be practical and get a fiberglass one. I was doing a lot of research, going to marinas, looking at 'boat porn' as I called it, and I met this old guy that was out working on his wood boat. I asked him the same thing you just asked me and his response was, 'They do take more work...but then so do pretty girls. And who would you rather be seen about town with?'" With a wink, she added, "That was the day I stopped considering fiberglass boats."

"Smart old guy."

She continued to walk the dock, slowly dragging her fingertips along the hull. When she reached the stern, she laughed aloud.

Leaning over the rail, Birdy peered at her inquisitively. "What?"

"*The Bird's Nest*. That's such a great name for your boat. I love it."

Birdy blushed at the compliment. "Thanks. Now, come aboard so you can see the green indoor/outdoor carpeting I had installed on this old pontoon." She reached down to help Sydney maneuver the small ladder.

"Yeah, right," Sydney snorted. "There's no way you would allow that stuff on this gorgeous boat," she said, gazing at the vessel admiringly one more time. "I brought berries and white wine for our lunch. How's that sound?"

"Wonderful."

She passed off the wine, "You do have a refrigerator on this thing, right?"

Birdy gasped, seemingly offended by the question. "Of course. This is the twenty-first century, isn't it? It's in the basement."

It took Sydney a second longer than it should have for the joke to register. "Basement?"

An impish grin grew on Birdy's face. "Busted. No basement. The fridge is in the galley." At Sydney's confused expression she clarified, "The kitchen. A galley is a kitchen."

"I didn't even know boats could have kitchens."

"Did you think I lived on a rowboat this whole time?"

Before Sydney could respond, the sound of crunching gravel caught her attention and she saw a truck parking at the end of the driveway. "Must be Uncle Al. I'll go meet him and bring him up."

"Good, I'll give you both the grand tour at the same time."

* * *

Two hours later, Al the mechanic left, having given Birdy a list of what needed maintenance and what needed to be replaced. She and Sydney had been crawling in and out of the engine room with him, holding flashlights and making notes. Both were streaked in grease and sweating.

Birdy pulled a couple deck chairs up to the railing at the stern facing the magnificent river and opposite shore. She plopped into the chair next to Sydney and handed her a beer.

Hoots, sensing the work was done for the day, lumbered up to the deck and began mewing at Sydney, who reached down and rubbed his head. "Hey, buddy. Nice to see you out and about." To Birdy, she said, "I thought he'd be under our feet all day checking out the engine. I don't think he's moved off your bed since I got here."

"Hoots loathes work, don't you, buddy? He prefers to stay far away until it's clear things can go back to how they should be, which means he's going to lie around like a pile until someone can pet him or feed him. He's such a man that way." Birdy gazed down adoringly at her cat, who was aggressively rubbing his face on Sydney's shin, claiming her with his scent. *You have good taste, sir. You have very good taste.*

Birdy tried to rein in her thoughts. "Thank you for your help, by the way. I can't get Brooke anywhere near this boat. I tried to get her to come help us today and she suddenly had very pressing errands to run." She paused for a moment, realizing how glad she was that Brooke hadn't wanted to spend the day with her. "It's nice enjoying this old pontoon with someone for once. And thank you for introducing me to Al. He was great. I really owe you one."

"No sweat. It's been fun. And since you brought it up, I know a way you could make it up to me."

"Oh yeah? I guess I walked right into that one. What do you got for me?"

Sydney made a strained face and said, "I'm moving. I found an apartment." At Birdy's playful groan, she rushed on. "I know it's everybody's least favorite thing to do, but I swear I don't have very much stuff." Sydney made a scout's honor hand signal that made Birdy laugh. "And I promise I'll make it fun. And I'll buy you dinner and drinks."

"I guess I do owe you. When does this great resettlement happen?"

"Next weekend. We'll start bright and early Saturday morning." Her cheerful smile only made Birdy groan. "And bring that Volvo station wagon of yours. It'll be way more helpful than those scrawny arms you've got."

Birdy rolled her head toward Sydney with an amused expression. "And you promise dinner? And drinks?"

"Yep."

"Good. I need all the free meals I can get with this list Al just gave me."

"How much is on it?"

"A lot. I was worried I'd have to replace both the engines but he said, even though they have a lot of hours on them, they're in decent condition. It mostly just needs a lot of little fixes. Spark plugs, a new carburetor, new plug wires, oil, filters. Small stuff but the list goes on and on. He said if I go through him rather than the marina, he might be able to give me a bit of a break on labor, which I'm going to need."

Sydney let out a low whistle. "Do you have the money to do it?"

"Technically, yes."

"But?"

"I've been saving it to buy an engagement ring."

A long, awkward silence fell between them.

Sydney abruptly stood and said, her tone perhaps a little too bright, "I'm still hot. Let's take a swim."

Birdy gaped at her incredulously. The shift had caught her off guard but now she was cycling through all the reasons this was a bad idea. Namely that Sydney didn't have a swimsuit which meant...

Sydney started to peel off her clothes. "What? That's the perk of living on the river, right?" Her grease-smudged shirt came off first revealing tight abs and muscular shoulders. Birdy especially liked how her dark ponytail brushed against her shoulder blades as she undressed.

The undressing part was her chief concern but she searched for another argument that would get Sydney back in her clothes and Birdy back on safe ground. She felt guilty enjoying the view so much. "It's going to be freezing! I do have a shower on the boat you know. With hot water."

"I'm sure it will feel great." Kicking off her shoes, Sydney stepped out of her shorts to reveal matching bikini-style underwear.

"Jesus," Birdy moaned, staring at Sydney's gorgeous body. She was like a wet dream come to life.

"I'm going for it." Quickly, she covered the few steps to the end of the boat before Birdy could object more.

She watched the woman dive gracefully into the water, standing at the rail just as Sydney resurfaced.

"Jesus Christ, you were right. It's freezing! But it feels great once you're in. Come on, get in here, Birdy."

Birdy hesitated. "Listen, the thing is…"

"What?"

"Well…I…I can't really swim…very well."

"Birdy, you live on a boat. What do you mean you can't swim?"

"I mean, I can swim. Like I wouldn't jump in and immediately drown but I get a little panicky under water. And I'm not very good at treading water, and…" The smile growing across Sydney's face stopped her excuses. The woman just looked so damn hot with her hair pushed back and water dripping down her nose.

"I'm a good swimmer. I was a lifeguard in college, so I won't let you drown, Bird. Get in here!"

Every bit of Birdy wanted to be in that dirty river with Sydney. She unbuttoned her shirt, happy she'd worn a cute bra with lace on it instead of her usual discolored, shapeless number, and stripped off her cut-off jeans. Without giving herself time to think, she raced to the edge and jumped in, holding her nose as she hit the water. She resurfaced quickly, the cold knocking the air out of her. But she was afloat and right now that was a small victory she was happy to celebrate. With her head above water, she slowly made her way over to Sydney.

"That's quite the doggy-paddle you got there," Sydney said with a smile.

"Shut it," Birdy replied with a small splash aimed at Sydney's face.

Sydney took the cue and sent a much larger splash back her way.

The cold water went into Birdy's eyes and up her nose, causing the familiar panic to creep in. Her hands went to her face to get the water out of her eyes and her feet seemed to stop kicking the way they should. Her head dunked under water but she pulled her face back up, spluttering. She couldn't resist the need to wipe the water from her eyes again, and when her arms stopped treading her face dipped back down under the brown water.

Oh Jesus. Am I seriously drowning right now in front of Sydney? This is really happening? Just get back above water again, Birdy, that's all you have to do. Why are my legs not moving?

Just as she began to really panic, flailing her legs around madly, strong hands grabbed her sides, lifting her head above water. Blindly she reached out, draping her arms around Sydney's neck. Still spluttering and trying to get the water out of her nose and eyes, she wrapped her legs around Sydney's waist tightly and clung to her. While attempting to catch her breath, she felt Sydney's warm body pressed up against her own and her nipples hardened against Sydney's shoulder making her very aware of how little fabric was separating their lower bodies.

As Sydney treaded water, pulling them closer to the dock ladder she could feel Sydney's powerful muscles contracting, her hip lightly grinding between Birdy's opened legs. Losing herself for a moment, Birdy molded her body more tightly around Sydney, which only pulled her center more firmly against Sydney's hip. Big mistake. Lacking control, she moaned softly. Water dripped from Sydney's parted lips and Birdy wanted nothing more than to lick the droplets away.

"Fuck," Sydney groaned hoarsely. She reached out a little wildly, grabbing hold of the ladder. Her eyes fell from Birdy's gaze to her mouth and Birdy felt a hand tighten its grip on her waist, holding her even more securely against the strong, hard hip still powerfully stroking through the water. She was breathing heavily, her chest rising, her nipples straining against the translucent lace. Positioned as she was, pelvis grinding into hip, chest heaving just above the water, she could easily follow Sydney's gaze and saw her own dark nipples barely obscured by sheer, waterlogged lace. She badly wanted to push the bra aside, or better yet, rip it off. She imagined Sydney drawing a taut nipple into her mouth, lightly biting Birdy's flesh while her other exposed breast pushed the torn fabric of the cup open.

Their eyes met and Birdy gasped at the desire she saw there. "Please, Birdy. Kiss me."

Reaching up, she felt Sydney's strong jaw against her palm. She wanted nothing more than to feel Sydney. To be completely taken by her. Her lips, her tongue, her fingers, every inch of her skin needed to be wrapped in Sydney.

She brought her left hand up to Sydney's shoulder, craving the connection. The small diamond glistened in the sun and her breath caught. Her chest tightened and reality came crashing back down on Birdy. She bowed her head in defeat, leaning her forehead against Sydney's. "I'm sorry, I shouldn't have…I can't do this." She pushed away from the warmth and security, and unsteadily climbed the ladder. She then rolled herself onto the dock, arms and legs splayed as she lay on her back in a growing puddle of river water.

After a minute, Sydney also tumbled onto the dock.

They each panted for a long moment, the spell broken, yet Birdy was still overly aware of the body next to her, unsure of how to steer away from the intense passion she was sure they had both felt.

"You were right," Sydney said, breathing hard.

"I know," Birdy replied, still gasping.

"That water is cold."

"Yeah."

"And you can't swim."

"Nope."

"And I don't feel any cleaner."

"I told you so."

"We should get you a life jacket."

"I have one. For swimming."

Chests heaving, Sydney reached over, covering Birdy's hand and lingering on top of it, which was not helping Birdy recover her breath. "But I had fun," she said with that crooked smile that always made Birdy's heart flip. Sydney squeezed her hand and quickly stood. "Now where's that shower you were telling me about?"

Birdy rolled her head, following Sydney's progression as she walked the length of the dock. Her eyes eagerly watching Sydney's ass, clad only in wet bikini underwear, until the guilt reclaimed her. *Friends, friends, friends,* she chanted. It was her new mantra. *Friends, friends, friends.*

* * *

"Why did you name him Hoots?"

The late-afternoon sun was golden and shimmering on the river as they sat on the deck taking in the view. They each had taken a shower and the berries were gone, along with cheese and a baguette Birdy had on hand. Sydney was swirling the last of the wine in her glass.

Sydney was enjoying this day with Birdy far more than she felt she should, considering the nasty business of a wedding looming on the horizon.

Hoots was also enjoying himself immensely, swirling between their legs as if weaving an invisible knot, tying them together. He had taken to Sydney quickly and spent much of his time loudly begging for cheese, and sitting on her foot.

"I got him from the Humane Society almost five years ago. He actually came with the name Hootie. He was a pathetic little creature and I fell in love with him immediately. They posted his picture on their website and he had crossed eyes and all his whiskers were curly and he looked fat and scared." Birdy hesitated and then continued. There was heaviness in her voice that hadn't been there before. "This was back when Brooke and I first started dating. I had mentioned, probably on our first date, that I really wanted a cat. Apparently right after that, Brooke signed up to receive alerts from the Humane Society. I didn't know it at the time but she had been combing through the postings to find just the right cat for me." Birdy paused, staring at the water and absently picked at the nail on her middle finger with her thumb. "Brooke was the one that emailed me the picture of him. The subject line said, 'You're his home' and then under the link in the email it said, 'I'll pick you up in fifteen minutes. Let's go rescue him.'"

Her jaw rippled, emotion visibly passing across the planes of her face, gathering in her eyes. Sydney was surprised to hear so much intensity in Birdy's voice. She had become accustomed to the casual tone Birdy usually adopted when talking about Brooke. She realized until this moment Birdy had kept her walls up, protecting her relationship with Brooke. Now, some of her true emotions were breaking free.

"When we got to the Humane Society, they brought him out. He was limping badly and his tail was basically a giant bald scab. They told me he had been thrown out of a car on I-5 in front of the Hooters, hence his name. Luckily, someone had seen it happen and was able to pull over in time to rescue him. He had these horrible scabs on the pads of his feet. When Brooke picked him up his feet bled on her pants. She was wearing one of her favorite suits," Birdy said distantly. "It was a light tan color and I remember her looking down at the rusty brown splotches of blood and not saying a word about it. She let Hoots curl up in her lap and stain her suit, and she just petted him and talked to him." She shook her head at that, seemingly releasing herself from the pleasant memory. "I'm sorry. I got lost in my head."

Hoots had apparently accepted the fact that Sydney didn't have any more cheese stockpiled out of his reach and moved on to Birdy, begging loudly.

She lifted him up to her lap, stroking his velvet fur. "The Humane Society said that he was healing nicely and in no time at all he would be a normal, healthy cat. I had already fallen in love so I brought him home. His name was a little too Hootie and The Blowfish for me so I changed it to Hoots, which is appropriate since he hoots like an owl."

He seemed to know she was talking about him, and let off an appreciative purr as he rubbed his face on the arm of her deck chair.

"The problem was, when I got him home, he wasn't healing up nicely. He wouldn't eat and he just laid in a corner all day.

He hardly moved at all. Brooke and I took him to the vet and they gave us prescription food but he still wouldn't eat. We tried canned food, but he was wasting away. Brooke took him to the vet a couple more times for blood tests. She knew how hard it was for me. I kept crying each time and I think I freaked out the vet techs." She gave a small, self-deprecating chuckle and then sobered just as quickly. "Nothing was helping so we went to the vet again and they said the next step would be a feeding tube or kidney failure. I couldn't even speak. My chin was wobbling and I was trying not to break down in the exam room for the fifth time. Brooke was amazing that day. She held me up, almost literally, and asked all the questions I couldn't. We decided that we couldn't subject Hoots to more procedures and that a feeding tube was just too much. She got Hoots and me situated in the car and then went back in to make a last appointment for him. She said she would take him and I didn't have to go if I didn't want to. We had only been together a few months."

The Brooke she was describing hardly seemed like the same brusque and cavalier woman Sydney had met at the print shop.

Almost to herself, Birdy added, "I've always been in awe of how supportive she was. It felt like we had been together for years and yet everything was still so new and exciting, but comforting."

As much as it hurt, after the incident in the river, Sydney knew she needed to hear this. She couldn't just go on dismissing Brooke as the villain, as if she weren't a person who mattered. A person who mattered to Birdy. She didn't know what to say so she waited for Birdy to continue.

Speaking louder, refocused, Birdy continued, "I had skipped breakfast and lunch that day, so she took my pathetic ass through a drive-through. When we got back to my place I sat on the floor, eating my chicken sandwich and sobbing. I was a mess. Hoots came out of his travel crate and he started nosing around me. He kept putting his face in my sandwich. I swear to you, I actually said, 'Hoots, stop trying to eat my sandwich!' Luckily, it clicked for Brooke. She took the chicken out of the bun and broke it up and he wolfed it down. He ate every bit of it."

"I think this is the first time in history fast food *saved* a life."

"No kidding. Brooke delivered chicken sandwiches every day for a week until I finally found a fancy cat food with whole chunks that he was willing to eat. He was seriously going to starve himself because he didn't like the food I was giving him."

Reaching over, Sydney picked up Hoots from where he was balancing on the narrow arm of Birdy's chair like an elephant on a circus ball. "Looks like all that fast food went straight to your hips," she said as she rubbed his ample stomach.

Birdy stretched over and patted his head, "You really are the most difficult cat ever, Hoots." Her hand drifted down his back as they both petted him. He purred blissfully at the attention.

Their hands briefly touched and Sydney felt a wave of happiness. Gently she covered Birdy's hand with her own, holding it against Hoots's side. After a long moment, he gave a loud meow and ducked his head into their hands, butting them apart, demanding attention.

Finally, Sydney cleared her throat and said, "So Brooke saved his life, huh?" She swallowed hard, uneasy with the conversation but needing to talk about it.

"Yeah, she did." Birdy seemed far away. "Back then, her love felt so palpable. The way she doted over him…it showed how much she cared about our life together."

"And now?"

"She barely notices that he exists."

The tension was there again on Birdy's face, the ripple of her jaw, the stern look. Sydney wanted to hold her, to feel the warmth of her skin against her lips, to comfort her. She couldn't stand to see the weariness etched in Birdy's face, the contemplation and confusion she wore like a mask.

Sydney scooped Hoots up by his armpits and kissed his nose, hoping to distract Birdy. She blew gently in his face, and he sneezed wetly across her mouth and then shook his head and sneezed again, his whiskers twitching. She wiped her chin with a grimace but couldn't hide her smile at Birdy's building laughter. "I guess I asked for that."

She didn't mind Birdy's look of amusement at her misfortune. Wiping her lips dramatically for effect, she silently congratulated Hoots on successfully lightening the mood.

"So what about you then, where did you get your name? I'm pretty positive I've never met a Birdy before."

"My mom gave it to me."

"Named after a great-grandmother?"

"No. The story is actually far more romantic than that." She paused, taking a sip of her wine. "My moms were partners for eight years when they had me. My birth mom, Jo, told my mother, Bea, that since I wasn't biologically hers, she wanted Bea to name me so she would feel just as connected to the birth as she was. They had also decided that Bea would adopt me and I would take Bea's last name so that I completely belonged to both of them. They didn't want to saddle me with a hyphenated name in the early eighties, which was probably easier. So, I was to be a Cartwright and not a Finch."

Sydney watched a blue heron glide above the water, congratulating herself for following through on her promise to research the birds of the area. She realized as she listened to Birdy's story that maybe she shouldn't have taken it upon herself to learn about *every* bird she set her sights on. Great Blue Herons wouldn't break her heart, but this Bird, this one definitely could. The heron finally landed and she shook herself from her thoughts. Glancing over at Birdy, she noticed how far away she seemed, completely lost in her own introspection. A small silence stretched.

"My mom tells this story much more dramatically than I can." It was obvious thinking about her mother made Birdy happy. There was a light in her eyes now and she seemed to have landed again much like the heron. No longer miles away but instead here with Sydney once more.

"When she tells the story she would always take several minutes to explain how difficult it was to decide on a name.

She really lays into it. The trials and tribulations of such a monumental decision. At a dinner party she can make mothers of six feel that no one could ever have faced a more serious and difficult task as Bea Cartwright did when she named little Birdy," she said laughing. "It goes like this. She would start by saying she read five different books with baby names, she studied the origins of each one she liked, she consulted family and friends and genealogy books. If I had been named after my great-grandmother, you would be talking to a Myrtle right now."

Sydney sympathetically twisted up her face, causing Birdy to laugh.

"My mother says she gave herself an ulcer over this decision. She had picked out a few names. Jessica, Amy, Amber…it was like a best of the eighties compilation. I could have been a Leslie, but she thought having two moms was already going to be hard enough and I didn't need a name that alliterated with lesbian. The current leader at the time was Megan. This is where my mom pauses and lowers her voice for dramatic effect so everyone has to lean in to hear her."

"Your mom's quite the performer, huh?"

"Yes. She loves a good audience. So the way she tells it she was lying in bed one night with my mom, who was nine months pregnant with me. Jo leaned over and kissed her forehead and Bea felt so much love in that kiss that she thought she was going to explode. She felt love for her partner, for their home and their life together, and she felt love for me, wrapped up in her partner's belly. She said she had never been happier than in that moment." Birdy patted her leg as an invitation for Hoots, who curled up in her lap.

"As she had every night for almost eight years, Jo said, 'Good night. I love you my little bee.' And Bea said, as she had every night for eight years, 'I love you too my little bird. Good night.' She said the next day she woke up and her 'ulcer' was gone. She knew that she wanted me to experience as much love in my life as she had with my mom—her Finch, her little bird.

So, she named me Birdy and has forever referred to the two of us as her birds."

"And what does Jo think of the name?"

Birdy twirled her wine, lost in thought. "Unfortunately, Jo died of cancer when I was two. I have no memories of her so I've never gotten to see my moms together. I've never seen the love between them, a love that I'm sure is greater than any love I've ever experienced. My mom has always been enough for me but I do wish Jo could be here for her."

Sydney felt overwhelmed. The story had been touching and had resonated with her deeply. Happiness and longing battled deep inside her. An ache settled in her chest and a hunger for Birdy she had never experienced before grew from that ache. It was far beyond sexual, she realized. She wanted to be with her, to be a part of her. She felt the love that Birdy's moms surely shared and knew then that she could easily fall in love with her.

Her hands clenched the arm of her chair so tightly her knuckles had turned white. She was falling for her but knew she couldn't be with her. But then, another passing thought grabbed her heart, making it race. *She may be engaged but that doesn't mean I can't fight for her.*

Sydney searched for something neutral, something to quell the ache in her chest, but what came out was the question she needed to ask most.

"Do you love Brooke as much as your moms loved each other?"

Birdy sighed, squinting out over the water and into the late afternoon sun. A light breeze picked up, lifting her dark hair.

Sydney ached as she watched the tension ripple through Birdy's jaw.

Finally, she quietly said, "I don't know. I'm scared that I don't." But then with more conviction, she corrected herself. "I'm scared that I *can't*. That their love was too big to replicate and maybe I'm trying to hold my real-life, in-the-trenches love up to an idolized giant. Maybe it's all been there right in front of me and I forgot to stop wanting."

Sydney rested her hand on Birdy's forearm, hoping to comfort her. They sat like that for a long while, Sydney's thumb occasionally rubbing her arm gently.

"She still gets the emails," Birdy said softly.

Sydney hadn't followed Birdy's train of thought.

"Brooke. She still gets the emails from the Humane Society with cats available for adoption. She unsubscribes from everything else. She's fanatic about an uncluttered inbox. But not those emails. She hasn't unsubscribed from those."

Sydney watched as a small, private smile grew across Birdy's lips while she thought about Brooke, and she pulled her hand away.

CHAPTER TWELVE

The small storage unit's door was rolled open when Birdy parked next to Sydney's Jeep. At the sight of Sydney wearing fitted olive shorts and a slim white T-shirt, she let out a long breath before forcing herself out of the car. Since last weekend, she had been obsessing about their encounter in the river. Knowing she needed to clear the air with Sydney but not wanting to broach the subject at work, she had gone to sleep last night resolved to address it first thing this morning before anything got out of hand. And before she did something she would regret. Again.

She kicked her car door shut, put her aviators on and spoke sternly as Sydney approached. "Listen up, Ramos. There are ground rules here. Number one: If there are two boxes and one is heavier than the other, you take the heavy one. Number two: If there is beer in your fridge, I will help myself to it. That rule applies beyond today as well."

Sydney did a poor job of smothering a smile. "Should I be standing at attention right now? You're pacing. And you have a very intimidating steely glint in your eye."

"I will crush you like the hardened General I am if need be, Ramos." Birdy had a hard time stifling her own grin as Sydney was beaming ear to ear.

"Anything else, sir, ma'am?"

Birdy's smile faltered and she took a deep breath. "Yes, rule number three. If I fall into a body of water, just let me drown." She stopped pacing and leaned heavily against her car. "I think it will be less torturous than that look you get on your face when you want to kiss me."

Sydney's eyes widened, as she had apparently not expected the seriousness of Birdy's request. "Bird, I'm sorry that—"

Interrupting her, trying to spare her the apology, Birdy said, "Me too. I want to be your friend, Syd, but that's all I can be." She exhaled, glad she had spoken her piece.

"What I mean," Sydney countered, "is that I'm sorry if I made you uncomfortable. But I want to be clear that I'm not sorry for the way I look at you or how badly I want to kiss you."

"No, no, no, no, no! That's the look. Right there." Birdy flattened herself against her car, realizing she had nowhere to escape as Sydney slowly advanced toward her. "Put that away right now, Sydney Ramos."

Taking another step forward, Sydney licked her lips with what seemed like deliberate sexiness.

So uncool, Birdy bemoaned to herself. As her final defense she flung her left hand up and flashed her ring. "I'm engaged. You can't look at an engaged woman like that."

Sydney gently brushed Birdy's hand away as she took yet another step closer.

They were less than a foot from each other now and Birdy gasped as Sydney began to lean in. Closing her eyes tightly, she willed herself to breathe. Two excruciating seconds later she felt Sydney's body barely brush against her own and her lips puckered the tiniest bit in anticipation. Another endless second passed and she heard a familiar thump and squeak. Unscrewing her face and squinting out of one eye, she saw Sydney's amused face and the car door that she had just opened.

"I think you better have a seat. All of these ground rules seem to have overstimulated you, General."

"I hate you," Birdy said grumpily.

"Maybe for now, but I think I'll win you over one day."

* * *

They were able to load up nearly all of Sydney's belongings in one trip. A mattress was tied to the Volvo's roof and the station wagon's large expanse was filled with boxes. A small love seat was sticking straight up from the open cabin of Sydney's Jeep.

Birdy followed the thirty blocks from the storage unit to Sydney's small studio apartment in a warehouse-style building in Portland's up-and-coming inner southeast neighborhood. Loading the two cars had been easy from the first-floor storage, but unloading was shaping up to be a challenge. The bottom floor of the concrete building had been converted to a trendy restaurant that shared an atrium with a realtor and an acupuncturist. The row of apartment-sized windows appeared to be at least three stories up. "Please tell me it's not up there."

"Okay."

"It's up there isn't it?"

"Yeah. Here's a box. Go get 'em, tiger." Sydney slapped her butt and then turned back to the boxes in the car. "I'll be right behind you."

Birdy entered the utilitarian concrete stairwell. She couldn't see around the stairs but she could smell bacon and assumed there was a door around the corner that provided direct access to the restaurant. "To think I could be having brunch right now." Then she smiled to herself, aware of the slight sting on her ass where Sydney had slapped her.

She trudged up the stairs, gasping for breath at each landing. She experimented with balancing the box on the railing and sliding it ahead of her but the box fell on her foot so she abandoned that method. The stairwell got hotter with every step and she slowed her pace even more, satisfied that Sydney hadn't yet caught up with her.

When she finally got to the top landing, she awkwardly balanced the box on her knee and swung the heavy emergency door open. The box slipped lower in her grip as she stumbled into the corridor, the metal door clanging shut behind her. Looking down the hall, she put her burden down in defeat at the sight of Sydney standing twenty paces ahead her.

Hands on her hips, she asked, "How the hell did you do that?"

Sydney laughed, pushing herself up from where she leaned against her apartment door, a much larger box at her feet.

"How did you beat me?"

"I used the elevator, tiger."

Birdy spluttered. "What elevator?"

"The one at the bottom of the stairs, obviously."

"You have got to be kidding me."

Sydney doubled over with laughter at Birdy's exasperation. "I thought you would see it! But then when I realized you took the stairs I assumed you were just getting some extra training in for that hike you're going to take me on soon." Her eyes sparkled with mischief.

Birdy lightly toed the box, scooting it toward Sydney. "This box and I are done. That would be *finito* to you."

"That's Italian. You mean *terminado*?"

"Yes, that's what I meant." Birdy huffed and pressed the elevator button, waiting for the doors to open but nothing happened. She tapped her foot impatiently and glared at Sydney, who was biting her lip and desperately trying not to laugh.

In mock seriousness Birdy said, "I'll be *terminado* with you if you don't cut it out." The elevator dinged its arrival and she marched in. When the doors slid closed behind her and the motor whirred into action, she smiled at the happiness she saw reflected in the brushed metal panels.

* * *

An hour later Birdy was thrilled to have all the boxes stacked along the wall that separated Sydney's living space from her bathroom. The move was finished, and unpacking was definitely not in her job description. The mattresses were sitting askew on the floor, while Sydney and Birdy sprawled comfortably on the love seat.

"See, I told you I didn't have very much stuff. Thanks for your help, Bird." Sydney squeezed Birdy's knee.

"You're welcome. It wasn't that bad."

"That's not what you said thirty minutes ago when you were cursing my belongings and whining about being dehydrated."

"Yeah, well, I was just trying to keep you entertained."

"Well, now it's my turn to entertain you. How about we start with the grand tour?" At Birdy's indulgent nod, she continued. "So, that wall over there is the kitchen, as evidenced by the three cabinets, miniature appliances and two full feet of counter space. Next to that is the front door where you bruised your arm when you ran into the doorjamb."

Birdy rubbed her arm for effect.

"The door next to that is the front, guest and master closet all rolled into one cozy, little shoebox, which they only added so they could pretend this is actually a livable space. The wall to our left, across from the kitchen is the master bedroom. You'll notice it already has a coat hook so it can double as a *foyer*."

"*Foy-er*." Birdy perfectly mocked her nasally French purr.

Continuing her bad impersonation of a maître d' at a posh French restaurant, Sydney said, "Oh-ho-ho, you like my accent?"

"*Oui*."

"You think it's-a sexy, ah?"

"I think you lost it. You sound more like the Mario Brothers now."

"I'll work on it for you. Mario's not sexy. Continuing the tour, we currently are sitting in the living room, which one could consider a sunroom since it contains the only wall with a window. The bathroom is to your right. It was designed to be a whole seven feet from the bed to afford maximum ventilation and air quality. What do you think?"

"My favorite thing about that tour is that I didn't even have to get up."

"Yes, that is due to the open concept which really maximizes the flow of the so-called living space, allowing the genuine hardwood floors to be bathed in natural light." Sydney accentuated the absurdity of the listing's features by curling her fingers into quotation marks around each. "Or at least that's what I was told when I rented it."

Birdy lightly slapped Sydney's stomach with the back of her hand and laughed, enjoying Sydney's humor. "It's actually really nice, Syd. Small." At Sydney's humph she corrected herself. "Excuse me. *Cozy* not small, but nicely updated and modern. You should have seen the hellhole I lived in before I got my boat. I'd say you found yourself a great place."

"Thanks." Sydney beamed with obvious pride. "So, how about that meal I promised you? Since we skipped lunch, I could go for an early dinner if you're up for it."

"Perfect. Brooke has a work event that goes late tonight at the convention center so I'm all on my own for the day. I'd starve if you left me to my own devices and didn't feed me."

"Do you want to go somewhere? There's a pretty nice looking café a couple blocks away we could try."

"I don't know if I'm up for a restaurant. I'm sweaty and dirty."

"How about we order a pizza?"

"Now you're talking."

* * *

Birdy was happily devouring her third slice of pizza when Sydney returned from rummaging in one of the boxes to sit alongside her on the floor, their backs against the couch.

"I promised you some alcohol too, didn't I?"

Her mouth full of cheese, she nodded excitedly.

Sydney put two shot glasses, a saltshaker and a small bag of limes on the open pizza box between them and then presented Birdy with a mostly-full bottle of tequila. "Thank God I had the forethought to label my Tequila Box."

"Geez, you weren't kidding. I thought you meant a beer or something."

"Or something," Sydney said as she poured two shots. "Hold on." She got back up and rummaged through a different box. She straightened and turned toward Birdy with a massive cleaver in her hand and a malicious glint in her eye.

"Jesus. I didn't see this plot twist coming," Birdy said, stuffing the rest of her slice in her mouth and feeling wholly unconcerned.

Sydney plopped back down and gently sliced a lime into wedges. After they prepared their shots she raised her glass before motioning to the room and saying, "To new beginnings."

"To new beginnings," Birdy repeated. She wasn't exactly sure what part of her life she was toasting. Her marriage was certainly a new beginning so that applied but sitting here with this beautiful woman, she didn't much feel like toasting her upcoming wedding. Sydney, and her friendship was a new beginning, so she decided she would toast to that.

She watched Sydney take her shot, marveling at her soft lips. The corner of her mouth pulled back sharply as the burn of the alcohol hit her and then she licked her top lip, leaving her tongue there in concentration as she started to cut another lime wedge.

Glancing up Sydney said, "You shouldn't be allowed to look at me like that either."

"Like what?"

"Like you want me to kiss you."

Birdy shook herself. "Don't be silly. I didn't look at you like that." Her eyes dropped to Sydney's lips, just to make sure they still appeared as soft as she remembered.

"You're looking at me like that right now." Sydney moistened her lips, a gesture that was cruelly unnerving. Another shot prepared, she slid it across the pizza box.

"Are you trying to get me drunk so you can take advantage of me?" She was relieved that her attempt to lighten the mood seemed to have worked, but then her breath caught when Sydney replied in a smooth, sexy and low cadence.

"No. I'm trying to get you drunk so you'll take advantage of me." And then Sydney licked the salt from the back of her own hand in a way that made Birdy jealous of everything that tongue had ever touched. She took the shot and then sucked slowly on the lime wedge, the juices making her lips glisten.

Birdy was painfully aware of another, even greater, flow of juices. She licked at the salt from her own hand, feeling more like Cornflake, her mom's golden retriever, than a seductress. After throwing back her shot she shoved the lime wedge in her mouth, then coughed and gagged on the liquid searing her throat.

Okay, that probably successfully killed the mood. She wasn't sure if she liked that or not.

Her coughing continued, prompting Sydney to rub her thigh, concern in her eyes. "You okay?"

She nearly moaned at the sensation of Sydney's hand on her bare leg and in a fleeting moment of sanity, she said the one thing she knew would kill the mood completely. "So...do you want to start printing those wedding invitations next week?"

Sydney removed her hand and picked up another slice of pizza. "Sure thing."

Yep, killed it.

CHAPTER THIRTEEN

Two weeks had passed with near radio silence from Birdy. Sydney arrived at work each morning hoping to reestablish their connection, to talk with her about something other than designs and prints. She decided to redouble those efforts after a weekend alone in her tiny apartment, and Monday morning she entered the office with renewed motivation. Before she could say anything though, Birdy signaled her over to join her conversation with Mare.

"Okay, Mare, spill it," Birdy demanded.

"I don't want to talk about it." Mare rubbed her reddening face, her freckles almost disappearing into the new shade of pink she was becoming. There were no customers in the office but it was clear Mare wished the little bell above the door would tinkle so she could avoid the questions Birdy was leveling at her.

Sydney had no clue what they were going on about.

Birdy noticed her confusion and filled her in. "Mare went on a date with my friend Saul this weekend. And now I want details. Come on, Mare."

Happy to be included in the conversation with anything that involved Birdy, Sydney excitedly rolled up a chair and sat in it backward, hiking her running shorts up a bit as she did so. She couldn't be sure, but she could have sworn Birdy's peripheral vision was hard at work taking in the length of her thighs. It seemed Birdy was trying unsuccessfully to look anywhere but at her legs so she shifted, letting her knees spread just a bit farther until she was sure Birdy's quick gasp was due to the several inches of newly exposed skin. She knew she shouldn't tease Birdy like this but it was just too much fun. She stifled a smile and turned to Mare. "Spill it."

Birdy noticeably cleared her throat, seemingly recovering from the view and chimed in, "That's what I said. Spill it, Mare. Leave no pebble unturned. We want details."

"*Juicy* details," Sydney added.

"Yeah," Birdy agreed. "Make it juicy." She and Sydney shared a salacious grin.

"You two are ridiculous. There aren't any *juicy* details. It was only a first date. Just a lot of awkward conversation."

"Well, what did you think of Saul?"

"He was nice enough. And I've always thought he was cute."

"Okay," Birdy said. "So what's the problem?"

"Oh, I don't know. He talked too much and he laughed really loud and he kept dropping his napkin on the floor. And then when he took me home, he didn't even make an attempt to kiss me. He shook my hand and practically ran back to his car." Mare covered her eyes and then threw both arms in the air. "He shook my hand!"

"It sounds like he was nervous," Sydney supplied. As far as she was concerned, nothing else made sense.

"I don't think so. I've always been really good at reading people," Mare said, causing Birdy to roll her eyes. "I could tell that he just wasn't that interested in me."

"Oh, Mare." Birdy wheeled her desk chair up closer to Mare and clutched her hand. "I've known you for a long time now and I love you dearly. I hate to be the one to tell you this but..." She trailed off, gazing out the window dramatically. "I have never, ever, in my entire life met someone who was less adept at reading people than you. Never."

"I am not bad at reading people," Mare said defensively. "I've always been told I'm good at figuring folks out. I'm good at reading between the lines and hearing what they aren't actually saying."

Sydney may not have worked at PDX Ink long but she knew that was completely untrue. One of the things she liked most about her boss was how easy she was to get to know, an open book. Every emotion and thought was telegraphed as if she was a walking billboard advertising her emotions. It was endearing, really. Sydney realized that even the least emotionally attuned people could tell what Mare was thinking, so why shouldn't Mare assume she could tell what they were thinking? She scooted her chair close enough to take Mare's other hand, remembering when Mare offered to set her up with Tony. Sydney had accepted the phone number, assuming Tony spelled her name with an "i" and not a "y". He did not. Now was a good time to remind Mare of this. "I wouldn't say you're exactly great at figuring people out. You thought I was straight."

"You're not?"

Birdy chimed in, "You give money to that crazy homeless man every week to help him go to Juilliard. You think that fifty-year-old homeless man is going to be a ballerina."

"Well, he said he got accepted…"

"He's in a wheelchair."

Sydney said, "You flirt with the Starbucks barista every morning."

"Well, he's cute."

"*She* is cute. And her name is Shelby and you've been hitting on a butch lesbian."

"Also," Birdy said. "Meth Mouth Michael."

"Oh, Michael." Mare dreamily stared out the window again. At Birdy's stern glance she said, "Okay, okay. What's your point?"

"Our point," Birdy said, "is that you are a horrible judge of character."

"The worst," Sydney added, nodding.

"And our other point is that Saul is crazy about you, and he is beyond nervous when he's around you. So you need to give him another chance and get it out of your head that he doesn't like you. Also, you need to stop doing that creepy, dreamy-eyed routine whenever I mention Meth Mouth Michael. There's no reason for you to like him. He was an addict and he wasn't even that nice to you when he worked here."

"Knock, knock." All three women looked up toward the door as Brooke cheerfully entered the office. "Hey, girls. I came to grab Birdy. Mare, is it okay if I steal her for an hour? I set up a consult with our wedding florist. It's the only opening he has this week."

Without waiting for an answer, Brooke tugged her out of the office, chattering about the flower arrangements she wanted.

"Speaking of dating people who aren't nice to you…" Mare shuffled papers on her desk and then turned to Sydney. "Wait, are you really gay?"

CHAPTER FOURTEEN

"Birdy, these invitations are beautiful!" Sydney leaned her hip against one of the platens on the manual press she had been working on as she studied the design again. In her time at PDX Ink, she had been continuously impressed with Birdy's talent. In college she had taken a couple graphic design courses. Never had she made anything so fine as what she held in her hands right now.

"Thank you. I've been working on them for the past week. I'm glad we get to print them finally so I don't have to stress about it anymore."

"How did you even come up with this? They're so detailed but feel so simple at the same time. The design is really extraordinary."

"Thanks, Syd. I actually got the idea from the Heathman Hotel where we're having the wedding. I don't know if you've seen it downtown." Sydney shook her head so Birdy continued. "Well, they always have uniformed doormen outside. I guess they're bellhops, but they essentially wear beefeater uniforms.

You know, the guards at the Tower of London? The uniforms are so intricate with their gold-embroidered jackets and flat hats with flowers around the brim that I decided to include them on the invitations."

The two tiny figures faced each other at the top of the card, acting as a keystone for the rest of the border that seemed to unfurl away from them in an intricate floral pattern that Sydney could only imagine represented the doormen's uniforms. Framed within the dark green border was black script announcing the details of the event.

"I love how regal they are. I feel like I'm printing invitations for the royal family," she said.

"Exactly what I was going for. I think Brooke will love them. They're elegant, sophisticated and very self-important."

Sounds exactly like Brooke, Sydney thought to herself. *Throw in controlling and bitchy and it would be a dead ringer.*

She shook herself from her antagonistic thoughts, and beckoned Birdy across the shop. "Let me show you what I've been working on all day. I think I have a good idea for these invitations."

They stopped at a long table covered with butcher paper. Every shade of ink imaginable was smeared on the surface, long-dried remnants of previous jobs. At one end of the table were open tubs of ink and a small electronic scale.

"I've been mixing inks trying to come up with the perfect colors for this design. Since your theme is emerald and ebony, I've been trying to find a way to portray the elegance of the colors without just presenting the guests with flat green and black." Sydney picked up a piece of cream-colored card stock with a strong texture that was rough to the touch. "They call this a burlap texture. I thought that it might add to the Victorian feel you have going on with the design while alluding to the color of Brooke's dress. Also, it's made out of one hundred percent recycled products."

Birdy examined the thickness and texture of the paper. "I love it. I think this is exactly what we needed. I had pictured a matte finish and hadn't thought of it this textured, but you're right. It adds age to the invitations and matches the design. It makes it feel even more stately."

Sydney beamed, pleased with the compliment. "Good. Hopefully you like the inks just as much. I made the pantone colors you suggested." She used her finger to smear first a thin layer of green in one corner of the card stock and then black beside it. "These are the colors you used when you designed it. I think they work really well but I have a couple suggestions for you. I mixed up a green just a little bit lighter than yours and added metallic silver to it, which gives it an almost iridescent quality."

"Iridescent? Like glitter?"

"Do you want glitter ink?"

"God, no. That is so not my scene."

"Oh good. I was worried there for a second." Sydney felt a smile spread on her face as she thought about a pleasant memory.

"What?" Birdy prodded.

"I was just thinking about this time with my nieces. I was supervising some arts and crafts and I asked my little four-year-old niece if she wanted to put glitter on her paper, and she blurted out that, and I quote, 'glitter is the herpes of craft supplies.' I almost died. Apparently my brother said it in front of them. It's a Demetri Martin quote. The comedian. And Dess just really latched onto it. Luckily my brother Matty assures me she does not know what herpes is."

"That's hilarious. She sounds amazing."

"Yeah, she's a precocious little bugger. She and her older sister, Sofia are the sweetest things ever. Definitely that hardest part about leaving Texas." Shaking herself from her memories, Sydney continued. "Anyway, we'll avoid any glitter STDs and stick with what I already mixed up. I combined the metallic with regular ink so it's not an intense shine. It just adds a subtle depth to the color. Just enough shimmer to make you think of the Emerald City, not a glitter bomb."

Sydney carefully spread a thin amount of her emerald ink on the opposite corner. "In order to balance out the green I added a little bit of brown to the black to warm it up some so it feels more like ebony wood instead of a flat black which is a little colder." Using a clean finger, she smeared her final color next to the green she had mixed. She flapped the card back and forth several times to help dry the water-based ink, allowing Birdy to see the true colors.

Birdy considered the paper for several minutes, folding it in half, isolating each pair of colors. Finally, she unfolded it, smoothed out the crease and pronounced her verdict. "Syd, these colors are beautiful. I absolutely love them."

"You're not just saying that to be nice?"

"No, absolutely not. I wish I had thought of this. They are perfect. Obviously even more than I could have imagined. They're not too far off my original colors but they add just a touch of sophistication and warmth that I was missing. Thank you so much. Brooke is going to flip when she sees this!"

Brooke is not the one I'm trying to impress, Sydney wanted to say but instead she said, "Are you ready to start printing?"

* * *

Birdy registered the rushed enthusiasm in Sydney's voice as she excitedly talked her through the process. It was nice to think she was having fun with their project.

"Okay, so what I've done is put six copies of the invitation on each screen so that when we print on a large piece of paper we've actually printed six invitations at once. It will lower printing time a ton and then we just have to cut them apart. Now since we're printing two different colors"—Sydney hurried across the shop, beckoning Birdy to keep up—"we have to print all of the invitations with green first and let that dry, and then we line up the black screen to one of the green prints." She picked up one of the two screens leaning against the manual press to demonstrate what she was saying. "Then as long as we put each piece of card stock on the registration pins, the black will print at a consistent location in relation to the green."

Recognizing the frenzied energy as that of an artist who enjoyed creating, Birdy had the feeling Sydney found the act of producing her art even more satisfying than the completed product.

Sydney stopped abruptly and gave her a sheepish look. "I'm sorry, I feel like you know all of this already. I'm not sure why I'm trying to teach it to you."

"It's okay. I know some of it, like I'm pretty familiar with lining up the designs and registering them to each other since that affects my job. I am curious about how exactly you get the design on the screen though." She had been at PDX Ink long enough to know almost all the ins and outs but she couldn't resist the temptation to listen while Sydney played professor to her student. Not wanting the lesson to end, she laid it on thick. "Mare walked me through it once when I first started working here but it was a long time ago. I can see you're a good teacher so I was hoping you could show me again…just so I can, you know, feel like I've been completely involved in the process."

I might as well be batting my eyelashes and twirling a lock of hair around my finger like a hapless coed.

Instead, she played it cool and leaned nonchalantly on an arm of the printing press, which spun out from under her. With a yelp, she fell sideways, supported only by the revolving press arm. Just as she thought her next destination would be a sprawled formation on the concrete floor, she was abruptly pushed back into a standing position, as if she hadn't just become an anthropomorphized Stretch Armstrong doll.

Sydney had grabbed the next board and was holding it in place, a quick action that saved Birdy from a guaranteed face-plant. On top of that, she was good enough to have an expression of concern on her face rather than humor, which Birdy was sure was just beneath the surface.

"That was…well, that was terrifying. Thank you for rescuing me."

"You're welcome."

Birdy was almost distracted from her humiliation and the fact that her right side now felt stretched a foot longer than her left by the way the corners of Sydney's eyes crinkled when she smiled. Almost.

"Want to see the darkroom now?" Sydney asked.

Birdy allowed herself to be led her through a thick black curtain into a small room built into the back of the shop. Once the curtain swung shut behind them, they were left in total darkness. She had been in this room before with Mare when the lights were on, but now in the darkness she felt disoriented and anxious. She tightened her hold on Sydney's hand, unwilling to lose her anchor.

"As you can see," Sydney began softly, standing much closer than Birdy had expected, "this is our darkroom where I work with the emulsion. It's light sensitive so we can't use the overhead light." After a breathless beat she added, "But we can turn on the safety light so you can see around."

Birdy's nerves tingled as she sensed Sydney stepping closer. It gave her the sensation of floating in a sensory deprivation tank, totally unaware of herself or her own body, as if she were levitating with only Sydney's touch and words to keep her grounded. Feeling Sydney's body press lightly against her, she was intensely aware of Sydney's breath on her ear and she found herself leaning in, expecting Sydney to kiss her in the exact spot her breath had warmed.

An eternity passed in the dark as she waited to feel Sydney's lips, but then a low buzz filled the room. She realized that even in a lightless room, she had closed her eyes in anticipation. When she opened them, the deep red light that filled the room slowly brought her out of the spell the darkness had cast. Peeking over, she expected to see Sydney inches from her face but instead she was a couple of feet away, still lightly grasping her hand. Her chest appeared to be rising and falling rapidly, though maybe that was just a trick of the deep glow of red light. After a gentle squeeze from Sydney, her hand fell to her side. The withdrawal of the warm touch left Birdy with a strange feeling, as if she had imagined the entire, intimate encounter that lasted only seconds but felt much longer. Trying to slow her quickened breath, she was unsure if the pulse thrumming in her neck was discernible in the red glow.

Sydney cleared her throat and continued with her explanation in low, measured tones as if she too were trying to gain control over her rapid heartbeat.

"The emulsion is a, uh, thick, gooey liquid that you spread in thin layers on each side of the screen—a screen like this one—with a scoop coater." She half-heartedly waved a long, silver V-shaped trough.

She can even make a scoop coater sound sexy.

Sydney then put it back on the table and it clattered loudly into the sink. "Whoops... So, uh, once the emulsion is dry you take the screen outside this room to the exposure table." Meeting Birdy's eyes one last time in the glow, Sydney opened the curtain, escorting her back into the brightly lit workspace.

Blinking rapidly to adjust to the light, Birdy attempted to clear her head of the intense attraction she had felt in the darkroom. She had obviously just envisaged it because no matter what reaction she had imagined from Sydney in the red glow, she saw no signs of it now in the harsh white light. The power of their fleeting connection in the cramped darkroom began to lift as it would after a dream she was not supposed to remember. Pushing the last vestiges of that warm glow away, she forced herself to pay attention to what Sydney was saying.

"This is where your designs come into play. You print them from your computer on transparent film, as you know, of course." Sydney coughed, seemingly embarrassed. "And I line up the film and screen on the light table. Light shines up through the design and screen. All of the emulsion exposed to light hardens while the emulsion behind the ink on your printout doesn't."

Was Sydney avoiding looking her in the eye? Perhaps she also had been affected by the red glow, a theory Birdy decided to test. With a step forward, she stood ever so slightly closer than customary and was rewarded when Sydney bumped awkwardly into the light table in her haste to put separation between them. And still she did not look up. Theory tested and confirmed. Eye contact was definitely being avoided.

Forcefully, Sydney cleared her throat and then absently fiddled with a knob on the machine. "Umm...when I spray the screen with water with a pressure washer all of the emulsion that didn't cure washes out of the screen so you're left with a stencil that is a perfect replica of the design you made on your computer. Pretty cool, huh? The precision of screen printing has always fascinated me." In her excitement Sydney had apparently forgotten her moratorium on eye contact and her smile faltered. "That sounded really dorky...Um, anyway, does that all make sense?"

Since leaving the darkroom, the stomach-clenching, palms-sweating moment in the red light seem farther away and less real, but the fact that Sydney also had seemed overwhelmed by the intensity of the experience kept those feelings from receding completely. Birdy was taken by how skilled Sydney obviously was and how sure of herself she seemed, which was really sexy.

Realizing she hadn't responded to Sydney's question, she cleared her throat and said, "Yes, that made perfect sense. Mare made it all sound so much more confusing. She went on and on about types of emulsions and varying exposure times for screens. I was lost immediately, but you explained it perfectly."

"Thanks." Sydney smiled, apparently reassured. "Mare is right, of course, there are tons of details that I didn't go into. That stuff is too complicated for our purposes, but this hopefully gives you a much clearer picture of how your designs get from your computer to our customers." Sydney visibly gulped. "I sound like a freaking textbook, don't I?"

"You're a regular Houghton Mifflin Harcourt."

"Huh?"

"Textbooks...ummm...they publish...never mind. And yes, that helped a ton. It's nice to see the entire process since I'm the designer *and* the customer in this case." A small snort escaped before she could stop it. *God, I'm so lame.*

Sydney brightened, apparently pleased that Birdy had stooped to an even nerdier level. "Oh, so does that mean you're paying me?"

"Hell, no. You're here out of the kindness of your own heart and don't you forget it," Birdy replied with a matching grin. "Now, where are my beautifully designed and perfectly exposed screens?" *The glow. The red glow. I'm blaming it on that. And I'm* never *going in there again.*

An hour later, the first screen was secured to the table in hinged clamps, the registration holes had been punched in the paper, and a thick, glistening glob of ink had been ladled onto the screen above the design. Sydney selected a long wooden-handled squeegee from the row hanging along the wall. "The key to an even print," she explained, returning to the worktable, "is to apply firm, even pressure with the squeegee as you pull it across the screen."

After removing the prop holding the screen up from the table, she laid the screen flat against the paper that was secured onto the registration pins. Squeegee in hand, she seated it in the green ink. "You have to keep your hands toward the outside of the handle and you should try to keep the squeegee at about a forty-five degree angle. Push firmly so you force the ink through the mesh but not so hard that you are bending the rubber blade too far back." Sydney checked to make sure Birdy was following. "Once you're ready to print you should put one foot behind the other so you can rock back with it."

Without thinking, Birdy rapped, "Rock back wit it. Uhhn yeah," she grunted rhythmically. "Rock back wit it, fool. Rock back wit it old school." She repeated the chorus three times, each time a little more enthusiastically, egged on by how Sydney's face scrunched up in confusion.

"What?"

"Oh, come on! Lucky Specialist?" Birdy ignored her puzzled look and continued, "You messin' in da booth…posting a five-five dive in light-up light shoes…Bitch, they call it Rose City… with my girl you know I don't dance like Diddy!…and I squeeze da john, even if da police on—"

"Okay, okay I know who Diddy is but light shoes?" Sydney interrupted. "And is squeezing the john what I think it is?"

"I really can't be sure. I never did a critical analysis but I think we can assume it's very dirty."

"Okay, well after you 'rock back wit it'"—Sydney carefully enunciated each word, much to Birdy's delight—"you gotta flood the screen…like a printing fiend," Sydney rapped with exaggerated awkwardness.

"I'm impressed with your commitment to that slant rhyme. Now, explain this 'flooding' business."

Sydney demonstrated pulling a print, a thin bead of ink rolling in front of the blade. "Flooding requires a bit of coordination."

Lifting the screen several inches above the table with one hand, she then used the other to push the squeegee and ink back across the screen, leaving a thin layer of emerald ink obscuring the design.

"And that is how you flood. Because we are using water-based ink, if we leave too little ink in the design it will dry out and then we would have to clean out the screen, which is a pain in the ass. Lean the squeegee at the far end against the clamps and then you can prop up the screen and check out the print."

"Seems easy enough," Birdy said.

"You ready to try?"

"Sure. Okay, so first I put the paper on the registration pins and then I lower the screen and hold the squeegee like this."

"Your hands are a little too close together."

"Better?"

"Yes, but now the angle is too high."

Birdy held her breath as Sydney lightly touched the small of her back. Already, the heat from her body was only too apparent as she reached around to guide Birdy's hands, and to that she added the spark of her breasts brushing against her arm. Her face was only inches away.

If Sydney was aware of her imminent combustion, she didn't let it show. Now holding her hand, she adjusted the squeegee angle. "Right there. Forty-five degrees."

As Sydney stepped away, Birdy released her breath in a rush of air, making it far too obvious she had been affected by the closeness. All she could manage was a pinched, "Okay."

With shaky hands, she drew the blade across the screen, trying her best to rock back as Sydney had instructed.

"Great," Sydney said. "Now lift the screen a few inches with your left hand."

Birdy released her grip and lifted the screen, watching helplessly as the squeegee fell back, the wooden handle nearly submerged in green ink. "Crap!" she said, trying to fish the tool out and getting green ink on her fingers and palm. Her hair came loose of its tie, and flustered, she pushed it away with the back of her wrist.

"Come here, let me help you," Sydney said with too much amusement. Was it possible she was oblivious to the effect she was having on Birdy's ability to send synapse instructions to her hands? She dug the squeegee out of the ink easily with minimal mess, scraped off the excess ink onto the screen and exchanged it for a clean one. After expertly flooding the screen she studied Birdy's print. "Seems easy enough, huh?"

Birdy huffed her way over to the sink to wash her hands.

"Your print looks pretty good, Bird. Just a little bit in the top corner that didn't come through." She lowered the screen and printed it again to cover the imperfection. "Come here and do the next one."

"I don't know. I don't want that disaster to happen again. I feel like I have ink up to my elbows."

"More like up to your eyebrows."

Oh, great. Birdy touched her face, feeling the semidry ink there. "You think this is funny, do you?"

"Yes, you look hilarious right now. Full camouflage war paint is definitely a good look for you. Just a few more smears and you could have fought in 'Nam."

Concentrating hard, Birdy was able to twist her smile into an angry slash and then dipped one finger into the ink. "'Nam, huh? You know what we did to traitors back in 'Nam, Ramos?" she asked as she slowly stepped toward Sydney, who looked ready to dodge an attack if needed.

Birdy was only a couple feet away when her lips parted and her eyes dropped to Sydney's mouth. That damned electricity was still flowing between them. Thick ropes of lust connecting them. Unconsciously she must have continued forward as they were now so close that she had to resist reaching out to pull her nearer. She was surprised when Sydney closed her eyes as if waiting.

What was that old saying about paybacks being a bitch? This was the same woman who had left her hanging in front of that dingy storage unit, waiting for a kiss like an idiot.

Taking advantage of Sydney's lapse in vigilance, she wiped the cool, thick glob of ink across her cheek.

The sensation must have startled her because she opened her eyes quickly and then leered conspiratorially at Birdy. Quiet and controlled, she vowed, "You'll pay for this, Bird."

As Sydney reached for her, Birdy spun away from her grip, putting the worktable in between them. "I can't believe you just stood there and let me do it! You never would have survived 'Nam."

"I wouldn't have been fraternizing with the enemy there." Sydney darted to the right of the table trying to reach Birdy. She had wiped the excess ink off her cheek and now held it aloft, ready to return the favor.

Birdy laughed and ran through the nearest open door into the break room. She threw herself on the couch and yelled, "Truce! I call a truce. I'm waving my white flag, Sydney. We're even."

"We're not even." Sydney walked slowly and deliberately into the room, her ink-smeared finger held aloft. "You did the first one to yourself."

As she neared, Birdy giggled and threw her hands up, flapping them erratically to ward off her opponent and keep the glob of ink at bay. She was caught off guard when Sydney put one knee on the couch, loosely straddling her legs. Her surprise made it easy for Sydney to seize both her wrists and gently hold them against the back of the couch above her head. Suddenly, struggling out of this position no longer appealed and Birdy instead sunk down lower on the couch forcing Sydney to lean over her. Sydney's newly exposed cleavage was in perfect view and somewhere deep in the red glow of her mind Birdy imagined tasting the revealed skin. She realized that neither of them was giggling anymore, but a small smile still played on Sydney's lips.

Softly, gently, Sydney ran her finger down Birdy's nose, no doubt leaving an obnoxious streak of green in its wake. "Now," Sydney said quietly, "we're even."

Birdy was left cross-eyed and panting as Sydney blithely returned to her print station. It wasn't fair that anyone could turn herself on and off with such irritating precision.

"These things aren't going to print themselves, Bird."

Right, my fucking wedding invitations. Resigned, Birdy caught her breath, washed the ink off her face and went back to the real world.

CHAPTER FIFTEEN

"Hold up, hold up, hold up. Let me get all this straight." Beth was sitting on the floor of Sydney's new apartment. She had recently taken up yoga and was now practicing her stretches and poses on Sydney's rug.

Needing to vent, Sydney had invited her friend over and somewhat reluctantly divulged the less than flattering series of events she had recently found herself a part of. She was finding it harder to disclose her feelings now that Beth had moved on from a basic butterfly stretch and was now addressing her more directly from a warrior pose.

"Hot girl you work with…"

"Birdy," Sydney interjected.

Beth lunged forward on her left leg several times. "Yeah, yeah. Hot girl you work with is in fact a lesbian, which you know because the two of you have been flirting ceaselessly. Also, hot girl is *engaged*."

"Right, but I didn't know that at first."

"Okay, so you guys print shirts together and flirt shamelessly."

"I thought she was flirting but it might have been just me," Sydney added quickly, feeling the need to defend Birdy.

"It sounds like she was flirting back. And then you find out she's engaged by accidentally meeting her fiancée?" Beth switched her pose, now leading with her right leg. As she lunged, her knee made a frightening popping sound, which she ignored.

"Yeah."

"But you didn't end it there?" Beth asked incredulously. "Instead you went to a concert and almost kissed, you went swimming and almost kissed, she helped you move and you almost kissed, you printed her goddamn wedding invitations and almost kissed... Jesus, Sydney. You're a real glutton for punishment. Can you do anything without almost kissing the girl?"

Already sitting balled up on the couch, knees pulled to her chest, Sydney held herself together even tighter at Beth's unsympathetic words. She covered her face in embarrassment. "I know, I know! Honestly, I have no idea what's wrong with me. I should be running as fast as I can from this woman. It's just that I really like her, Beth. She's gotten under my skin and I don't know what to do about it."

"Does she feel the same way? Or is this just physical for her?"

Sydney was relieved when Beth sat back down and resumed a butterfly stretch position. It was hard to spill her guts while Beth attempted yoga. "I don't know. I think—or hope—she might have some real feelings. Like, I don't feel she's just toying with me, you know? Or fucking around with me because she can. I'm getting so many mixed messages from her, but I get the feeling she's confused... Like maybe she could have feelings for me but she's in too deep in her relationship to see it."

Beth held both her ankles and attempted to extend her legs while pulling her heels away from the ground. She looked like an egg rolling around on the carpet.

"Maybe you should respect that, Syd. If she's in that deep, you can't dive in after her. At some point she's going to have to surface for you."

"I know. I feel like I'm drowning."

"You need to let her go."

"How can I do that? I work with her for God's sake. I have to see her every day."

"Cold turkey is always my preferred method, but as hard as it's going to be, I think you have to try to be friends. Only friends."

"I don't know if I can. I don't know if I even want to."

Beth released her ankles and sat still finally. "If you keep this up, you could really fuck things up for her. You realize that, right? This isn't just about you. You're going to get hurt. It's so painfully obvious, but if you keep playing with fire like this, you're going to hurt Birdy too. She could lose everything. You're both on a crash course toward mountains of pain."

"Gee, thanks for the optimism."

"Optimism is your job. It always has been. I'm the realist and I'm here to tell you it's time to get your head out of the clouds. You need to get your feet under you again."

"Grounded to the cold rock that is pessimism? Come on, Beth. You gotta give me something."

"Strap on some sturdy boots and stay there awhile. You need a dose of reality."

"Speaking of, Birdy and I have plans to go hiking his weekend."

"Jesus, Mary and Joseph. You can't quit smoking if you keep buying cigarettes. Is there no hope for you?"

"I don't know, but that's exactly what I'm looking for. Hope."

Beth resumed her egg position, this time on her knees with her face pressed into the rug.

"What are you doing now?" Sydney asked.

"Child's pose. I'm going to stay here forever so I don't have to see you ruin your life."

CHAPTER SIXTEEN

"Hey babe. I'm here!" Birdy said as she pulled her key from the open condo door. "And I have a surprise for you."

"Baby, come here! I'm in the bedroom and I've been waiting for *hours*," Brooke said with a dramatic whine.

At the end of the hall, Birdy dropped her bag in the doorway of Brooke's bedroom at the sight of her fiancée lying naked in bed, the covers pushed to her hip. "I've missed you."

Sex had never been on their list of problems. Sometimes she thought it might be the glue that held them together, and right now she needed that glue to strengthen their bond.

Pulling her shirt over her head, she ambled toward the bed. Her attraction to Sydney had gotten out of control, but that was just out-of-control pheromones, she told herself. This, what she had with Brooke, was love. It was more than desire and good chemistry. The connection they shared and the deepness with which they felt for each other was the real deal.

Whereas the lust she had for Sydney was just a distraction.

Unbuttoning her jeans, she let them drop to the floor. Brooke opened her arms as she approached, and Birdy snuggled in. She decided at that instant she didn't want to be distracted from this anymore and melted into Brooke's kisses. She just needed to focus on this moment, to be truly here with Brooke so she could reset her compass and remember why she was on this path.

Not one bit of her was thinking about Sydney Ramos, nope. She was here with Brooke and she was Sydney-free. She wasn't thinking about Sydney's touch, just as Brooke's hands traveled lower down her body. Definitely not. A shiver coursed through her body that belied her internal dialogue.

Birdy gasped, thrown by the vision of Sydney touching her as she was about to have sex with her fiancée. "Fuck."

"Yeah, you like it when I touch you, baby?"

At this point Birdy wanted anything that would drive the thought of Sydney's mouth and hands from her mind. She shook the vision, forcing herself to stay in the moment. "Yes."

Brooke reached around her and unclasped her bra, taking one of her nipples into her mouth, licking the tightened skin. At Birdy's small moan, she reached between them, pushing her panties to the side.

Closing her eyes, a picture of Sydney holding her wrists and hovering above her on the break room couch swam into her thoughts. It was so vivid and delicious she couldn't clear it from her mind. She thought of each time she and Sydney almost kissed, at the beer fest, in her new apartment. So many close calls, except now in her imagination, she finished each moment with a breathtaking kiss that turned her on even more.

Brooke's lips found her breasts again as her mind settled on the memory of Sydney holding her in the river, water dripping down her face. Imagining the chill of the water on her nipples being replaced with the warmth and softness of Sydney's mouth. She could vividly picture the look in Sydney's eyes, her mouth devouring her breast. It was a look of fierce passion and hunger.

"Wait." Birdy rolled away from Brooke and lay on her back on the other side of the large bed, willing the vision out of her mind.

"What's wrong, babe?"

"I…ummm…" Birdy searched for something to say, something that would give her space to figure out why all of a sudden she was looking for an excuse not to have sex with her fiancée. This wasn't supposed to be one of their problems. "Your surprise! I want to give you your surprise." She scrambled out of bed.

"We're kind of in the middle of something here, Birdy. Can't it wait?"

"No, definitely not." She found a pair of Brooke's sweatpants and pulled them on before shimmying back into her T-shirt. She needed the physical separation so Brooke's hands wouldn't end up right back on her.

"Does this surprise really require you to be dressed?"

"No, I just…got cold. Aren't you cold?" Birdy tossed Brooke her sleep shirt. "Here, put that on so you don't get cold."

"I'd rather you come back to bed and warm me up again."

"Surprise first." Birdy rummaged in her work bag, removing the thick stack of invitations she and Sydney had printed. There it was again. Sydney. This was ludicrous.

The invitations safely tucked behind her back, she sat on the bed once more, this time as close to the edge as possible. Brooke reached for her leg and Birdy thrust out the stack of cards to distract her from her pursuit. "I finished our invitations. I designed them myself and even helped print them. What do you think?"

Brooke gave the top card a quick once-over. "They're cute." She tossed the stack on her bedside table, two of the invitations sliding off to the floor. "Now where were we? I'm pretty sure all of those clothes were gone and you were right here." She lifted the covers indicating the space along her body. Her very tight, fit body.

Birdy still found her insanely attractive but knew it would be impossible to make love with Brooke while thinking about someone else. A little more time, that's all she needed to get herself straightened out, to get her head back in the game. If she had to fake a few headaches in the meantime, it would be worth it to be fully immersed again in both the physical and emotional connections they once had. Complete connections that left zero room for thoughts about Sydney Ramos.

"They're cute? Come on, give me more than that. What do you think of them?"

With a frustrated huff of resignation, Brooke dropped the covers over herself and reached for a card, studying it more closely. "Yeah, they're cute."

"That's it?"

"I don't know, Birdy...You know I'm not artsy like you."

"What does that have to do with anything? What do you think of them?"

"I guess they're kind of quaint and...rustic."

"That sounds like a dirty word the way you say it. Do you like them?"

"I mean, they'll work."

"Of course they'll *work*. They're wedding invitations. I'm asking you if you like them."

Brooke hesitated, seemingly unsure how to proceed. "They're not exactly my style, obviously." Apparently recognizing Birdy's expression of hurt, she rushed on, "I was just imagining something a little more polished. Glossy maybe. It could have our picture on it or maybe some sparkly, curly script or something. Some bling, you know?"

Birdy thought back to the way she and Sydney had laughed about her niece comparing glitter to herpes and couldn't help the small smile that spread on her face.

Unfortunately, Brooke seemed to take the grin as mocking, as she was suddenly glowering.

Birdy rushed to apologize. "I'm sorry. I'm not laughing at you."

"What then?"

"Nothing. I was just...it's nothing. I like your idea," she lied. "I'm just not sure there's enough time to have more printed."

"I know. They're fine, really. Thanks for printing them. I'm sure they'll grow on me." Throwing the covers back with a sigh, Brooke got up and wrapped a towel around herself before roughly kissing Birdy on the cheek. Before leaving the room, she delivered a parting shot with her usual unfeeling sting. "I just can't believe they're the reason I didn't get laid."

Birdy retrieved her invitations from where Brooke had discarded them on the nightstand and slowly ran her thumb over the ink, feeling the slight embossment it made. She could hear Brooke start the shower in the en suite and allowed herself the luxury of thinking of Sydney, her lips pursed in concentration as she pulled the squeegee to print black ink on top of the green. Those same lips close to hers, hovering only inches away. She rubbed at the text, as if trying to scrub away the memory, and then left the bed to put the stack back in her bag.

CHAPTER SEVENTEEN

Sydney drove to Birdy's, enjoying the hot August sun on her shoulders. She had taken the soft top off her Jeep and removed the doors, something she rarely did since she had to haul them up to her apartment, where they now took up every free inch of her floor.

She was looking forward to her day with Birdy. They were going to cruise along the Columbia Gorge and go for a hike. Birdy had offered to plan the day, wanting to show her one of her favorite spots. Lunch and beer were also promised and Sydney had to constantly remind herself this wasn't a date. It had been over a week since they printed the wedding invites. They had talked regularly at work but she was having trouble shaking Beth's words, and was therefore trying to give Birdy a little bit of distance so they could both gain some much-needed perspective. They'd had too many close calls.

She wanted Birdy to dump Brooke and be with her but she wasn't sure exactly how far she was willing to go. Beth was right, she knew, but she wasn't yet ready to concede defeat. She did, however, admit that kissing a nearly married woman seemed like a line she wasn't willing to cross.

Exacerbating her inner turmoil even more, Birdy had texted the night before to tell her when to pick her up and had also added, "Make sure your backseat is free. I have a surprise for you. ;)"

Sydney had reread the message twenty times, unsure of what to think or how to respond. The winky face made everything that much more confusing. She had finally typed back a hesitant "...okay..." and ran downstairs with a handheld vacuum to clean the seat and floorboards.

She pulled up to Birdy's dock, checking one last time to make sure her backseat was clean before catching her reflection in her rearview mirror. Rolling her eyes, she admonished herself. *You're scared to even kiss her. It's not like you're going to have sex with her in your backseat.*

She straightened her mirror and turned to get out of the Jeep, finding herself nearly face-to-face with a very large dog, its very large dog paws on her doorframe. The dog immediately started licking her arm from wrist to shoulder.

"Well, thank you. I knew my shower hadn't been enough. Apparently I needed a bath as well," Sydney said to the dog, moving her arm out of tongue's reach.

"I see you've met your surprise."

Sydney whirled to find Birdy standing at the passenger side of the Jeep with her arms stretched upward on the truck's roll bar. Her stance highlighted her toned arms, and Sydney couldn't help but admire the way her breasts jutted forward.

She had on fraying corduroy cutoffs and a loose, striped tank top. Her dark chin-length hair was tucked behind her ears and a pair of oversized aviator sunglasses accentuated her delicate features in a very sexy way.

Sydney sucked in her breath. How was she supposed to behave herself when Birdy looked like that?

"That's Cornflake. She belongs to my mom. I'm dogsitting for the weekend. Is it okay if she comes along? I brought towels for the backseat if you're all right with it."

Sydney glanced back at Cornflake, who took the opportunity to take a swipe at her face again with her giant tongue. She wasn't used to being around dogs, especially large ones, but she wasn't willing to disappoint Birdy. "Of course. Should I have left the top on? Will she jump out?"

"Nah. She wouldn't, but I also have a harness for her so we can seatbelt her in."

They got Cornflake settled in the backseat with a towel beneath her, which Sydney was thankful for since the dog was drooling like a waterpark. Then they took off, heading east toward the Washington State side of the gorge.

Along the scenic route on Highway 14 toward Stevenson, they admired the landscape that reached skyward all around. Sometimes it sloped back toward the river with tree-softened drops, other times dramatic cliff faces stood exposed. The wide, glistening river was always present, adding dimension to the intense colors that washed over the region.

Their conversation was pleasantly sparse as they focused on the roar of the wind and the sun-dappled road ahead. Occasionally Birdy would point out a landmark like the Vista House or the most famous waterfall, Multnomah Falls, which could barely be seen across the river. Usually, though, she would just glance back and check on Cornflake before catching Sydney's eye and smiling as she turned around. It was in those moments that Sydney most wanted to lose herself, to ignore all the warnings and give in to the feelings she knew would make her happy. She had to keep both hands on the wheel to avoid reaching over and letting her hand rest in Birdy's lap.

In between daydreams, she worried their backseat passenger might jump out onto the road. But every time she checked the mirror, she saw Cornflake's tongue hanging out of a mouth that seemed to be turned up into a contented smile. Occasionally the dog's ears would catch the wind and fan out, and Sydney thought she looked ready to take flight with her own happiness. Being with Birdy gave her a similar feeling.

Trying to rein in her thoughts, she reminded herself of the reality of the situation. "Where's Brooke today?" she asked, attempting to eradicate any hesitancy or nervousness in her voice. She was trying to be a friend to Birdy, though she knew she wanted much more. Asking about her fiancée was a good step. Granted, a step that made her want to shoot herself in the face.

"She had to work today. The giant Comic Con is this weekend. She's an event manager at the convention center so she has to help plan and manage stuff like that."

"It sucks she has to work on weekends. A Comic Con, huh? That should be a pretty fun event to coordinate though."

Birdy's loud snort was carried away through the open Jeep top. "Brooke hates Comic Con. Hates with a capital H. Far too much whimsy in the air. Capes, elf ears, *cosplay*." She laughed more, giggles taking over. "She has to suck up to a guy who refers to himself as a mage while she's wearing this tiny little cape clipped to her power suit."

Sydney could imagine Brooke, the Queen Bitch, plastering on a schmoozing smile when a Comic Con official walked near. She relished the thought of her sucking up to anyone dressed like a Jedi.

An hour out of Portland, Birdy instructed her to turn right onto an old steel bridge that spanned the width of the Columbia. They passed under a sign that read "The Bridge of the Gods." It felt like an ominous name, and as her tires drifted left and right on the steel grating, the feeling grew, like she was no longer in control, another force propelling them across the bridge's narrow lane.

Once safely on the other side, they paid their dollar toll and backtracked slightly on the Oregon side of the gorge until they reached the trailhead for Wahclella Falls. Birdy unbelted Cornflake, who nearly fell out of the Jeep with excitement. She danced at their feet, willing them to hurry until she was distracted by a smell, which she hunted down and peed on.

Sydney was wearing a soft gray University of Texas T-shirt and short khaki shorts, which had seen plenty of hiking trails already. She pointed down to her closed-toe hiking sandals and asked, "Do I need to change into my boots?"

"It's only a mile in. It's probably not as much as you're used to so you should be fine in those. Plus, Cornflake will definitely be swimming. I'll probably wade in with her."

Sydney shouldered her small hiking pack and Birdy added a tennis ball and waste bags for Cornflake, who was once again bouncing all around.

"You ready?"

"Yep. Let's hit it."

The path began as a wide gravel road that followed the edge of a rocky and shallow creek. Cornflake bounded into the water at her first opportunity and lay down at the deepest section she could find. She cooled her jets while snapping at each leaf that drifted past, flouncing in the water, and tripping and sliding on rocks. Occasionally, she dunked her entire face in the water.

"She's a regal creature, that one," Birdy deadpanned.

"I can tell. Such grace and poise. Watching her is like the first time I saw the ballet or tasted a fine wine. Also, she's pooping in the river."

Birdy groaned and Cornflake goggled at them, her back hunched and her mouth drawn in concentration.

"Well, I guess that's one less bag I'll have to use."

Cornflake bounded to the shore victoriously and shook the water out of her coat at Sydney's feet.

"True grace."

"A vision of elegance," Birdy agreed.

They hiked on past a small dam, where the trail narrowed dramatically and climbed higher along a ridge. Soon they had a gorgeous view of the creek below and the wind-carved basalt rock face on the other side of the narrow gorge. Though the hike was easy for Sydney, Cornflake plodded along behind them, panting heavily from the climb.

At a fork, Sydney followed Birdy, who also seemed to be breathing a bit faster. The trail steepened considerably. Eventually, the roar of rushing water registered and Sydney tried to locate it. They rounded a bend and she nearly plowed over Birdy, who had stopped abruptly in the narrow path. Recovering, she sidled up alongside and took in the view.

"Bonus points," Birdy said.

"Huh?"

"You said I got bonus points if our hike ended at a waterfall."

Sydney was awed by the falls, which were still a hundred yards or so ahead of them. It was a tiered falls, the upper section caked in richly colored mossy rock over which the lower falls spilled. Trees towered over the water along the rim of the rock, adding to the magnificence of the scenery. She could not yet see the plunge pool at the very bottom but the mist rising up from the rushing water caught the late morning sun and glistened above the lower falls. A small rainbow was visible in the weightless water droplets.

"Definite bonus points. This is gorgeous."

Birdy was obviously pleased with herself. "Come on, let's go see it up close." She tugged at Cornflake's leash, willing her up from the strip of shade where she had plopped herself. The path sloped downward now, leading the three of them to the base of the falls.

Cornflake picked up steam when she saw the giant pool of cool water ahead. They carefully climbed a large pile of downed timber that had been pushed up against the embankment opposite the waterfall until they reached a rock outcropping that stood only twenty or thirty feet from where the stream crashed into the pond. The dog dove in and seemed surprised by the depth of the water. When she resurfaced, she paddled about more cautiously, if not more gracefully, while picking out sticks to chomp on as she swam.

Standing on the rock, Sydney let the mist rain down on her, cooling her heated skin. She reverentially took in the beauty of her surroundings and felt content. Unwilling to think beyond this moment or to consider her near future, the one that didn't include Birdy when she went to sleep tonight or when she woke up in the morning, she allowed herself to just enjoy the moment.

Birdy joined her on the rock and took off her sunglasses to wipe the water droplets away with the hem of her shirt. She squinted up at Sydney. "When's your birthday?"

"April. Why?"

"Just felt like I should know. April what?"

"Twenty-seventh. What's yours?"

"May tenth. We're pretty close. What's your favorite color?" Sydney looked around, taking in all the rich hues that surrounded her. "Green."

"Red."

"Complementary colors," Sydney said quietly.

Birdy nodded, understanding. "They are. They bring out the best in each other and make each other more vibrant," she said almost to herself before calling out to Cornflake, who subsequently pushed her entire wet body between Birdy's legs. Though too late to save herself from getting soaked, she lightly nudged the dog away. "You hungry?"

"Me or Cornflake?"

"You. Cornflake's always hungry." At Sydney's nod, she added, "Let's head back."

They looped back on a trail that hugged the western bank of the creek before crossing the water over a wooden bridge. At the end of the mile, Cornflake was fairly dry so they loaded her into the backseat on her towel and drove east again to the base of The Bridge of the Gods.

"This is Cascade Locks, a pretty cute little town with an awesome brewery. The view is incredible. Turn left up here." Birdy directed her into a park and then along a lane until they reached a brewery that was nearly in the shadow of the bridge. Finding a shady table outside, they ordered sandwiches and a tasting flight of beer.

Their table overlooked a sharp bank that dropped into a set of locks built into the river over a hundred years ago. Just past the lock canal was an elevated strip of land that served as a picnic area for some. Beyond that, Sydney could see the entire width of the Columbia River and across to Washington State, where impressive rock outcroppings peeked out above the trees. The afternoon light glistened on the water, adding golden hues to the shaded blues. Sydney hoped she would never forget this day.

"You think the view is beautiful?" Birdy seemed to guess her thoughts. "Wait until you try these beers."

She explained each of them in the tasting flight and encouraged Sydney to take the first sip. They talked about the beer and their hike, their conversation eventually drifting to Birdy's boat, the Northwestern climate, their work…all easy topics. Conversation was breezy for nearly an hour until Sydney found she was frustrated by the small talk. It felt like a barrier had gone up between them. Beth's words had caused her to reexamine her desire to win Birdy's heart, but in her effort to be Birdy's friend, she was slowly building a wall between them. A wall constructed out of fear, uncertainty and pedantic small talk.

A lengthy silence spread between them as they studied the river, and not the comfortable silence Sydney was used to with Birdy. This one crackled with unspoken words they were afraid to say, like a smoldering log, waiting to take flame. After a moment of uncertainty Sydney asked, "How are your wedding plans coming along?"

Birdy's head snapped up. She was noticeably caught off guard. "Surely you don't want to talk about that."

"No, not particularly, but we have to talk about more than beer and work if we're going to be friends."

"Is that what you want? To be friends?"

Contemplating the question, Sydney sipped her beer. "Depends. Do you make out with your friends?"

"Home-wrecker," Birdy said, a tinge of humor in her voice.

Sydney lit up at her words and pushed her fist in the air, singing a few lines from Miley Cyrus's "Wrecking Ball" toward the sky.

Birdy covered her face, looking around in a show of embarrassment.

Unperturbed, she nudged Birdy's arm. "Admit it. I do a pretty cute Miley rendition, don't you think?"

"Adorable."

"You're picturing me swinging around naked on a wrecking ball. I can tell."

Birdy reddened. "I wasn't but now…"

"Work boots make my calves look good too."

"I don't doubt it." Birdy ran her finger around the rim of the glass in front of her.

"Come on, I make a pretty tempting home-wrecker, don't I?" She finished the cream ale she had been nursing and pulled another beer from the wooden tray. "Oh, God. This must be the IPA. Yuck."

Birdy snatched the drink from Sydney and took a long sip before sighing, satisfied. "That just means more for me. And you would be a tempting home-wrecker as long as you don't sing. Is that why you're single? 'Cause you sing dated Miley Cyrus songs to people?"

"Nope. You're the first one to be blessed with my angelic voice."

"So then why are you single, Miley? Girls must be breaking down your door to watch you twerk."

"I'm single because you're the only girl besides Beth that knows where I live, and so far you haven't knocked down my door." With uncharacteristic seriousness, she took a chance and quietly said, "I wish you would though."

Birdy paled and looked away uncomfortably.

Immediately Sydney regretted her sincerity so she hastily attempted to lighten the mood. "You can borrow my wrecking ball if you need it." The comment barely earned a small chuckle from Birdy.

She knew her flirting was only tolerated because she masked it all in a perpetual lightness. Laughing and joking suggestively was fun but she constantly yearned for more, and exposing that desire had been a mistake. She wanted so badly to show Birdy her serious side but was worried the intensity would scare her away. Now her concern had been proven to have merit.

Her mind drifted to earlier in the afternoon and how wonderful it would have been to wrap Birdy in her arms and kiss her with the waterfall crashing behind them. She wanted that easy intimacy with her as well as the scorching passion she knew they were capable of. Wishing to take Birdy home with her and feel every inch of their skin connecting was a pointless dream. Obviously Birdy was unobtainable but still she hoped that someday, she could have her.

Soon after, they finished their beers and agreed to head back to the city.

When they arrived at the dock, Birdy clipped Cornflake's leash on as Sydney vigorously scratched her ears, feeling much more comfortable with the large dog than she had at the beginning of the day. "Thanks for the surprise. The day wouldn't have been the same without this goof."

"Yeah, she's pretty easy to love."

She's not the only one.

"I had a great day," Sydney finally said, breaking the tension building between them after they stood for an anxious moment.

"Me too," Birdy said quietly and then she turned to go.

Sydney reluctantly got back in her car, wondering if her relationship with Birdy had forever changed. Friendship no longer seemed plausible and love impossible. If her feelings for Birdy were proving to be all or nothing, she realized that nothing, the most painful choice, would be her only choice.

* * *

As Birdy led Cornflake toward the boat, she was unsure why today had felt so dissatisfying. It was as if a wall had cropped up between them. The easy flow was replaced with tension and their usual shared humor replaced with edgy seriousness. Sydney had seemed reserved at times. Occasionally her old self would shine through and Birdy was always awed by the attraction she felt. In some ways, today had been easier as there was less guilt-inducing flirting and fewer butterflies in her stomach to swat away. But there had also been less laughter, less openness, and Birdy missed the connection. And she had to admit she missed the flirting.

She stopped on the dock, letting Cornflake sniff the post where a bird had just been perched, when she heard Sydney call her name.

Standing in her Jeep, her forearms draped over the top of the windshield, Sydney called out. "You never told me if Brooke liked the invitations. She loved them, didn't she?"

Birdy couldn't stand to tell her the truth. "Yeah, Syd. She loved them."

"Good. How could she not? You made them!" With a final wave, Sydney started the ignition and swung the Jeep toward the road.

Birdy's smile faltered as the taillights faded into a dusk that threatened to suffocate her.

CHAPTER EIGHTEEN

Sydney unbuttoned and then re-buttoned her white dinner jacket as she pressed the elevator call button in the lobby of Brooke's building. The early October night had chilled the silk lining, raising goose bumps along her bare arms. After four months in Portland, Sydney was getting her first taste of winter outside of Texas.

She pushed the call button again, feeling impatient in spite of her reluctance to reach the twelfth floor. She hadn't expected to be invited to the engagement party, but then Brooke had no cause to think there had ever been anything brewing between her and her fiancée.

When the elevator opened, she stepped in and checked her reflection in the closed doors, which were so polished they mirrored an unadulterated view. The invitation had requested formal attire, so she wore skinny black tux pants that ended at the ankle and shiny black power pumps. Under her white, tailored dinner jacket, she had left her sleeveless white blouse open at the collar to reveal a delicate gold necklace her nieces had given her last Christmas. Her dark hair was pulled back tightly into a chic ponytail, and she had very carefully applied a thick line of eyeliner. Made up like this, she looked the part for a formal dinner party, but the barely concealed nervousness and sadness in her eyes hinted at her apprehension to be in the same room as Birdy while she celebrated her engagement to another woman.

The elevator arrived at the twelfth floor, where the picture window at the end of the hallway overlooking Portland's downtown and the Hawthorne Bridge made her feel miles away from her squat, comfortable studio apartment, which she could nearly see crowded among the buildings to the east of the bridge. The suit and pumps gave her a sense of control in the wholly awkward situation, but the smallness of her home made her feel dejected and lost. She looked as if she fit in but knew this—an opulent building, a celebration of happiness was not where she belonged. The desire to be anywhere but here consumed her but mostly she longed to be on Birdy's boat, just the two of them, with their flip-flops kicked off and their feet propped on the railing.

She had stood at the window longer than she meant to. Barely registering the sound of a door opening farther up the hall, she didn't turn until a man joined her at the window.

"God, I love this city," he said, gazing into the distance.

She could only nod, still lost in her thoughts but feeling strangely at ease next to him.

"Are you Sydney?"

Finally, she turned her full attention to him.

"Yes."

He smiled warmly. "I'm Saul, Birdy's friend. I've heard a lot about you."

"I believe I've heard a thing or two about you too." Most of what she knew had come from Mare, not Birdy.

"Nothing good, I hope. I have a reputation." He squinted one eye at her, mouth downturned into a frown.

She couldn't help but laugh. "Don't worry, it's all been bad."

"Good. You, on the other hand, I can't say the same for. Mare can't speak highly enough of you and Birdy nearly swoons when she talks about you."

"Oh." Sydney gulped. She hadn't expected that, but she was elated that Birdy thought about her.

Saul's overly familiar look made Sydney wonder how much he knew. She suddenly wanted to tell him everything.

"And you've met Brooke, the host of this little fête?" His tone suggested he was feeling her out while keeping his own cards close to his chest.

She nodded glumly, deciding she didn't give a damn if Saul knew she was less than thrilled about being here.

"Then I'd say you're looking forward to this dinner party just as much as I am," he said sarcastically. Offering Sydney his arm with the resignation of troops headed to the front lines, he pushed open the heavy beige door to Brooke's condo.

"You two have met!" Birdy's eyes were alight with happiness when she saw Sydney on Saul's arm.

"We're already inseparable," Saul said, giving her a tight one-armed hug that seemed as much for Birdy's benefit as hers.

She was thankful for the contact as she desperately needed something to ground her. The dress Birdy wore was stunning. It was a short, navy blue lace sheath with a scalloped V-neckline that flattered her figure perfectly. Sydney found herself at a loss for words.

With great effort she finally spoke, saying the first thing that came to mind. "You look beautiful, Bird." She was unable to hide the breathiness in her voice.

"You do too." Sydney held herself stiffly as Birdy looked down her length, noticeably gasping when she took in the pumps that made her several inches taller. She couldn't help but bite her lower lip nervously at Birdy's appraisal of her appearance. As soon as her teeth pressed into her lip, Birdy flushed and whimpered. Apparently Birdy found her mouth distracting. If they were anywhere else, Sydney could have some fun with that.

Finally, Saul cleared his throat and Birdy looked away, obviously flustered. "I'll give you two a minute," Saul said, gracefully exiting the conversation.

"You didn't have to come…" Birdy said.

"I guess I was feeling especially masochistic tonight. Plus, I look killer in this tux."

"I can attest to that."

"Is it okay I'm here?"

"Yes! Definitely yes. I invited you, didn't I? I'm glad you're here. I mean, it's nice to have more friends here. Brooke has so many." Birdy bit her lower lip and surveyed the party with an unusual wariness. She seemed uncomfortable and self-conscious. Turning back to Sydney, she said more quietly than before, "I didn't think you would come. I thought it might be… hard for you or, well, awkward."

"I guess I just needed to see it for myself, you know?"

"What if you don't like what you see?"

"Hey, we're going to be friends, right?" Sydney gulped, not feeling as confident as she sounded. She hadn't yet figured out how to be just friends with someone who made her crazy with desire. "As your friend, I wouldn't miss it."

"Right. Friends."

They gazed at each other and a heavy sadness crept into Sydney's heart. She wasn't sure she had made the right decision. She shouldn't have come, shouldn't have decided to play witness to this monumental life event. This party represented the loss of her own dream, her hope for what her life could be and who she could spend that life with.

What she hadn't said to Birdy but had to admit to herself was that she needed to know if she should fight for Birdy, if she *could* fight for Birdy and to lay her indecision to rest.

Grappling for words, she opened her mouth and then shut it again when another partygoer pulled Birdy into an enthusiastic hug and demanded to hear all of the details of the engagement. She stood awkwardly a few feet behind them as Birdy professed her excitement over the "big day" to this overly exuberant girl, whose wide, flat features made her look as if she'd had a facelift only hours ago. Sydney hadn't meant to eavesdrop but the girl's piercing voice made it impossible not to hear their conversation.

"Oh, my God," Facelift exclaimed, still holding Birdy's arms. "You two are like the cutest couple. Your love for each other is just *so* obvious. It's like, tangible, you know? I'm just so happy for you!"

"Thanks, I'm so glad you could make it tonight."

Obviously trying to extract herself from the conversation, Birdy's exit was delayed when the girl spoke to her again. "You know, you and Brooke are totally my Bette and Tina."

Birdy looked taken aback. "Huh?"

"You know, *The L Word*? You guys are totally a Bette and Tina power couple. Well, before Bette cheats on Tina of course."

"Of course."

Sydney didn't know whether to laugh or gag.

"Anyway, congratulations! You two deserve all the happiness in the world. It's obvious you two were meant for each other. Brooke adores you."

Birdy gave the girl a genuine smile for the first time and then her eyes wandered the room until resting on Brooke, who happened to glance up at the same time. Brooke held her gaze and their smiles grew.

Sydney thought dejectedly that this must have been what they looked like when they first started dating, giddily staring at each other from across the room. A current of love flowed between them and Sydney wanted to die.

Saul suddenly reappeared, offering his arm to Sydney once more. "I think it's time I take you around the room for some introductions." He steered her toward Mare and said, "I take back what I said earlier. I think you want to be here *even less* than I do."

* * *

For an hour, Sydney smiled and hugged anyone Saul introduced her to as Mare chattered into her ear, exposing any juicy tidbits she had about Brooke's friends.

Saul pointed across the room. "That's Birdy's mom, Bea. She's a hoot. Want to meet her?"

"Honestly, no." Sydney already felt like a fraud among all these cheerful well-wishers. Considering the way she felt about Birdy, she thought meeting her mother in this setting would be a new low, so she came up with an excuse to ease her bluntness. "I may be an extrovert but I'm feeling a bit socially overwhelmed. Maybe I'll get a chance to meet her later."

A cute little Pomeranian sniffed around Sydney's feet and she crouched down to pet it, taking the opportunity to avoid any more explanation as to why she had no interest in meeting Birdy's mother. She realized the dog must be Brooke's and she gave it a soft growl that made her feel remarkably better. Unperturbed, the enemy dog scuttled off to another group, who offered napkins full of appetizers.

Finally dinner was served and Sydney found herself mercifully seated with Mare and Saul, far away from the celebrating lovebirds at the other end of Brooke's impressively long dining table. The meal had been catered, and she had already snacked on her own plate of delicious hors d'oeuvres. While the main course was being served, Brooke stood with a glass of champagne in hand, smiling at her guests and waiting for their complete attention.

"First of all, Birdy and I would like to thank you all for being here. I know several of you traveled far to be with us and we appreciate your friendship and love. I hope you all will be able to make that trip again in January for the wedding. Don't think you're off the hook just yet." She paused, basking in their laughter.

Sydney straightened her silverware anxiously and prayed she wouldn't be invited to the wedding.

Brooke went on, "All of you represent some of the most important people in our lives and we couldn't imagine taking this monumental step without you." She regarded the table, making eye contact with several of her guests. Each one lit up as though feeling special at gaining Brooke's personal attention.

"There's one person here in particular I want to acknowledge. Bea Cartwright, Birdy's mother. You and Birdy are my only family in Oregon, and I appreciate you taking me in and accepting me as your future daughter-in-law. With my family living out of state and my father's poor health making it impossible for them to travel for this event, it means so much to have you here as Birdy's parent as well as my own. Birdy is my entire world and I plan to take very good care of her. You giving us your blessing means more to us than I ever could explain."

Birdy put her arm around her mother and gave her a tight squeeze.

"Thank you for raising such a perfect daughter." Brooke delivered one more beaming smile toward Bea and then shifted her attention to Birdy, who looked brilliantly happy.

Sydney felt a raw surge of jealousy barrel through her veins.

"We are all here to celebrate the love I have for this woman, Birdy Cartwright. It hasn't always been easy for her, and she's put up with a lot from me over the years. Those of you who know me can attest to how difficult I can be." Brooke's friends looked at each other, laughing and seemingly thinking about shared memories.

One of Brooke's more boisterous friends chimed in. "We knew you were worth it!"

Brooke smiled and tipped her glass toward her friend. "Thank you, Em. But more importantly, I'm lucky that Birdy seems to think so too, since she has agreed to be my wife."

A loud cheer came from the attendees as they hooted and whistled their congratulations. Indulging them with a large smile, Brooke waited for the noise to die down before continuing. She looked to her side, all of her focus now directed solely at Birdy.

Sydney was amazed at the power of Brooke's charisma. How she could quiet a room with a smile and so easily make others hang on every word. In a crowded room surrounded by sameness, she had the unique ability to make one feel special. All of that power was now directed at Birdy, who beamed back with love in her eyes—and Sydney was helpless to do anything but watch.

"For five years I have adored you, Birdy. For five years I have loved you, and for five years I have been the luckiest woman because you have loved me. You are the reason I live, and I look forward to each new day of our lives, with you by my side as my wife. Thank you for your love and loyalty." Tears welled in Birdy's eyes and Brooke spoke to the rest of the table, raising her glass. "To Birdy, and our future together."

"Hear, hear!"

As everyone took a sip of champagne, Birdy stood abruptly, her chair falling back as she wrapped her arms tightly around Brooke's neck and kissed her fervently. Tears spilled down her cheeks, and she smiled as Brooke wiped them away, planting a kiss at both corners of Birdy's mouth before turning back to the table with joy and pride on her face.

Sydney finally pulled her eyes away, heartbroken and ashamed that she had been chasing a woman who so obviously didn't want to be chased. She wished she could sink down into her chair and disappear. Or find a way to excuse herself and then make a run for it. But deep down she knew she deserved this. She deserved to hear and see exactly what she had spent several months wishing didn't exist.

After Birdy retook her seat and the rest of the group finished toasting the couple, Brooke picked up a stack of papers from a nearby sideboard. Once again she scanned the room, her smile asking for quiet, which fell immediately.

"Before you all enjoy this meal, which was made by a professional chef—don't worry, I had nothing to do with it, so it will be delicious—I have something to give each of you." She held up the invitations Sydney had printed. "My talented fiancée designed and printed these invitations by hand, and I am happy to say that each of you will be the first to be formally invited to our wedding." She again smiled warmly at Birdy. "These invitations are a tangible reminder of your love, patience and forgiveness, and I would be a fool to be jealous of your vision and talents. Do you think you can forgive me once again?"

Sydney looked around the room, much as all of the other guests were doing. She sensed they were all witnessing a moment that was meant more for Birdy than it was for them.

When Birdy nodded, smiling through her tears, Brooke raised her glass once more, "To Birdy."

"To Birdy," the group chanted. "Cheers!"

Sydney couldn't bring herself to do anything more than half-heartedly raise her glass.

"Now let's eat," Brooke called over the well-wishers, taking her seat and kissing Birdy tenderly once more.

Sydney felt small and pathetic. Seeing them together smiling and holding hands, she knew she had to allow Birdy to be happy. She had to bow out gracefully from the race in which, she now realized, she hadn't even been a contender.

* * *

The table had been cleared and the caterer sent home for the night. Birdy was relieved to finally be alone with Brooke and cuddling on the couch. A few champagne flutes, still half full, sat scattered around the room, the remaining bubbles sluggishly rising to the surface. She sighed contentedly and laid her head on Brooke's shoulder.

"That was a great party," she said, nuzzling closer.

Brooke pulled her in tightly. "You think everyone had a good time?"

"Definitely. You're a good hostess. Attentive, outgoing. You're really good at making people feel special. That's why I love you so much, because you make me feel special."

"I love you too." Brooke kissed the top of her head and gave her one more tight squeeze. "I'm totally beat. Ready to go to bed?"

"Soon. You go ahead. I'm going to clean up a bit more and wind down." She gave Brooke a lingering goodnight kiss and then pulled her feet up under her as she watched her disappear into the bedroom. Pumpkin jumped up on the couch and in an uncharacteristic display of affection cuddled next to her, his front paws resting on her leg.

"You're not so bad when you're not snapping at my ankles, you know? And you are really cute, but don't let that go to your head. You already have way too big of an ego for such a little dog." She stroked his fur, enjoying how soft his ears felt under her palm. He licked her hand before resting his chin on his paws. "Be nicer to Hoots, okay? We're going to live with you soon."

Tonight had been exactly what she needed in her relationship with Brooke. A reminder of what she had and what she would be giving up if she continued on this dangerous trajectory toward Sydney. Despite Saul's earlier assurance that she had not cheated on Brooke, she knew in her heart that she was guilty of emotional infidelity.

She thought of a time in college when she had been sitting with a group of friends on the floor playing Never Have I Ever. Someone said, "Never have I ever…cheated on someone." Only one person put their finger down, ticking off one of her five allowed admissions before she lost the game. The girl, Lindsey, happened to be Birdy's current crush, and Birdy was shocked by the confession. Everyone whooped and demanded an explanation. Lindsey calmly shrugged her shoulders and said simply, "Shit happens."

Something about that overly simplified explanation had always struck her. Yes indeed, shit happens. It was shit that she allowed herself to be swayed by her feelings for Sydney. She was finally beginning to understand the detached frankness in Lindsey's tone. She had always viewed cheating in a black and white matter—either you are a cheater or you are not—but a world of gray was attacking her naivety, and it was overwhelming and confusing. The enormity of that uncertain grayness made Birdy want to shrug her shoulders and say, "Shit happens." She wanted to give up and make it all go away. Everything made sense in her old life and she just wanted that back. Tonight felt like a step in the right direction.

She thought of Hoots. "A place for everything and everything in its place," she murmured, her hushed tones barely reaching her own ears. She clearly had a place here with Brooke, a defined role. She just hadn't realized until now how much comfort that role gave her.

Surely she owed it to her relationship with Brooke to try to bridge the crevasse that had been forming between them. She had made a commitment, hadn't she? She was to be married in just a couple months. Invitations had been sent, down payments placed, arrangements made.

She quickly readied for bed and climbed under the covers and cuddled up against Brooke's back. Her arms wrapped around her fiancée and held on to their love as tightly as they could.

CHAPTER NINETEEN

Brooke entered the Halloween party at Mare's house guns a-blazing, literally. She leveled her toy rifle at the nearest partygoer, who happened to be Sydney. "*Chk-chk, kapow!* Gotcha!" With a maniacal cackle, she shouted over her shoulder to Birdy, "Go retrieve my fallen prey while I get us some drinks."

Birdy, dressed as a brown Labrador, gave Sydney a small wave as Brooke continued on toward the kitchen for a drink, not her first of the evening.

"She's a sexy duck hunter," she explained needlessly, having searched for something innocuous to say. It was hard not to feel silly in her dog costume.

"And you're her retriever."

"Yeah, it's sort of becoming a theme. Last year she was a sexy construction worker and I was a jackhammer," Birdy said dryly. "The year before that, she was a sexy tennis player and I was a tennis ball. I think I'm moving up. At least I'm not an inanimate object this time."

"Well you look absolutely adorable in that costume." Sydney checked out her oversized brown onesie, which had a large white oval stitched on the stomach and a cartoonish dog's face on the hood. She also made a show of checking out Birdy's ass and shaking the tail attached to it. "I would be drooling but I guess that's your job."

"Hilarious. Who the hell are you supposed to be, anyway?"

Sydney was dressed much as she always was—short black running shorts, a vintage striped tank top and Nikes with long white tube socks that ended with two red stripes just below her knees. Her dark hair was pulled up in a ponytail, but on her upper lip was a bushy, sandy-colored mustache. "I'm Pre."

"Who?"

She raised her hands in exaggerated disbelief. "You know, Steve Prefontaine?"

"Oh, isn't he that runner guy?"

"Runner guy? He was a legend! You're from Oregon. He's one of your most famous athletes. How could you not know this? He held records in, like, every long-distance running event and went to the Olympics."

"I think I saw a movie about him on TV," Birdy said with a dismissive wave of her hand. "But you do look pretty cute with that mustache, Pre."

"Thanks, Fido."

With a chuckle, Birdy excused herself to find Brooke, not surprised that she hadn't made her way back with the promised drink. She found her in the kitchen, an empty shot glass in hand and a lime wedge in her mouth.

"Hi, baby," Brooke said, pulling her in for a kiss.

The tequila on her breath and the salt and lime on her lips weren't entirely unpleasant. A couple years ago she might have lingered, running her tongue along Brooke's lips, enjoying the lewd churn of their hips.

With Brooke's heavy arm settled around her shoulders, Birdy realized that they rarely did anything more than peck in public these days. Not like the old *horny days* when they couldn't keep their hands off one another. They would make out passionately, hands trailing over each other's bodies, flirting with the far boundaries of "appropriate public behavior." She wondered when that had stopped. Did it gradually die as lust often does? Did they just become more aware of the eyes around them, in turn becoming less aware of each other? Tonight it was all for the best because the only set of eyes on them seemed to be Saul's, rolling as they were.

He was leaning against the counter on the far side of the room, holding his cocktail napkin in front of his face, pretending to vomit. Birdy stuck out her tongue and then downed the shot of vodka Brooke handed her.

Mare approached and slid her arm around Saul's waist. Seeing them together and watching Saul giddily pull her even closer still made Birdy smile, even though they had been dating for a few months now.

She tugged Brooke's hand. "We need to go say hi."

"I don't want to talk to that asshole."

"Just be nice." She gently urged Brooke toward their hostess. Half a step behind Brooke, she caught Saul's eye again and gave him her best "don't fuck with me" look. For good measure, she mouthed the same words she had just said to Brooke, asking him to be nice.

Though Birdy hugged them both enthusiastically, Brooke hugged only Mare. Her greeting to Saul was a barely civil nod. "Saul."

"Brooke. Always a pleasure." His sentiment wasn't quite dripping with sarcasm, but there was a dampness to it that made Birdy cringe inwardly.

She sensed Brooke was winding up to pitch a snide retort, so she jumped in to cut her off. "Saul, you're dressed exactly like you always are. Where's your costume?"

"I'm wearing it. I'm going as a middle school guidance counselor this year."

"That's what you wear every year. It's not a costume when you just wear your usual work clothes," she said, whacking him on his shrugging shoulder. "What about you, Mare? You look like a mountain climber."

"Yeah, I'm going for a granola Laura Croft Tomb Raider look." She wiggled her toes in her contoured, minimalist shoes and showed off her khaki shorts and lavender tank top. "Plus this way I can put vodka in my CamelBak." Mare sucked her drink through the straw that was clipped to her shoulder. "It tastes like hell, though."

"I heard those shoes are really bad for you," Brooke said rudely, pointing at Mare's feet. "They were supposed to, like, *revolutionize* barefoot running but apparently it was all a scam. They just settled a class action lawsuit. I can't believe so many people were stupid enough to buy those ugly things. They can really fuck you up and ruin your body."

"Yes, well, apparently so can tequila," Saul countered pointedly, looking Brooke up and down. He hugged Mare to his side protectively as he stood to his full height, which was several inches above Brooke.

Brooke's face turned crimson as she took a step toward Saul, a sign she was about to erupt with anger. Birdy had seen it many times, enough to know that she didn't want to see it now. She grabbed Brooke's elbow and tugged her back. To head off any further friction, she said in her most innocuous voice, "You two are looking awfully cute together."

Saul smoothed his plaid shirt and adjusted his knit tie. The fidgeting was a nervous habit, but he got it under control quickly, lifting his shoulders and chin with pride. "Yes, well, we're pretty happy, I think." He looked at Mare for confirmation. "We're going out for fondue tomorrow night to celebrate four months of dating."

"Wow, four whole months," Brooke slurred sarcastically. Her color was down but the bitterness was still clear in her voice. "I think that's a record for you, Saul."

"Brooke, stop it," Birdy hissed quietly into her partner's ear.

His chin still high, Saul snapped back, "Four months in a *healthy*, *caring* relationship. I think that would be a record for you as well, if you ever actually reached it."

The drinks had dulled Brooke's usual quick wit and razor-sharp tongue. She opened her mouth, hesitating and then muttered, "Asshole." Then she roughly shook off Birdy's grip and returned to the bar to fix another drink.

"Shit," Birdy said, watching helplessly as Brooke left the kitchen, sloshing her overfilled cup. "This could go south fast if we don't go talk to her and try to calm her down."

"Birdy, I love you," Saul said. "But there's no *we* to it. This is the ticking time bomb I'm always on you about, and you keep getting blown up trying to disarm it. For better or worse, till death do you part."

Aggravated at Saul, Birdy turned to Mare, who opened her eyes impossibly wide and whispered dramatically, "FOR-EV-VER."

"Super helpful, guys. Thanks."

In the living room, Brooke was now talking animatedly with a group of women. She had apparently moved on quickly from her confrontation with Saul, most likely thanks to the alcohol.

The women who were clustered around Brooke appeared to be enthralled with her karaoke story, each of them smiling and laughing in unison, like a chorus of twittering birds. Brooke was most in her element when surrounded by people, feeding off their energy and charming them completely. It was that special brand of charisma that had driven Birdy to fall in love years ago.

She thought back to that night of karaoke legend, remembering how Brooke had worked the stage. She had rapped every word of Vanilla Ice's "Ice Ice Baby" with complete femme sex appeal, never once looking at the monitor. Frat boys and their girlfriends had thrown themselves at her, jumping up to dance onstage, singing along to the chorus, never taking their eyes off her. She was energetic, surprising and sexy as hell. When the song finished, she came back to the booth smiling radiantly, and possessively put her arm around Birdy's shoulders. In a stunning surprise, she completely claimed her with a lustful kiss that left Birdy panting.

Birdy had felt so special that night, enveloped in Brooke's world of intrigue and charm. That was Brooke's gift—creating a world you felt lucky to have been invited into. No matter how much turbulence they had endured, she had never flown higher. At times, she feared the only thing holding her up at this altitude was Brooke. Her vivacious, difficult Brooke.

Next year, she thought, Brooke should dress as a snake charmer and Birdy would be her willing, fork-tongued victim.

She pulled herself out of her reverie, watching as one of the girls clutched Brooke's arm, laughing a little too long and a little too loudly. Birdy noted that she was dressed as a seventies glam rock groupie with pink-lensed glasses, fur coat and dramatically flared jeans. Her costume was appropriate as she seemed to be Brooke's biggest fan. Covering the woman's hand with her own, Brooke winked at her. A moment of heat passed between the two women, and something flashed in Brooke's eye—something Birdy hadn't seen in a long time. Awkwardly, she looked away from her snake charmer, unwilling to shed light on the niggling feeling in her stomach.

When she raised her gaze again, taking in the rest of the room, her eyes immediately met Sydney's as if she were a compass finding true north. She was sitting on the couch, her lean runner's legs crossed, ankle to knee. She had been shredding the label off a beer bottle in her lap, but it sat forgotten now. Birdy felt as if she were suddenly drowning in her forbidden desire. Lost in the moment, she immediately forgot about her previous resolution to think of her as nothing more than a friend. Now, nothing could draw her attention away from the yearning she thought she saw mirrored in Sydney's face. Not Brooke's bad temper or flirting, not Sydney's ridiculous mustache that was perched above soft, parted lips and not the woman whose massive tits were pressed against Sydney's arm.

Okay, maybe the tits could distract her. Birdy aborted her slow, possessed walk across the room and finally blinked, breaking the spell long enough to examine the woman pressed up against Sydney on an otherwise empty couch. She was dressed as a doctor—scrubs, lab coat and stethoscope. Heightening Birdy's annoyance, she wasn't even dressed as a *sexy* doctor. No, this was much more convincing and significantly more intimidating. Nobody's tits should look that good in scrubs.

Dr. Tits swirled her forefinger in Sydney's ponytail, lightly tugging it. The woman crossed her legs, letting one of her well-worn Nikes rub against Sydney's left shin. Great, Birdy thought, she's probably a runner too. She probably knows *exactly* who Steve Pre-fucking-fontaine was.

For a moment, Sydney looked as if she were plotting an escape to join her, checking to see that Brooke was still otherwise engaged. Then something the doctor said drew her attention.

Birdy felt the loss instantly. Refusing to watch in case Sydney returned the woman's flirtations, she returned instead to Brooke, only to find that the gaggle of giggling girls had mostly disbanded. Three of the women remained but Brooke was nowhere to be seen.

Figuring she had probably gone for another drink, Birdy made her way to the kitchen. In a less crowded corner of the room, she spotted her fiancée talking animatedly with the rock band groupie. Birdy noticed that they were standing farther apart than before, and while no arm squeezing was taking place, the woman was still laughing wildly, throwing her head back, her dirty blond curls bouncing around her face while she clutched her necklace, inviting Brooke's eyes to take in her cleavage. An opportunity Brooke would never miss.

Birdy registered a touch of jealousy but the winning emotion was relief. At least Brooke was in a good mood again.

She continued her way back to the kitchen, seeking out her best friends, who always provided advice—albeit usually unsolicited—and comfort.

The only comfort they seemed capable of providing tonight, however, was to each other, as they greedily attacked each other's faces with their mouths. Mare pushed Saul against the counter roughly. He desperately clutched his glasses as they threatened to fall off while his other hand grabbed Mare's ass. She rubbed his chest and wrapped his tie around her hand, aggressively pulling him closer.

Birdy couldn't contain her smile. She found the display a little nauseating but still, she was happy for her friends. She pulled a beer from the fridge after shoving Saul not so gently down the counter so she could open the door. He didn't seem to even notice the intrusion so she leaned against the fridge, watching the awkward battle of tongues with curiosity.

Finally, on the verge of laughter, she cleared her throat loudly. "Okay, you two. You only have a couple more hours to entertain us all and then you can continue your...gentle lovemaking without audience."

Saul righted his glasses while Mare giggled and kissed him again. As if suddenly conscious of their public display, she straightened his tie and pulled her shirt back down from the dangerous heights it had risen.

"Sorry," she said, still giggling. "I just can't keep my hands off this sexy man."

"I'm happy for you. Disgusted, but happy. I'm just not used to seeing straight people make out. It feels so...unnatural." She gave an exaggerated shiver and then laughed with her lust-struck friends.

"How's the party out there?" Mare turned in Saul's arms and playfully wiggled her butt against him. "I've barely left the kitchen all night."

"Everyone seems to be having a lot of fun," Birdy said. Through the parting waves of people she could see Sydney methodically peeling the label off the beer again, tearing each shred of paper into tiny pieces and then feeding them into the opening of her empty bottle.

Dr. Tits, however, was keeping her hands busy another way. She was languidly rubbing Sydney's neck, running her fingers in a circuitous route through her hair and down to drift just under the strap of her tank top, lightly squeezing the muscles in her neck.

"Some seem to be having more fun than others," she added bitterly.

Saul followed her eyes and let out a low whistle, nodding appreciatively like a dog on a dashboard. "Who's the doctor? That mustachioed chick is definitely getting some tonight. I'd like to see where that stethoscope ends up. Oh, shit. That's Sydney." Quickly he looked at Birdy and mumbled a quick apology. His frown turned into a doughy-eyed grin, though, when Mare smacked his stomach and then twisted her hand once more in his tie.

Mare said seductively, "Oh, you'd like to spend some time with a doctor, huh? Maybe I could schedule an appointment for you tonight. We can do a routine checkup so I can evaluate which parts of you need my attention most." She planted a long, sloppy kiss on him that again sent his glasses into lopsided disarray.

"Stop!" Birdy pleaded. "I'm going to puke. I'm happy that you're happy but I will puke all over you if you don't stop."

Mare finally pulled away, though unembarrassed and unapologetic.

"For real, though, who's the doctor, Mare?"

"Yeah, the one with the tits," Saul supplied helpfully.

"That's Michaela. She works out at my gym. I invited her to meet Sydney, now that I know that she's gay." Mare gave Birdy a no-thanks-to-you look and continued, "I delved into my lesbian Rolodex so I can hook her up with some ladies."

Saul leaned over Mare's shoulder and whispered into her ear. "I love that you have a lesbian Rolodex. That's pretty hot. Is she actually a doctor?"

Birdy sputtered, "Of course she is, Saul! Only a doctor would wear a non-sexy doctor outfit to a Halloween party. She was probably so busy saving lives that she didn't have time to change into her sexy Playboy bunny costume." She huffed, crossing her left arm around her stomach and propping her drinking arm on it so she could take a long, jealous draw from her beer bottle, nearly killing half of it in one go.

As if she had a right to be huffy about anything. Two weeks ago at their engagement party, she had made a commitment to herself to stop flirting with Sydney and to truly focus on her relationship with Brooke. That meant Sydney had every right to do whatever she wanted with Dr. Tits or anyone else. But no amount of rationalization could stop the emotion building inside—a jealousy she had no power to stop.

Oblivious to Birdy's inner turmoil, Mare added the coup de grâce, "Actually, I think she's a gyno."

* * *

Sydney was very aware of the breasts pressed against her arm and the ceaselessly moving hand that had explored every inch of her neck and shoulders. The touching and massaging felt good, she had to admit, but too often her eyes traveled across the room in search of Birdy.

She had watched the exchange between Brooke and the fur-clad rocker chick. Birdy too had witnessed the flirting, showing little reaction except for a slight reddening of her throat and cheeks.

Sydney had almost left the couch then, wanting to console her, to hold her, to make her forget that Brooke was even in the room. But she thought back to the engagement party and the speech Brooke had made. The love she had seen in Birdy's eyes in that moment had made her rethink the impossible plan to win her affections. Watching them kiss had made her feel like a predatory bitch. Her days since had been a constant battle between head and heart. A part of her still wanted badly to fight, but her head told her she had to let Birdy go. Birdy was so deeply invested in her relationship that Sydney wasn't sure she could reach that far while leaving her character and morals intact.

Birdy was in the corner surrounded by Brooke's friends, all of whom were behaving like Brooke was homecoming queen and they were her court. When Birdy abruptly left their circle for the kitchen, Sydney realized Michaela was asking her a question.

"Sorry, what?" she asked, trying to refocus on her blind date.

When Mare had called her into the office last week to say she was inviting a friend for her to meet, Sydney's immediate reaction was to refuse the date or even threaten not to come to the party. She also considered locking herself in her apartment or maybe just moving back to Texas. The possibilities were endless as her mind ran wild with avoidance techniques. No way was she going on a blind date. The only person she wanted to date was Birdy. Instead of blurting out that she would rather be celibate, she forced herself instead to actually consider the possibility of dating someone else. In the end, she had accepted, albeit with reluctance.

As much as it hurt to be here, she reminded herself of why she had come—to at least make an attempt to let Birdy go. Maybe this blind date would be a good first step.

It wasn't as if she had expected much. Having heard stories from Birdy about Mare's rather bizarre taste in men, she assumed her taste in women couldn't be any better. Michaela was distinctively attractive with full pouty lips, hazel eyes and slightly pointed nose. She wore trendy, thick-rimmed glasses that solidified her doctor look. Or a stripper with sexy librarian appeal. Sydney could get behind either of those options, since neither reminded her of Birdy.

"You work with Mare?" Michaela repeated, continuing to play with the fine hairs that curled against Sydney's neck.

"Oh, yeah. I'm a screen printer so Mare's my boss actually."

"Screen printing. That's cool. A couple years ago I went to Pittsburgh for a conference and checked out the Andy Warhol Museum. Isn't he the one that kinda made it famous?"

Sydney was actually impressed. She was more accustomed to getting a "What's that?" in reply. It was refreshing to meet a woman—a nice looking woman, no less—who actually knew a little something about it.

"Yeah, he did make it famous in the sixties. That print of Marilyn Monroe really set it in motion. I've never been to the Warhol museum but I've always wanted to go."

"It was great! Super interesting. I'm just glad I remembered a little something about it. I thought they called it silkscreen at the museum. Is there a difference between that and screen printing?" There was genuine interest behind those sexy doctor glasses.

For the first time that night, she actually found the woman she was with to be rather exciting. *Well, why wouldn't you, Syd?* She asked herself. *She's attractive, has a great career and is obviously into you.* Thoughts of Birdy still swam in her mind. *You can't have her, Syd. She's getting married.*

"It's the same process, really, it's just that back then when Warhol was doing it they used actual silk to make the screens.

Now they use a synthetic fiber mesh. Some people still call it silkscreen though. The technical name for it is serigraphy so file that one away and you'll be a real hit at parties," Sydney gave a self-deprecating chuckle. This was actually the first time her screen printing knowledge had been a hit at a party and she didn't feel like a complete dork talking about it. Well, other than when she explained it to Birdy.

She wanted to kick herself. *I can't even make it thirty seconds without thinking of her.*

"Maybe I'll just take you to my next party and you can impress everyone for me. It helps that you're so cute too."

Sydney admitted to herself she was flattered. Stroking the bushy hair that was stuck to her upper lip, she said, "Just let me know when. I'll trim my mustache for you."

Michaela ran her thumb over the mustache, letting it trail lightly over Sydney's top lip. "No need. You look really cute with it. Plus, I think it might make kissing you pretty fun."

Michaela bit her lip in a way that was so sexy Sydney assumed she must practice the move in front of a mirror each night. After a long moment she squeezed Sydney's knee and then firmly grabbed the beer bottle she was still clutching in her lap. "I'm going to go wait in that impossibly long line for the bathroom and then get us another drink. You stay put. Okay?"

"Okay. Thank you," Sydney said, relinquishing her empty bottle.

Smoothing her mustache and straightening her tank top, she wondered if she really had the heart to pursue something with Michaela. She wanted to fight for Birdy but here, surrounded by all of these people, including Birdy's fiancée, she couldn't see what purpose it would serve. Yes, she could play the martyr, celibately waiting for Birdy to finally see her, run to her, be with her, but could she do that to herself? Subject herself to the futile chase, the heart-crushing pain of unrequited love? She knew her decision to back off now, to let Birdy be happy with the woman she chose and to let herself be happy with someone else, maybe someone like Michaela, was the smart, practical thing to do. That's what her head said, but her heart was having trouble letting go.

Suddenly self-conscious about her costume, she peeled off her mustache and sought out Birdy, who was standing in the kitchen watching her. Martyr or not, she couldn't help the way her heart fluttered, or the way her breath quickened. She couldn't help the warmth and wetness that surged between her legs. Seeing the rise and fall of Birdy's chest, it was clear she too was mired in emotion. She had to bite the side of her finger to stave off the moan that nearly escaped, and she crossed her legs at the knees, squeezing her thighs tightly together.

After a long, heated moment, Birdy turned back to her friends seemingly in response to a question, and Sydney quickly dropped her gaze. Maybe out of guilt, her eyes immediately found Brooke's. She was no longer with the other woman but instead stood alone, staring at Sydney.

Her icy glare flicked back toward the kitchen, indicating she had been aware of the moment Sydney had just shared with Birdy.

When she once again focused on Sydney, her eyes held a glassy-eyed drunkenness as well as an unnerving, prowling coquettishness. She took a small sip of her drink, licked her lips slowly and sauntered to the couch. Some of her drink spilled on her hand but she ignored it, looking instead at Sydney with devilish intent. "She's pretty hot, isn't she?" Brooke asked, giving no clue to whom she was referring.

"Who?" More than anything, Sydney wished she had a drink in her hands, something that would help hide the twitching of her fingers.

"Your doctor friend. I hear she's a gyno. I wouldn't mind her in my cunt," Brooke said crudely, letting her thin black bar straw drag seductively across her lower lip. "Actually, without that silly mustache on, I think the three of us could have a nice time. We'll both be her patients. If you don't mind sharing."

In a shocking move, Brooke pressed herself against Sydney much in the same way Michaela had. But where Michaela had been soft and inviting, Brooke felt hard, as if she were challenging Sydney to speak.

Sydney glanced toward the kitchen, thankful to see that Birdy was engaged in conversation, oblivious to her fiancée's scene.

Reaching brazenly for Sydney's thigh, Brooke drunkenly sloshed her drink in Sydney's lap. She wiped at the now wet shorts with the palm of her hand. "Just a little prelude. I could make your shorts much, much wetter," she said breathily, leaning closer. Her hand then aggressively gripped Sydney's upper thigh, and a finger crept under the hem of her loose shorts.

Sydney straightened and leaned away, trying to put distance between them without causing a scene. It would be best to not awaken the beast she had a feeling Brooke could be. She moved Brooke's hand from her thigh under the pretense of looking at her ring. "That's quite the rock you have there."

Without humor, Brooke laughed. "You think so? This is nothing. I deserve better than a chip. But then, I settled, as you do in relationships." She leaned in even closer, breathing into Sydney's ear. "I have a feeling though, that sleeping with you would be far from settling. Even without your doctor, I bet you could do a *very* thorough examination. I think I'd make a satisfied patient."

Sydney bit back her anger, swallowing her disgust. "And this relationship?" Sydney asked, motioning to the ring.

"Is about give and take. And I have learned that one person can only *give* you so much and I really, *really* love to take. And when I take you, *neither* of us will be thinking about Birdy." Brooke raised her eyebrows knowingly, a moment of clarity in her drunkenness. Sydney had the impression she was being challenged rather than seduced. Then Brooke departed as purposefully as she had arrived, slowly dragging her fingernails across Sydney's bare shoulder.

CHAPTER TWENTY

A week into November and Birdy wondered if this would be the year the Portland rain would finally kill her. As she bolted from the city streetcar to the downtown public library, she said aloud, "It's too early to hate the rain. You still have at least four more months of this, Bird."

The nickname made her think of Sydney, made her flash back to the way Sydney had looked at her at the party. Then just as quickly her idyllic memory dissipated as Dr. Tits crowded in, boobs first.

Once inside, she jogged up the beautiful marble steps of the library's main branch to the second floor. This building, the richness of the air and the golden glow throughout, felt like it had lived deep inside her since she was a child, having first come here with her mother. For a moment she pictured herself descending the stairs in a lace wedding gown, a lush bouquet cascading from her hand. She tried to picture Brooke waiting for her at the bottom of the stairs, an antique, leather book tucked under her arm, the one in which they would write their vows. Her vision of the book was clear, patina burgundy leather and fading gold bars on the spine. Crisp, yellowing pages that smelled of this library, somehow stronger and more reassuring than the scent of her bouquet. The smell of age and permanence, far sweeter than the fleeting perfume of cut flowers.

Lost in the romance of her vision, she reached the bottom of the stairs and came level with Brooke, the bearer of her book. Suddenly her imagination grew hazy. Brooke's smile was gone. The hand reaching out for her, the clothes…they weren't Brooke's. They belonged to someone else, a face she refused to bring into focus.

Instead, she willed her mind to form a clearer picture of her future bride. Training her thoughts on what Brooke had wanted for their wedding, she saw her in a glamorous ballroom, the Heathman Hotel of Birdy's imagination in a feathered, brilliantly white gown. Her arms were filled with a rich, virile bouquet spilling forth, and she was surrounded by people. But when Birdy tried to step into the picture, she felt small and insignificant. The loneliest girl in the room.

As the fantasy played out, she had managed to wander deep into the stacks, her fingers brushing the varying textures of books old and new. When she reached the end of the long row, she dragged herself from her melancholy. The weight of the daydream still upon her, she couldn't help but feel sorry for herself. She'd had a crummy week.

Her attempts to talk about the need for Brooke and Saul to get along had been completely dismissed by Brooke, who had gone on as if nothing had happened at the Halloween party. While still not thrilled about the union, Saul had heartily agreed to stand next to her during the ceremony as her best man. She had long given up on the two of them becoming friends but had hoped a truce could be reached soon. Brooke's unwillingness to discuss the night's events made Birdy feel the armistice might be harder won than she imagined.

Her lack of meaningful conversation with Brooke, though, was not weighing as heavily on her as the absence of conversation of any kind with Sydney. Work had been a flurry of designing publicity posters for bands and printing T-shirts for a Thanksgiving Day half-marathon. Sydney had not sought her out since the party, and Birdy, unable to think of a single question that didn't involve the possibility of an entanglement with Dr. Tits, hadn't approached her either.

The whole week had provided nothing but loneliness and dissatisfaction. Brooke had invited her out with friends tonight, the usual catcalling their way through various clubs. It was something Birdy did on occasion, camping out at the bar when Brooke didn't drag her into the throng to dance. But she was not in the mood for throngs of any sort tonight, no sir.

Instead she was letting herself fall into a rabbit hole of daydreams, which included library weddings. The big, beautiful etched stone steps were to blame. And leather-bound books. Those were definitely to blame too. Birdy knew she was being schmaltzy. A sloppy, soppy, sappy schmaltz. And she was loving every minute of her misery, dammit.

If Brooke was out with her friends, chasing each drink with a new bar, and Sydney was likely being blown by Dr. Tits, Birdy at least could be in the library feeling as wretched as she goddamn wanted to be.

One flight down she studied the newly released hardcovers with shiny plastic sleeves and checked on some old favorite paperbacks, like Steinbeck's *Cannery Row* and Elizabeth Berg's *Open House*. She had read them many times before but still liked knowing they were there waiting for her when she wanted to visit them again. A sort through bins of CDs she knew she would not check out left her with nothing more to do. Descending the main stairs, she distracted herself from her earlier romantic vision of this grand entryway with her iPhone and earbuds. A gloomy, post-rock playlist...the perfect fit for her mood.

Pulling up the hood of her North Face raincoat, the winter one that was both insulated and stormproof, she left the lobby and the comforting glow of the library. The building was closing anyway, so her brooding would have to continue in the misting rain. Allowing herself to feel like an outsider, she weaved around groups of people. Girls in glittering dresses who dodged puddles and shared cigarettes caught her eye as she wandered with her head down, getting lost in the streetlights, rain and music.

Looping her way through Portland's downtown for an hour, she arrived back at the now-closed library and the streetcar stop that would take her to the Southwest waterfront and Brooke's condo. Just ahead was a dimly lit restaurant where couples were bathed in soft red light, reminding her of the glow of the darkroom she had experienced with Sydney. The couples stared into each other's eyes, sharing crepes and sipping wine.

A table stood flush against the window, mostly cleared of the remnants of dinner. A couple was finishing off the last of their wine. Birdy looked up from the flickering candle and found herself falling into too-familiar light brown eyes. She gulped for breath, her step faltering as she stared at Sydney. The streetlight lit her features and the words painted on the restaurant's window fell like gray stencils across Sydney's mouth. Everything felt gray as the world slowed, bleaching the color from Birdy's vision except for those eyes. Those eyes that embraced her, held her and warmed her in the cold night. Her heart thudded and she felt light-headed, ethereal.

Sydney held her gaze without blinking. Her eyes showed surprise but also something else. They showed wanting, much like Birdy's, but there was something deeply rooted there as well. Something Birdy wasn't willing to name. Something that made her stomach flip dramatically and deliciously.

The truth in Sydney's expression scared her and she pulled her gaze away, finally noticing the woman sitting on the other side of the table. At first she didn't recognize the pleasant face that offered her a small smile. The woman's hair was down, a reddish hint in the soft brown curls which were being held back on the sides by glasses that were pushed up on top of her head. She had friendly hazel eyes and high, strong cheekbones. Birdy's gaze dropped to her chest. *Ah yes, Dr. Tits.*

Politeness dictated that she should smile back. Maybe give them a carefree wave and walk on with a jaunty tip of a make-believe cap, but she couldn't. She couldn't breathe, couldn't blink, couldn't think. Her only rational move was to leave. She ran away, hurrying out of the streetlight that exposed her emotions and left her feeling raw and naked on that wet sidewalk. Scared of the look she saw in Sydney's eyes and scared of the intensity with which she hungered to see it always.

She ran back toward the library, wishing it were still open so she could be comforted by the warmth and distracted by the books. The last thing she wanted was to think about Sydney on a date with Dr. Tits.

Michaela, she corrected herself. After all, she had seemed perfectly wonderful tonight as they regarded one another through the window. Perfectly friendly and perfectly beautiful and perfectly perfect, which made all of this so much worse. The woman wasn't a villain just because she wanted what Birdy couldn't have.

She took off her headphones, needing to hear the sound of the rain as she ran up the front steps of the library toward the golden light that glowed through the metal and glass doors. It was locked, as she knew it would be, and she felt lost with no other beacon of hope to run toward. She touched the handle, pulling lightly on the bolted door and let her shoulders slump, not yet ready to turn around to face the city in defeat.

"Where are you flying away to, Bird?"

Her heart sped up again as she spun, seeking out the owner of the voice at the bottom of the steps. The glow of a streetlamp was mirrored on each of the wet, stone steps, creating a fragmented path leading to Sydney, who stood tall and straight, a messenger bag strapped tightly across her body.

Birdy couldn't shake the vision that had been crowding her thoughts in the library. Slowly she descended the stairs, now seeing Sydney waiting for her at the bottom so clearly, as if she had always been the other half of the dream.

Running her thumb over Birdy's eyebrow, Sydney caught some of the water that dripped down her face. She asked again, "What are you flying away from, Bird?"

"You," was all Birdy could manage. She couldn't help but push her cheek into the warmth of Sydney's hand.

"Why?"

"I…" Birdy faltered, but she was so lost in the moment and in Sydney's touch that she could think of nothing but the truth of her feelings. "I can't stand to see you with Dr. Tits."

Sydney gave her the lopsided smile she had adored since the moment they met.

"Dr. Tits?"

"She has *really* big tits," she said, her decent side feeling at least a little ashamed that she had reduced the woman to a sexual caricature.

This time Sydney threw her face back into the rain and laughed, a sound she loved. But in that split second, she missed the feel of Sydney's hand on her face.

"They are pretty big," Sydney admitted with a grin.

"Have you been going out with her a lot?" Birdy tried her best to sound only vaguely interested in the answer.

"This was our first date, if you don't count the Halloween party."

She wanted to sound removed, even disinterested, but her voice was too strained, her questions too searching. "What do you see in her? I mean, other than her boobs?"

Sydney only shrugged and sucked in one cheek, biting it. It was a vague gesture that made it hard to tell if she was skeptical about Michaela or annoyed that Birdy had asked.

"I'm sorry. That was rude. Are you going to see her again?"

This time, she chuckled cynically. "Seeing as I threw some money and a hasty 'sorry' at her as I ran from the restaurant to chase after you, I'd say it's safe to say that, no, I won't be seeing her anymore."

After a moment of sheepish silence while she scuffed her toe against the wet pavement, Birdy managed to mutter, "Sorry I ruined your date."

She shook her head and took Birdy's face with both hands. "No, you're not."

Her hood having fallen back, Birdy squinted up into the rain. "Then I'm sorry for all the mixed signals."

Sydney sighed and then, seemingly having made up her mind, nodded. "I want you, Bird. But the message I get is that

I can't have you, and it's killing me. You've made it clear you want somebody else. I vowed to myself that I'd stop chasing you and let you be happy. I promised to stop thinking about touching you and kissing you, but I can't get you out of my head. All the time I think about making love with you. I'm not strong enough to fight this"—her eyes fell to Birdy's lips—"and I'm not even sure you want me to."

With her stomach now doing somersaults, she felt a hot, consuming need for Sydney's lips. A powerful, intense desire warmed her body, and she stepped forward, her body brushing against Sydney's.

Sydney cupped her head, signaling her intention with slow and deliberate movements. "Do you want me to stop fighting for you?"

Too scared to say aloud what she actually wanted, she managed to shake her head. She had made promises too and not just to herself. Accepting Brooke's ring had been a promise, reaffirmed at their engagement party when Brooke had given her speech. But as frightened as she was—and as much as she knew she shouldn't—all she wanted was to be kissed by Sydney, touched by Sydney and completely taken by Sydney.

Searching Birdy's eyes once more, Sydney slowly drew her in, their bodies pressed against each other. Rain dripped down their noses and Birdy surrendered, finally meeting the lips she'd dreamt about her entire life. She moaned into the softness of the kiss, loving the feel of Sydney's tongue as it slowly ran along her bottom lip.

This was exactly what Birdy had been wanting—and fearing. Having finally taken this enormous leap into a black void of sexual attraction, she was even more unsure of where she stood than ever. For months she had been so sure a step in this direction would put her firmly on the path she should not travel, but now that she was spinning in a lust-filled abyss, her thoughts stretched no farther than the woman who held her tightly. The fears to which she had been clinging became too blurred to remain in focus. The only thing that remained crystal clear to Birdy right now was this kiss.

Her lips slid against Sydney's and she gently bit down on the lushness of her lower lip to keep them anchored together. Right now the only instinct she was able to obey was to cling to this sensation that made her heart feel too large for her chest.

Completely enveloped by her hunger for Sydney, she no longer felt the rain against her skin. Now the only wetness she felt was her own. Her legs were no longer steady enough to support her so she wrapped her arms around Sydney's neck more tightly and leaned heavily into her.

Gasping, Sydney pulled away and murmured, "We have to stop."

Birdy was still swimming in her need for Sydney. The words, completely incongruous with her own thoughts didn't register and she pulled Sydney to her again, their lips meeting even more firmly than before.

Sydney crushed her with a kiss, almost harshly before breaking away again. With a steely resolve, she said, "I can't sneak around while you're still with her."

The fog of desire cleared from Birdy's sex-saturated mind as quickly as it had rolled in and Sydney's words finally entered her consciousness, pinging painfully around her brain.

Her legs however still felt leaden from the rush of desire and she couldn't help but continue to lean heavily into Sydney. She remembered her fears, her uncertainties and most importantly, she remembered Brooke. She was so overcome with emotion and guilt that she was nearly ready to cry. Pushing her emotions down, as she had done so expertly for months, she finally composed herself enough to reply with a simple, "I know."

With another kiss to her forehead, this one plain and chaste, Sydney told her, "You're going to break my heart."

"I'm sorry. I really do want you."

"Want isn't enough, Bird. I *need* you. And I need you to choose me," Sydney pleaded, a hint of desperation entering her voice. "I'm falling for you so hard. But as much as I want to be with you, what I want most is for you to be happy. Are you happy? Because if you say you are, I swear I will walk away for good and let you be. Are you happy?"

Birdy didn't take time to think. "No."

Sydney bit her lip in frustration, looking away until she seemed to make a decision. "I know I'm setting myself up here to get hurt in the worst way, but I'm going to keep fighting for you until you tell me you don't want me to anymore. I'll wait for you, Bird. As long as it takes."

Birdy closed her eyes, unable to bear the naked devotion she saw. "Sydney, I…" She placed her hand in the center of Sydney's chest and feeling like a coward, pushed her away. She knew she should release Sydney, tell her not to wait for her. After all, she had made a promise to Brooke. The kiss had shaken her resolve, but she was still caught up in the momentum of her five-year relationship and the wedding that was soon to be.

"I'm sorry," she said weakly. Everything about her was weak and she hated herself for it. On weak legs and with weak resolve, she turned and ran away from Sydney and the love in her eyes.

CHAPTER TWENTY-ONE

It had been two weeks since The Kiss. Two long, tortuous but emboldening weeks since her lips had touched Birdy's. Two weeks since they had held each other, their bodies and lips demanding attention. Sydney had to shake herself as she felt a rush of heat between her legs, something that had become all too familiar lately.

She groaned softly, unable to keep herself from thinking about the fantasy that had left her quivering each night, causing her to wake up much later with her hand still buried in the heat between her legs.

Her mind flitted through the fantasy. Each time she touched herself she perfected the image of Birdy in the chair on the deck of her boat, wearing only the white, lacy bra that was still wet with river water. Her feet were on the boat railing, her thighs squeezing Sydney's head as she knelt in front of her, slowly and deliberately tasting her. Scooting lower in the chair, Birdy would offer even more of herself. Moans dripping with sexual need floated unrestrained across the river. Birdy's hand guiding the back of her head, selfishly and forcefully holding her face where she needed her most.

Sometimes in the fantasy she would slowly penetrate Birdy with one, then two fingers, bringing her to an intensely satisfying orgasm while Sydney continued to suck on her swollen clit. Recently however, her hand would graze past Birdy's belly, pushing her bra up, fully exposing her to the river. Birdy's head was flung back, her breasts pushed together by arms that reached fervently for her.

The large dark nipples she had seen through Birdy's wet bra always made her come hard and too fast, her walls pulsating and kneading. Needing Birdy.

Sydney licked her lips. She felt flush and wet and swollen. She really needed to leave these thoughts at home.

Because at work, unfortunately, it seemed Birdy had been avoiding her. She and Birdy had not talked about The Kiss yet, though Sydney had made a point to invite her to lunch most days. Birdy turned her down each time, choosing instead to eat at her desk.

Pulling her thoughts back to her work, she printed the last layer of red on a limited edition tour poster for a local rock band before shelving the paper with the other forty-nine posters that were drying on a nearby rack. This was a fairly simple print with light blue and bright red ink contrasting sharply on the paper with black details. Once all of the red was dry she would be able to print the final layer of black, adding definition to the images and words.

Finding a rhythm in her work, she was able to let her thoughts roam, relying on muscle memory to plod through the task of printing the posters. Paper, screen, tap, pull, lift, flood, paper. The repetition kept her on track while her mind drifted. Right now her thoughts focused on the predicament her heart was in and the woman at the center.

There was no easy way out of it because giving up was not something that came easily to Sydney Ramos. She blamed her parents for that, if blame was even the right word. They never let her quit anything she started, instead encouraging her to push through it miserably until a logical end. She had been forced to play at her two-year piano recital before they conceded that she disliked it long enough to move on to a new interest. Senior year, she signed up for calculus, mostly because Mandy Lexington, her swimming teammate and secret high school crush, had signed up. While Mandy had no problem grasping calculus, Sydney struggled continuously. Her parents reasoned that she had committed to the class and needed to see it through.

They had instilled in her a drive to succeed, which she had used to excel in swimming and softball. As a natural athlete, her unwillingness to give in to the fatigue and pain had made her a true competitor. Now, it was part of her identity. Never a quitter, she committed through to a logical end. And now she had fully committed herself to loving Birdy.

Unfortunately, there was no such thing as a "logical end" when it came to love. Nothing logical about the way she relived that kiss, that demanding, excruciatingly hot kiss over and over each day. There was a vision seared into her mind, one of Birdy staring at her with yearning through the restaurant window. At least she hoped it was yearning. It was completely illogical that she focused now on that moment rather than the way her eyes had clouded with fear, or the sight of her running away. She stubbornly pushed those images from her mind and zeroed in on the love she thought and hoped she saw in Birdy's eyes.

Sydney had fears as well. Paralyzing fears that she was on the precipice of heartbreak like she had never experienced before. Above all, though, she was imbued with hope. The way Birdy had kissed her, had given herself completely for those few moments in the rain, ensconced in golden light, breast to breast and hips reaching and wanting…it gave her a hope that made her resolve to fight for Birdy.

She was neither a quitter nor a coward. The potential of a relationship with Birdy, The One, far outweighed the fear of soul-crushing, life-altering pain. No matter which, her life was about to change dramatically, and she could only hope it would be for the better.

The shop door opened and Sydney glanced up from her work. Seeing Birdy, she smiled and hoped that maybe she finally was ready to talk about that night. The distance had been killing her and she so badly wanted to put it behind them and go back to that comfortable relationship they had before. She had to admit she wanted more too, like what she imagined in her fantasies, more than just comfort, but she desperately needed Birdy's friendship most.

Birdy didn't return her smile, dashing her hopes.

But then Brooke paraded through the door behind her, talking loudly and happily, obviously finishing a conversation they had been having in the office. Her hand clutched Birdy's elbow and they walked across the shop until Brooke noticed Sydney watching them. Her eyes were much more alert than they had been at the Halloween party, but the same seductive glance lurked there. Obviously for show, her hand traveled down the inside of Birdy's arm until she firmly intertwined their fingers. As if rubbing Sydney's nose in it, she lifted Birdy's hand to her lips and kissed the ring on her fourth finger.

Sydney took pleasure in seeing Birdy pull her hand away quickly before nervously smoothing her shirt, but she was less happy with the devilish intent in Brooke's expression. It held the same mix of seduction and aggression as at the party. Her hope that Brooke had been too drunk to remember the look she had shared with Birdy was dashed as Brooke once again regarded her as if challenging her to make her move. Apparently the woman held her alcohol better than Sydney thought. *If she remembered that, does she remember hitting on me? Does she remember practically confessing her affairs as well?*

Sydney lifted her chin, silently accepting the challenge Brooke had laid at her feet. "Brooke, nice to see you."

"They still have you slaving away back here, I see. It's stifling in the summer and freezing during the winter apparently." She shivered dramatically. "They really should pay you better, since they sit up there in a climate-controlled office. But then I guess that's what manual labor jobs are like."

Mare came bustling into the shop just in time to save her from making a snide remark. "Birdy, I forgot to ask you what I need to bring to your mom's for Thanksgiving. You're sure she doesn't mind me coming with Saul, right?"

"No, of course not. She'll be thrilled. Saul's eaten with us every year since his parents moved to Arizona. She's so happy you're coming. And seriously, don't bring a thing. That woman is a machine in the kitchen and probably has everything planned out already. Maybe just come early and you can help us with the turkey."

"Oh, a real turkey! Thank God," Mare exclaimed. Turning to Sydney she explained, "I usually go to my friend Gina's place. She has a big shindig with half of her yoga studio. She makes beautiful, gorgeous meals that are completely vegan and completely inedible. I usually try to stuff myself with rolls and flaxseed oil butter but this year they've all decided they're going to be gluten-free too. Which is just stupid if you ask me. Thank God Birdy invited me to her mom's this year. Are you coming?"

Sydney was caught off guard. She'd already turned down the very same invitation from Beth, who was part of Gina's yoga group. She hadn't realized Mare was too. Beth, though, hadn't bothered to mention this gluten-free business. "Oh, well, I...no. I have a quiet day planned with a book and a turkey sandwich."

"That's no way to spend Thanksgiving!" Mare cried. "I'm sure Birdy would love to have you join us, wouldn't you Birdy?"

Birdy stuttered after what looked like a stunned silence. With Brooke still clutching her hand tightly, she finally said, "I...I'm sure Sydney wouldn't want to be around me and my mom all day."

Brooke flashed a smug look.

"Are you kidding? I would love to meet your mom. And a home-cooked meal sounds amazing. I would love to come." Sydney looked innocently at both Birdy and Brooke. "That is, if you don't mind having me."

Unaware of the tension nearly crackling in the air, Mare waved her hand dismissively and said, "Of course she wouldn't mind."

Taking a small step from Brooke, Birdy pried her hand away from what appeared to be an increasingly strong grip. "We would love to have you. I'll text you my mom's address. Come over around one."

As Mare and Birdy left the shop floor, Brooke hung back and shot Sydney one more glance. It was strangely competitive and seductive, telling Sydney the offer from the other night was obviously still on the table. "Bring wine," she said. "You'll need it. Her mom's a bitch. Or, maybe we'll find another way to distract ourselves." Her lips puckered slightly into a pout and she winked suggestively before turning to follow her fiancée out of the building.

CHAPTER TWENTY-TWO

At one o'clock on Thanksgiving Day, Sydney parked her Jeep behind Birdy's wagon and took a moment to collect her thoughts. She wanted nothing more than to spend the day with Birdy but felt guilty walking into a family's celebration with less than innocent motives. She would do everything in her power to win Birdy's heart even if it meant playing nice with her nutcase fiancée.

Prior to the Halloween party—and The Kiss that followed a few days later—Sydney had been convinced that Brooke was madly in love with Birdy and was sure the guilt of pursuing Birdy under those circumstances would wreck her. Her assumption had since proven to be a vast misjudgment of character, and because character mattered to Sydney, she worried she was ruining her own with this quest to win Birdy's heart.

Late at night, with nothing but her thoughts, she harbored misgivings about her plan to persevere. She was a strong, confident woman—she knew that—so why was she fighting, nearly begging, for a woman who wanted her but would not fight for her in return? It hurt. Sometimes excruciatingly so but then reason would prevail, resulting in a willingness to cut Birdy some slack. Birdy had been planning her life with this woman for years and had spent all of that time trying to keep herself tightly woven into her volatile lover's life. Unexpected and uninvited, Sydney had entered that delicately balanced life and tried to demand her heart, which was already very invested in Brooke.

For a prize like Birdy, she could put her pride in the backseat for a bit longer and see this through to the bitter end, which she realized was exactly what she was careening toward. A logical but bitter end. If only she could preserve a small chunk of her heart when this all shook out—even if it were Brooke who walked away with the prize. She had always been a sucker for a good underdog story. Maybe she was writing her own now.

Her own intentions were clear but Brooke's gave her pause. The woman displayed her infidelity to Sydney without apology or shame. Surely Birdy was unaware.

Always attentive, even doting, Brooke only flipped the switch when Birdy wasn't watching. There was a confident aggression when she looked at other women, claiming them as if she had every right to do so. The woman was certainly alluring, even charming...as long as you're into living on the edge of reason with a sadistic psychopath who could eat your heart at any moment without remorse.

Shuddering at the thought, she wished Birdy could see Brooke for what she was. On several occasions, she had almost told Birdy about the propositions and implied cheating, but talked herself out of it each time. Sure, Birdy needed to know, but that didn't mean Sydney had to be on the other end of that conversation. One thing she had learned in life was to never tell your friend that you dislike their significant other. The friend always chooses them over you.

Besides, Sydney didn't want to fall prey to Brooke's games. She had a feeling that telling Birdy about the come-ons and pick-up lines was exactly what Brooke wanted her to do. It would ensure she'd lose Birdy and, in Brooke's eyes, lose the game.

It was this competitiveness in Brooke that made Sydney especially uneasy. As soon as Brooke realized Sydney cared for Birdy, she had turned up her game and tried to seduce Sydney, as if needing to claim her before Birdy could. There was insecurity behind Brooke's actions, in contrast to the confidence she overtly displayed. Despite that, the woman scared the crap out of her.

Still sitting in the driveway as she gathered her nerve to go inside, she shivered, the soft-top of her Jeep doing little to keep the car's warmth in. Brooke intimidated her, but she wasn't going to let that show, or she knew Brooke would eat her alive.

Forget Brooke. You're here for Birdy. And turkey. Her stomach growled. *Don't forget the turkey.*

Sydney collected her paper grocery bag from the backseat and bravely walked to the door where her evil adversary, her unobtainable crush and her crush's mother waited for her. *Trifecta!*

She rang the doorbell, breathing in the cold air and feeling anxious until Birdy opened the door, her small smile fading as her lips parted. Sydney couldn't help but think of the kiss they had shared and the way those lips had parted for her then. She ached to touch her, but for now would have to be satisfied with studying every detail of her face as they stared at each other. Both were a little breathless, the cold day showing their desire through quick bursts of clouded air.

Birdy was wearing a loose-fitting men's white Oxford shirt, lazily tucked into light, slouchy jeans without a belt. The sleeves were rolled up and Sydney could see goose bumps forming on her arms.

"Are you cold?" she asked quietly.

Birdy shook her head and sucked in her lower lip, nervously biting it.

"We should talk about it you know? About last time."

Birdy glanced over her shoulder. Apparently deciding the coast was clear, she said, "I know."

"But you don't want to?"

"I don't know. I seem to be rocking that avoidance thing lately. It feels like it's the only thing keeping me afloat."

"I guess that's good since you really can't swim."

Birdy chuckled quietly. "It's my emotional life jacket."

"I'm sorry I pushed so far last time. I meant what I said though. I'm still going to fight for you."

Swallowing noticeably, Birdy said, "I know I shouldn't want that. But I do."

Sydney's heart leapt despite the expression of hopelessness on Birdy's face. She nearly gave in to the urge to sweep her into a hug, wanting to comfort her, to reassure her.

Before she could, someone inside the house called out, "Birdy! Come help me with the potatoes. Is Sydney here?"

"Yeah, I'll be right there," Birdy answered over her shoulder and then noticeably shook herself out of her serious mood. A much brighter—if not forced—smile lit her face. The emotional life jacket back in place. "I guess you better come inside now. Let me take your coat and then I'll introduce you to my mom. Mare's been talking about you nonstop so she's excited to meet you. I think you'll really like her." Birdy hung her coat in the hall closet and led Sydney through a large, comfortable living room.

Cornflake lifted her head curiously from the couch cushion she was sprawled out on and then lunged forward when she saw Sydney. She snaked her way between Sydney's legs, licking her hands whenever she reached to pet her head.

"I think she missed you," Birdy said, and then added solemnly, "She's not the only one."

"I've missed you too, Bird." Their serious conversation was broken when Cornflake nudged Sydney's hand, demanding to be petted. Sydney laughed and bent down to ruffle the dog's fur. "Yes, I've missed you too."

When the attention stopped, the dog bolted excitedly to the kitchen as if to trumpet Sydney's arrival.

"I guess we'd better follow."

As soon as Sydney entered the kitchen, she was confronted with Brooke's smirking expression.

"Ah, the illustrious *artist* has arrived," Brooke said, her voice dripping with condescension. "Saul is going to have to watch his back. By the way Mare talks about you, I think she's in love.

I swear, no one seems to be able to hold a conversation around here without a mention of your virtues."

"That is, when you weren't discussing your own virtues," Bea retorted succinctly. "Sydney, I'm Bea. I'm really happy you could join us."

Sydney liked her immediately.

Clearly jealous of the attention, Brooke tried to reclaim control of the situation, taking in Sydney from head to toe and gesturing to the grocery bag in Sydney's hand. "I hope you brought wine like I said." Despite her apparent assuredness, her cheeks were still flushed from Bea's remark.

Sydney doubted it was easy to make Brooke blush, but Bea seemed to have a mark on her hubris. The seductive look she proffered to remind Sydney of her earlier proposition had much less power when she was so obviously rattled.

"Not exactly." She drew a bottle from the bag.

"Oh, champagne," Brooke practically purred. "I underestimated you, Sydney. That's likely to go straight to your head."

"Actually, no. It's sparkling grape juice. I would rather keep all my faculties tonight." Then turning to Bea, she added, "So I can fully enjoy this delicious meal. It smells fantastic."

Bea's lips pursed with pleasure at the compliment.

"Sparkling grape juice? I haven't had that since I was seven," Brooke said patronizingly, while swirling her glass of white wine. "A little childish, are we?" She obviously hadn't been taught to give up either.

Saul bristled while Birdy took a step toward Brooke, one ready to rumble, the other to calm.

With all the forced politeness she could muster, Sydney replied before Birdy had a chance to speak. "Childish? Funny you should say that. That's exactly what it is." She turned her smile to Bea and Birdy and proffered the bottle. "This is a bit of a family tradition that I thought I would share with all of you. Every Thanksgiving I usually have the honor of accompanying my two nieces at the kids' table, and the deal is they save me a seat as their personal guest of honor. In return, I bring the bubbles, as they call it. This is my first Thanksgiving away from them and I miss them terribly, so I hoped we could all have a glass of bubbles tonight in their honor."

"Aw, that's adorable!" Birdy and Mare squealed simultaneously.

"I would be delighted!" Bea said with a sweeping glance that included Saul, Birdy and Brooke. "Some of us could stand to drink a little less wine today anyway."

Saul practically guffawed at Brooke's fallen look, and raised his glass of wine to Sydney in a small toast to her victory.

"Here, let me put that in the fridge to chill," Bea said, taking the bottle from Sydney.

"Thank you. What can I do to help?"

Brooke gave a disbelieving snivel and left the room, phone in hand, but Bea didn't give her a second glance. "First, pour yourself a glass of wine so there's less for Saul. I hope you like pinot noir. It's all we seem to buy around here."

"Sure beats that sauv blanc shit Brooke tries to get us to drink," Saul said, taking a long sip of his wine. At Birdy's disapproving sigh he shrugged his shoulders. "What? She puts ice cubes in it, for God's sake." He was obviously unconcerned if Brooke could hear them, though it hardly mattered. Brooke's peals of laughter as she talked on the phone suggested she couldn't have cared less.

"Be nice, Saul," Bea said, her tone a motherly scold.

"That's rich coming from you, Bea. Pretending to be a proper lady now that we have guests?"

The woman giggled. "I thought I would try it on for size for once. Here, Sydney, help me peel these potatoes and we'll talk about you instead of Brooke."

Sydney caught a thankful glance between Birdy and her mom before Birdy punched Saul in the arm. Though the impending interrogation made her nervous, she was happy now to have something to do with her hands.

"Besides your nieces, who are you missing today?"

Thoughts of her family brought a smile. So did the fact that Birdy had moved her cutting board closer, perhaps because she too cared about her answer.

"Well, my older brother Mateo—everyone calls him Matty—is the one with the two girls, Sofia and Dess. We're pretty close and I always like joking around with him at the holidays. We usually just steal a lot of food while his wife Gabby helps my mom cook."

"What about your dad?" Mare grunted as she put a heavy pot of water on the stove to boil. The group effort to get dinner on the table was familiar to Sydney, and one of the things that made Thanksgiving so special.

"Dad's the classic man that sits in the other room watching football with my uncle. To be honest, he and I haven't been very close since I came out."

"How old were you?" Birdy asked.

"I knew in high school but I waited until college. I hadn't really even planned on telling him. I told my mom when I started dating my first girlfriend during freshman year at the University of Texas. Hook 'em Horns." She signed the team's slogan with her thumb and pinky. "Anyway, she was really cool about it. Matty had already warned her, I think, so she had some time to process it. Really, it didn't seem to surprise her. My dad, though, was a different story."

"Have you told him?" Bea asked.

"Not exactly, but he knows."

"That sounds juicy. I love a good coming out story if you're willing to share."

"You're really putting me on the spot. I don't want to hog the conversation."

"We'll take turns. Except Mare, we all have coming out stories," Bea said.

"Hey, what about me?" Saul exclaimed indignantly.

"You had to come out as straight, honey," Bea explained. "When you were in sixth grade, we all just assumed you were gay."

All of the women snorted with laughter as Saul huffed.

"You first," Bea said to Sydney.

"Okay, in college I was a fine arts major, which my dad hated. But I also played softball, which he loved. He would come to my games sometimes and then take me out for pizza after. One time he decided to surprise me and came to my game. I had no idea he was there."

"A surprise visit. I have a bad feeling about this," Birdy interjected.

Sydney nodded. "I played third base and fielded a grounder, fired it to second. They got the runner out at first and we wound up getting a double play, ending the game. I was ecstatic and Jamie, my girlfriend at the time, leaned over the fence by third base, and I planted a huge kiss on her. Of course, as you can guess, I looked up and saw my dad watching." She sighed at the memory. "He still came to some of my games but always let me know ahead of time that he would be there, and he never took me out for pizza afterward. But I have Mom and Matty, Gabby and the girls. They pester me all the time about finding a girlfriend. So overall, coming out was fairly painless for me."

"That's great that you have so much support," Bea said. "I always tell Birdy she has no idea what it's like for most lesbians. She had it easy since her two gay moms effectively weeded out anyone that wouldn't be accepting. Plus, in Portland, she's always been in this little bubble of social liberals, which I'm thankful for. I'm glad it wasn't as hard for her as it was for her mom and me. It's good to see things are changing."

Bea grew a bit misty-eyed as she spoke, prompting Birdy to give her a gentle kiss on the ear.

"It's probably just the onions I chopped earlier," she said, dismissing her watery eyes with a wave of her hand. "Where are you from, Sydney?"

"Houston, though I've been living in Austin since college."

"That's a long way away. No wonder you miss them all so much," Bea said.

"I'm flying back for Christmas. Mare gave me an extra week off so I don't have to go too much longer before I get to see them all again."

"That's nice." Bea started to say something more but Saul interrupted with his own question.

"Are you single?" He seemed to be looking more at Birdy than her, which made Sydney laugh.

"You guys are so nosey!" Birdy said, her attention rapt on the celery she was dicing to a near pulp. Her face seemed a little flushed. "She's probably tired of all of your questions."

"Not tired at all. And yes, I'm single."

Bea gave an interested little "hmm" and Saul raised his eyebrows at Birdy, who reddened even more.

Brooke chose that moment to return to the kitchen, still talking and laughing loudly into her cell phone as if to underscore that she wasn't satisfied with present company. After adding two more ice cubes to her wineglass, she refilled it with sauvignon blanc before retreating to the living room.

There was no mistaking that everyone in the room stiffened when Brooke entered, and relaxed again when she left. Knowing she was laying it on thick, Sydney asked with an innocent smile, "I finished the potatoes, what else can I do to help?"

"Suck up," Saul said into his wineglass as he winked at her.

* * *

"It feels good to sit down," Bea groaned as she sank into her overstuffed sofa and put her feet on the coffee table.

Birdy handed her one of the two steaming mugs of coffee she carried. She had put hers in her favorite Christmas mug that she had used for hot chocolate as a child. Now that all the leftovers had been packed and their guests had left, she was free to relax with her elf mug. The day had been an exhausting balancing act between her friends, her fiancée and Sydney. Trying to keep everyone happy and feeling included had left her drained. Needing time to herself now, she had told Brooke she wanted to stay the night on her boat with Hoots. Since Brooke always refused to sleep on the boat, it was a convenient way to be alone for the night.

"Sydney sure is nice. I like her a lot," Bea said.

"Yeah, she's nice." Birdy stretched out on the couch, putting her feet in her mom's lap.

"And pretty too."

"I guess so."

Bea chuckled. "You guess so? Anyone with eyes would be interested in her. Makes me wish I was thirty years younger."

"Well, you're both single. Maybe you should throw your hat in the ring...your very old, antique, dusty hat. Maybe she's into cougars." She giggled as her mom slapped her feet out of her lap.

"Admit it though. You have a crush on her," Bea said playfully.

"No, I do not! I mean, I like her and all, but I don't have a crush on her."

Bea took a long sip of her coffee, her silence a deliberate trick to get Birdy to say more than she should.

"Okay, fine. Maybe I have a tiny crush. An itty-bitty one."

"I knew it!" Bea declared triumphantly.

"Yeah, well it's not exactly something to celebrate seeing as I'm getting married in January."

"You have two in your bush."

Birdy spat the coffee she had just sipped back into her mug. Her mother had *not* just made a lewd reference to her vag. "What?"

"Two in the bush. That's your problem." Seeing that Birdy wasn't following, she continued. "Didn't anybody ever teach you your proverbs?" A bird in the hand is worth two in the bush."

"Is the old age getting to you, Mom? What are you talking about?"

She held out an open palm. "You have one in the hand—Brooke. She's the safe option, but you have the opportunity for an even bigger prize. That one is risky, though, because you'd have to let go of the safe option and try to capture the unknown." She stretched forward and clapped Birdy's knee. "How's that for old age, pipsqueak? You can't move me into a home yet."

"Mom, cut it out. No one is in my bush except Brooke." Birdy felt herself pale at her words as her mother erupted in laughter. Covering her face in mortification, she continued, "You know what I mean. I'm getting married. To Brooke. And I need you to deal with that."

Bea sobered. "I'm sorry. Honestly, I am. Brooke really impressed me at your engagement party. It's obvious how she feels about you. It seems like she's mellowed out a lot and is taking all of this very seriously. I promised myself after that night that I would stop criticizing her. Supporting you but not your relationship is not good enough, and Jo would rip me a new one if she were here. I want to be your biggest cheerleader. It's just…" She hesitated, obviously waging an internal battle over whether or not she should say what she was thinking.

"It's just what?"

After a deep sigh, she went on, "It's just that she…Sydney… she reminds me of your mom. She looks at you the same way Jo used to look at me. What do I know, though? I'm just being a silly old woman who worries about you. You tell me Brooke makes you happy. I'm glad you've found someone to do that, sweetie."

Birdy leaned into her mother's one-armed hug, accepting the peace offering.

As if she couldn't help herself, Bea added, "You can have anyone in your bush that you want." And then she fell into another fit of giggles.

CHAPTER TWENTY-THREE

After throwing the rest of her needed belongings in a suitcase Sydney sat back on her couch and drummed her fingers on the arm. Her flight wasn't until tomorrow afternoon, she was finished packing and had no plans for the night. She had just resigned herself to an evening of romantic comedies and leftovers when her phone buzzed against the fabric of the couch. A text message from Mare invited her to join them at a bar. They were already heading out the door.

Happily, she typed back a reply confirming she would be there. Not wanting to be too transparent, she didn't ask if Birdy was coming, but assumed she would be out with her two best friends. She just hoped Brooke wouldn't be there with her. Because pretending the fiancée didn't exist was obviously the healthiest thing to do. It was clear that Birdy wasn't the only one wearing the emotional life jacket named Avoidance and Denial.

Forty minutes later, she walked into the bar in North Portland. Good thing she had started following the Portland Trailblazers this season, because apparently this was a popular place to watch their games. The majority of the patrons were sporting Trailblazers gear, much like the tight black Damian Lillard jersey she wore under her fitted leather jacket. She had worn her hair down tonight and knew the skinny jeans made her ass look good—in case a certain person was there to see it.

Pushing through the crowd made up mostly of straight white guys yelling at the TV screen, she was happy to see the wall of whiskies that she had read this bar was known for. Birdy may know beer, but Sydney knew her bourbon. With her eye already on a favorite, she shimmied her way into a gap at the bar. Bourbon and basketball. Now this was her scene.

She yelled over the crowd to place her order for a Bulleit on the rocks. With a cheerful thanks to a bartender who was too busy even to look up, she left her tab open and then turned around to scan the bar, searching for Mare but hoping to find Birdy.

From across the small bar, Saul stretched on his tiptoes to wave her over. When she made it to their table, he and Mare each gave her a big hug. Not seeing Birdy nearby, she sighed heavily at her absence.

It was too loud to carry on a decent conversation, so she only exchanged a few words with Saul about the game, which he was following attentively. Sipping on her bourbon, she cheered with the crowd as the Blazers nailed a three from way behind the line. The cheers died down when they turned over the ball on their next possession and a familiar cackle echoed from farther back in the bar. Her heart sank, realizing Brooke was there. But that meant Birdy was too.

A quick survey confirmed it. Her back was to Sydney as she listened to Brooke entertain a small group of people. Not surprisingly, Brooke's arm was wrapped possessively around her waist with a hand shoved in her back pocket.

"Disgusting, isn't it?"

Sydney hadn't realized the quarter had ended and that Saul was behind her, watching the same display of affection she was.

"I'm definitely not the most appreciative audience."

"Brooke doesn't care as long as she *has* an audience. Look at the way they're all hanging on her every word," he groused, gesturing to the group of women surrounding Brooke and Birdy. "Can't they see she's a manipulative bitch?"

"I guess they're too manipulated to care. She does put on a pretty good show."

As if Brooke had heard them over the impossibly loud din of the bar, she looked past Birdy and spotted them, first Saul then Sydney. A playful smile grew on her face as she withdrew her hand from the pocket and returned it to the same spot. Now in plain sight, she flexed it several times to squeeze Birdy's ass. With a sardonic wink, she turned back to the group of adoring women.

Saul made a vomiting noise and pretended to catch it in his glass.

Sydney laughed as best she could, though there was nothing funny about Brooke's exhibitionism. "I hate her."

"Welcome to the club," Mare said, raising her glass in a salute to both of them.

Saul toasted as well. "Let me buy you another drink and we'll make a list of everything we hate most about the evil bitch."

For all her misery, Sydney at least liked Birdy's friends very much. She was lucky to have a boss like Mare.

"Save our spot," Mare said. "I'll help him carry the drinks... after we make out for a while, that is. Stay here."

"Will do." Taking the nearest stool, Sydney focused on the drink in her lap. She shook the ice and threw back the remaining bourbon. Powerless to resist, her eyes scanned the bar again and found Birdy quickly. Once again, Brooke was regaling her friends with stories, now gesturing with both hands. At least with her hands busy, she wasn't still groping Birdy.

Then all thought left her head and her breath left her lungs as Birdy turned, her eyes immediately meeting Sydney's. They held each other's gaze for several seconds, barely blinking, neither willing to break the contact. Finally, Birdy turned back to the group, holding her empty pint glass up as she excused herself to get another drink. Brooke barely acknowledged her, continuing her story. The group closed ranks as soon as Birdy stepped away, leaving Brooke with her back now completely turned to Sydney.

Maybe Birdy was walking in slow motion or maybe all of the romantic movies Sydney had ever watched were affecting her perception of time and space. Whichever it was, it seemed as if the crowd parted in an orchestrated dance, allowing her to make a slow, breathless walk toward Sydney without impediment.

Sydney was shocked when Birdy reached her barstool and rested her fingertips on her leg for a moment that passed all too quickly. Emboldened by the intimate gesture, she swiveled to allow her knees to lightly press against Birdy's hips until Birdy bit her lower lip and scanned the crowd guiltily, checking for Brooke. Sydney sat up straighter, pulling her knees away, creating the space between them she knew was appropriate, even though it was the last thing she wanted.

"Hi." One of the shortest words in the English language, but considering Birdy had abandoned her fiancée to deliver it, it spoke volumes.

"Hi, yourself. I've been thinking about you a lot."

"You have?"

"Constantly."

Birdy pulled her lips tightly together as if trying to hide how happy the admission made her. "My mother hasn't stopped talking about you since Thanksgiving. For a month it's been nothing but Sydney this and Sydney that. She told me to tell you to have a good trip."

"Your mom is great. I hope I get to see her again soon. Or more specifically, I hope she cooks for me again."

"I'm glad you liked her. And she would cook for you anytime. She's in love with you, so you can add her to your lengthy list of admirers along with Saul and Mare."

"And here I thought Brooke was the charming one." Sydney flashed her a smile.

"I guess you're giving her a run for her money."

Sydney sat forward and asked earnestly, "Am I?"

Birdy was about to answer when Saul and Mare arrived at her side. He put his arm over her shoulders while Mare, looking a little disheveled, handed Sydney a fresh drink.

"I thought maybe you two had gotten lost." Sydney took a sip of her bourbon, realizing at once she hadn't specified the premium brand. Beggars weren't supposed to be choosers.

"Oh, I think they got lost, all right," Birdy said, poking Saul in the ribs. "Lost in each other's mouths."

Saul leaned in, making sloppy, smooching noises in Birdy's ear as she giggled and pushed him away.

"Am I going to have to fight to keep you off Birdy too, Saul?" Brooke asked as she joined the group. Her eyes were on Sydney though, and Birdy instantly stopped giggling and paled. She took a small step back, putting even more space between herself and Sydney.

Rolling his eyes, Saul turned back to the TV, deliberately ignoring her.

Brooke laced her fingers in Birdy's. "I need another drink. Come with me, baby."

Sydney watched them leave. "I really hate her." She took another slug of her drink and distracted herself with the second half of the basketball game.

* * *

By the fourth quarter, she had lost track of how many drinks she had bought. It didn't help that Saul was in a generous mood since the Blazers were playing over their heads against a better team, and he topped off their usual orders with several rounds of shots. Brooke was across the room doing the same, taking shots of cinnamon whiskey with her friends.

Trying her best to focus on the game, Sydney cheered with the crowd with each basket and groaned when the other team hit a big shot. Birdy had kept her distance, usually staying next to Brooke and chatting with her group of friends.

The Blazers hit a three at the buzzer to win the game, causing the crowd to erupt with excitement. In fact, two total strangers hugged her, and she took another victory shot with Saul before slumping back on her stool, realizing how drunk she had become. The crowd began to thin and she saw that

Birdy had joined Mare and Saul at the bar. As they laughed, she was happy to see the light back in Birdy. She was much more animated and engaged now than she had been with Brooke's circle of friends.

The alcohol had dulled her senses, so she wasn't aware of Brooke's approach until she was standing before her.

Gently, she pushed Sydney's knees apart and stepped between them. She took Sydney's drink out of her hands and took a long pull from it. "Bourbon, huh? You like it sweet? Yeah, you look like the slow and sweet type." She leaned, putting her drink on the ledge behind her, and allowing her breasts to push into Sydney's shoulder. Her hand had dropped to Sydney's leg, and her thumb traced a slow circle along her inner thigh, very close to the seam of her jeans. "Bourbon's never been my drink. I tend to go for scotch but then I guess I like it a little rougher than you, but I could teach you to like it rough."

It infuriated Sydney to think about how this woman had so expertly manipulated Birdy, had her thoroughly hoodwinked while so willing to sharing her bed with another woman. Specifically, with Sydney. The thought of Brooke, hard and aggressive, touching her was sickening and Sydney shuddered in disgust.

Brooke, however, seemed to take her shudder for arousal. She peered at her through hooded eyes, a cocky grin on her face. "Your place or mine?"

Sydney felt drunk and slow-witted. "What about Birdy?" She realized her question sounded like she was acquiescing, ironing out the details of Brooke's plan.

Brooke obviously misread her tone as well and moved her thumb inward, now directly pushing against the seam of her jeans. "Oh, I'm sure she'll manage. She can stay with Tweedle-Dee or Tweedle-Dum over there." She cocked her head, gesturing to Mare and Saul.

Grabbing Brooke's wrist, Sydney pushed her hand away and sprang to her feet, forcing Brooke to stumble backward. For the first time, she was able to see past her own drunkenness to realize that Brooke was also trashed, maybe even more so. "Back off, Brooke. I will *never* sleep with you," she hissed. She made sure this time that her tone showed her disgust.

Brooke's eyes flashed with anger. "Your loss, bitch," she said and then reached behind Sydney, grabbed her bourbon, and threw back the rest of the drink in one large gulp. She shoved the empty glass roughly into Sydney's chest, forcing her to take it and then stormed back to her group of friends, teetering drunkenly in her heels on the way.

Sydney joined the others at the bar just as they were hugging goodbye. Saul pulled her into a warm embrace as well. "We're going to get out of here. We have a little victory dance to do at home, if you know what I mean."

"You're going to pass out as soon as you get in the cab." To Mare, she added, "Take care of him."

"Oh, she always knows how to take care of me," he said with a lascivious grin.

"Come on, big boy. Take me home." Mare waved her fingers and steered him out of the bar.

Birdy smiled as she watched them leave. "I think we're going to head out too. As soon as I can get Brooke away from her friends."

Leaning heavily against the bar to keep herself from wobbling too obviously, Sydney signed the tab the bartender had put in front of her. She snorted at seeing Brooke take another shot with the group of women. "More like her harem," she slurred.

"What do you mean?"

Still watching the group, Sydney said, "I'd be shocked if she hasn't slept with at least one of them." She turned her attention back to Birdy and realized what she had just said.

Birdy's face had fallen and she looked pale and angry. "Fuck you, Syd. That was low." She pushed past, heading for the door.

"Goddammit," Sydney said through clenched teeth and turned unsteadily to chase after her.

Birdy was outside on a mostly empty front patio, where Sydney grabbed her arm to stop her from crossing the street. "Wait, Bird. I'm sorry. I'm really drunk. Don't listen to me. I'm just being stupid and jealous." The cold air helped clear her mind a little as she tried to sort out the situation she had gotten herself into. The tiny part of her that was sober knew she shouldn't tell Birdy anything about Brooke. It would only drive her away. But the drunk side, which was unfortunately the louder voice in her head at the moment, told her to fight fire with fire. Maybe she could beat Brooke at her own game if she told Birdy how insidious her fiancée could be.

No, she couldn't hurt Birdy like that. She bit her tongue, hoping Birdy would accept her drunken apology and ignore her thoughtless comment.

Instead, Birdy narrowed her eyes at her. "Tell me what you know."

"What do you mean?" Maybe this was a good time to play dumb.

"You obviously know something about Brooke or you wouldn't have said that. What aren't you telling me?"

Sydney knew a trap when she saw it. Birdy was angry and there was nothing she could say that would help the situation. But she was drunk and in love, so she stepped off the cliff. "She's cheating on you, Bird."

Birdy shook off the hand that was still gripping her arm. "Brooke would never do that."

To Sydney's ears, Birdy wasn't convinced by her own words, which spurred her on. "She came on to me. She wanted me to have sex with her tonight." Sydney was desperate, pleading with Birdy to see the truth.

"Oh, this is low, Sydney. Really fucking low. You can't have me, okay? Get over it. Don't try to fuck up my relationship just because you can't get what you want." Shoving Sydney aside, she headed back toward the door.

Sydney called out to her, "I'm sorry, Bird. I was just trying to be your friend."

Spinning around to face her, Birdy spat, "If that's your idea of friendship, then I don't want it. This has just been a game to you, hasn't it? You had to beat Brooke. Well, guess what. You've lost. You really are just a home-wrecker, huh? Trying to get what you can't have? You're pathetic and deceitful and I wish we'd never met. Just stay the hell out of my life. Got it?" Birdy flung the door open and stormed back into the bar.

Stunned, Sydney froze as an icy pain numbed her limbs. Through the large front windows of the bar she could see Birdy wrap her arms tightly around Brooke's waist, imploring her to leave. Brooke angrily cut her off and turned away, shaking her from her arm.

Defeated and exhausted, Sydney slinked away from the bar, cursing herself as she got in a waiting cab.

CHAPTER TWENTY-FOUR

Birdy was livid. And scared. She knew Brooke was a flirt but she didn't think she would actually cheat on her. Brooke would never do that to her.

She might.

No, she decided. Brooke was vivacious, charming, maybe a flirt. But she was faithful. She wouldn't risk their relationship for a fling.

Luckily, Birdy had avoided the shots Brooke had been buying all night so she was moderately sober when she finally managed to drag Brooke away from the bar. She had seen her drink heavily many times and took care of her frequently when she came home trashed. Tonight, however, was a whole different level of drunkenness for Brooke. She had been irritated and aggressive at the end of the night in the bar, and as soon as they got in the cab she was inexplicably angry, pushing Birdy away from her.

Not that Birdy cared right now. Her hands still shook from the confrontation with Sydney, the ugly words from her own mouth echoing in her ears and making her sick to her stomach. Sydney was obviously drunk. Maybe she hadn't realized what she saying about Brooke, or how much it would hurt to hear it. But she hadn't deserved to be treated like that. A little cooling off time…that's all they needed.

Having grown accustomed to how emotional Brooke could be when she drank, Birdy was still surprised when she started crying before they had even gotten out of the cab. After paying their fare, she helped her into the atrium of her building and guided her into the elevator. When the doors shut, Brooke pulled her into a tight hug, sobbing into her shoulder.

"It's okay, baby. I'm here. I'll take care of you."

Brooke was blubbering incoherently. "I'm sorry."

"It's okay. You didn't do anything wrong. Just a few too many shots."

"I'm sorry. You deserve so much better than me."

Birdy couldn't help but hear her mom's voice. *Emotional roller coaster.*

"That's silly, Brooke. I love you. Come on, this is our floor." She guided her through the door and Brooke collapsed on the rug just inside the condo door.

"I'm sorry. I'm so, so sorry. I'm disgusting and I hate myself." Brooke sobbed, looking pathetic with snot and spit on her face.

"Let me just get you some water and you'll feel a lot better."

Still crumpled on the floor, Brooke obediently drank half the glass, spilling some on the rug. Birdy knew it was pointless to analyze Brooke's words and feelings while she was this drunk. A drunken tongue does not always speak a sober mind, she told herself. But still, she couldn't shake Sydney's accusation. And she had a sinking feeling that this emotional mess was related. Throughout most the night, Brooke had been unusually demonstrative, always pulling her close and including her in conversations. Then later, without warning, she had become edgy and angry.

With Sydney's accusations still ringing in her ears, she needed to understand Brooke's sudden shift of emotion, even as she dreaded the answer. "What's going on?"

Brooke buried her face in her hands and began sobbing again.

"Tell me what's wrong. I just need to know...then we'll go to bed."

She swiped at some of the spittle around her mouth with the back of her hand. Between sobs she choked out, "I...I had sex with someone else."

Birdy shuddered as a cold emptiness burned in her chest. Slumped against the wall, she stared at the rug, not understanding. A picture of Sydney was her clearest thought. *She's cheating on you.*

"I'm so, so sorry. It only happened once. It was a woman from my gym and she came on to me and it meant absolutely nothing." Her words were slurring and her voice was thick with mucus. "I'm so sorry, baby. I love you. Please forgive me. It will never happen again."

Brooke grabbed Birdy's head, attempting a kiss that she resisted by turning her face to the side.

"I'm so sorry. I'm...oh, God." Brooke lurched forward, scrambling to her feet and then stumbling as she rushed down the hall.

Birdy's senses were numb and her stomach hollow. She barely noticed the retching sounds from the bathroom. Her thoughts were trained on Sydney, with Brooke little more than a disturbing distraction. After several minutes, the sound of quiet sobs filtered into her consciousness from the bathroom.

She felt empty, and out of habit went to Brooke to comfort her. Sitting beside her on the floor, she held Brooke's head in her lap while she cried. Her heart ached with resentment for how Brooke had made this moment about her, for needing to be taken care of when she'd just torn Birdy's whole world apart.

A part of her wanted to get up and leave the apartment—and Brooke—maybe forever. But her own hypocrisy kept her painfully rooted to the bathroom floor. Hadn't she cheated too? Maybe she and Sydney hadn't had sex, but emotionally Birdy had been cheating on her fiancée for months. The only difference was that Brooke had the courage to admit what she had done wrong. Birdy had not had the courage to do that. She had decided to stick this out and make their relationship work despite her own infidelity. Did she even have the right to be hurt considering her own wrongdoing?

Eventually Brooke sat up, her face a mess.

Not wanting to hear any more explanation, Birdy turned on the shower and helped her undress. She guided her under the warm spray while she cleaned up the bathroom and scrubbed the toilet.

Her thoughts urged her to leave immediately and then just as quickly she found herself rationalizing Brooke's unfaithfulness. The words that kept circulating to the front of her thoughts were damning: *You cheated too.* By the time Brooke turned off the shower, she had resolved it was time to stop being weak. Time to take responsibility and be an adult, one who didn't shy away from her commitments. She needed to be strong for once. To own up to her mistakes and forgive Brooke for hers. Only then could they make their marriage work.

Swaying, Brooke leaned heavily on the counter as they both brushed their teeth. She was unsteady but somewhat sobered, enough that she was able to make it to the bedroom, where she threw back the covers and sprawled naked across the bed.

Birdy dutifully put Brooke's clothes away. Then with nothing left to do, she sat on her side of the bed as Brooke molded herself to her back. *You cheated too.*

"I'm so sorry, baby. I love you."

A hand moved up her stomach, cupping her breast under her shirt. Birdy still felt numb. She hadn't cried. She hadn't really even let herself feel since Brooke's admission. Her breast was being kneaded more insistently, but she was far from aroused.

Brooke breathed heavily—whiskey and toothpaste—and kissed Birdy's neck and licked her ear. "Let me show you how much I love you."

Birdy sat unmoving. She wanted Brooke's love. She wanted all of this to go away. Maybe Brooke could make it go away by touching her. Maybe she could love Brooke again.

Brusquely, Brooke pushed aside her bra, but at the rough touch she jerked away. Scooting to the foot of the bed, she righted her clothing, needing a barrier between them.

Sleepily, Brooke lay back on the pillows and asked, "What's wrong, baby?"

"I can't do this."

"Sure you can...we'll get through this. I know I fucked up but you still love me, right?"

Birdy sat for a long time, considering the question. Finally, she broke the silence. "There's something I need to tell you, Brooke. Something about Sydney." She waited for a response but there was none. "Brooke?" Finding her asleep, she pulled the blankets up over her naked body and went home to her boat.

CHAPTER TWENTY-FIVE

Birdy woke up cold the next morning. Hoots's little body was curled at the foot of her bed and she pulled him up to her chest, with only a small, sleepy meow to signal his protest. He settled himself again, this time under the covers against her stomach. The December morning was deeply overcast, making it impossible to know how late she had slept. The dreariness of the sky mirrored her mood. Numb, flat, dulled. Her mantra from last night of *You cheated too* had changed once Brooke tried to touch her. Now, ringing in her ears were the words, *I can't do this.*

It was over.

She needed to officially end it with Brooke but was too detached and unwilling to face her emotions. Brooke's confession had been pushed to the back of her mind, something to process later when her head was clear. Instead she had dumped herself in bed and fallen asleep immediately, thankfully not remembering any of her dreams.

The way she had left Sydney gnawed at her. Lashing out had felt like her only option when faced with Sydney's heart-wrenching words. And now Sydney was on a plane to Texas. She thought about texting her. Apologizing and explaining. Telling Sydney her relationship with Brooke was through, but she stopped herself. She had been the worst version of herself last night and had accused Sydney of unforgivable things. There was no way they could bounce back from that. Maybe Sydney's departure was for the best. It would give her time to end this chapter of her life with Brooke and mourn the loss of writing any future chapters with Sydney.

Cold and lonely, she realized a profound need for someone to take care of her. The full chicken soup and warm blanket treatment. Bumps rose on her skin as she quickly dressed and then she loaded up Hoots and an overnight bag and prayed that her mom was home.

* * *

"Spill it." Bea sat back on the couch, peering insistently over the top of her glasses.

Birdy couldn't even bring herself to feign ignorance. She had immediately burst into tears when her mom had opened the door and had allowed herself to be wrapped in a tight hug before being led to the couch.

Hoots had been released from his carrier and was now settled on Bea, who gently prodded Birdy again once her tears had slowed down. "What happened, baby?"

Birdy didn't know where to start. She was terrified of her mother's disapproval but she had to tell someone. The weight had grown too heavy.

With the impending admission, her eyes welled up again. Her mom nudged Hoots from her lap, slid over beside her and pulled her into a tight hug that made the tears spill over.

Through her sniffles, Birdy tried to explain. "Brooke cheated on me."

"What?" Bea cried. "I hate her. I'm sorry, Birdy, but I hate her. How dare she do that to you!"

Birdy held up her hand weakly to silence her ire. "I'm no better, Mom. I practically did the same to her." At the admission, the arms tightened around her shoulders, giving her courage to continue. "Except, for me it wasn't meaningless sex. It wasn't sex at all, it was just a kiss, but maybe I'm worse than Brooke. That kiss meant something. Emotionally, I've been cheating on Brooke for months with Sydney."

"Oh, honey. What are you going to do?"

"I have to end it with Brooke. I can't go on after something like that even if it does make me a hypocrite. I'm so sorry about the wedding. I know you've already paid for the food. I feel terrible that you're going to lose money. And all those people that had to buy plane tickets. I don't know how you even cancel a wedding."

"Don't worry about the wedding. Do what's right for you. You didn't bankrupt me. But you might have to wait a while for the next one."

Birdy sighed. Anxiety still prickled at her scalp but she immediately felt a weight lift off her.

"What about Sydney?" Bea asked.

"I said horrible things to her. I was nasty and cruel and I don't see how she could ever forgive me. And even if she does, which she won't, it's just terrible timing. She deserved better than to feel like a rebound, and I think I need some time to sort myself out. Closure with Brooke, time to heal. Sydney doesn't get back until after New Year's so I'm going to lay low. Take some time to be alone and figure things out. Decide how I could ever make Sydney forgive me even though I don't deserve it." Birdy scooped Hoots up, needing his warm comfort. The rush of emotions left her feeling drained and shaky.

"You'll win her back," Bea said assuredly.

"You weren't there. You have no idea how terrible I was. She'll never want me back." Birdy buried her face in Hoots's fur.

"What's Sydney's last name?"

"Ramos. I've told you that before."

"Do you know what that translates to?"

"No. You know I got a C in Spanish."

"Branch. It means branch, honey." Bea looked at her meaningfully. "She might be a pretty good place to build your nest, Birdy."

* * *

Birdy gave herself the rest of the weekend before she felt ready to confront Brooke. She had received multiple text messages and voice mails from her but had ignored them all.

Returning to work Monday morning, she felt somewhat renewed. It was late December, Christmas—easily her favorite holiday—was right around the corner and she had a new sense of hope after talking with her mom. Maybe she could make Sydney forgive her. Maybe Sydney was her home.

It would be a Christmas miracle but perhaps there was a way to claw out of this pit she had sunk them into that night with her hateful, awful, vengeful words. Humiliation and shame had burned within her and she had railed against Sydney. In hindsight, the truth she had found in Sydney's warning had been the accelerant, though she had been unwilling to recognize it at the time. It was like she had been a wounded animal, lashing out at the person she needed most. With any hope, Sydney would understand that and still have a place in her heart.

Not one to chalk anything up to fate, she now considered it a tempting possibility. Maybe they were meant to be together and would find each other against all odds. The first step was moving on from Brooke. She dreaded the confrontation but was even more anxious to put it behind her. Sydney would be back to work after the New Year and maybe they would have a second chance. She just needed time with Sydney again. Easy and casual time working side by side to reestablish themselves as work buddies and then let it build from there.

She was almost giddy with hope, her heart racing along with the insistent ringing of the office phone. Mare had made a quick run to the bank, leaving her to cover. She distractedly answered on the fourth ring.

"PDX Ink, this is Birdy. How can I help you?"

"Yes, I'm calling for Mare Lentz."

"She's not in the office right now. Can I take a message?"

"Yeah, this is Paul Steele over at Steele Threads Printing. I received an application from Sydney Ramos and I'd just like to get a reference from Mare. Could you have her call me back today?"

And with that every ounce of hope in Birdy's body wilted and died. Screw fate. Screw Paul.

Just stay the hell out of my life. Yeah, there's really no bouncing back from that, Birdy admitted. It had been silly to allow herself to hope. Hope was for those who deserved it. She filed Sydney away for now, her mental 'Regrets' folder now bulging, and turned her attention back to the phone call.

"Sure," Birdy managed to squeeze out of her constricted throat to Paul, the killer of Christmas miracles. "I'll have her call you. Goodbye."

Would she get a chance to say goodbye to Sydney as well?

* * *

Having left work early, she now sat in Brooke's condo, steeling herself for her return. She had let herself in long before Brooke was due home from work and had given Pumpkin an extra-large bone to keep him busy so she would have time to gather her thoughts. At work she had spent the day compartmentalizing her thoughts. Those of Sydney she attempted to bury deep, saving them for later. Likely tonight when she would be lying in bed bawling her eyes out. Right now, though, the only compartment she allowed herself to consider was Brooke and the conversation they needed to have.

Taking refuge at her mother's house over the weekend had been a good idea. One that came with a lot of delicious meals and the comfort of her childhood bedroom. For what must have been the thousandth time since she was a kid, she had stared at the tiny flowers that dotted her wallpaper. Finding comfort in the familiar pattern, she had allowed her mind to analyze her situation for the first time.

After the engagement party, she had thought she owed it to herself to rekindle the love she had once felt so strongly for Brooke but came to the realization that she had merely been paying penance for her guilt and giving emotional reparation to a love that was dead. She was tired of feeling lifeless and empty.

Brooke's emotional roller coaster no longer made her feel alive, it only gnawed at her, chewing her up little by little, until she finally looked down and realized she was only half.

She had thought all this time that it boiled down to a choice between Brooke and Sydney but she realized now that she had been wrong. It was a choice between Brooke and herself. Between Brooke and happiness.

She had no interest in working out their problems as she felt she had tried long enough. There was just nothing left to give. She was giving up Brooke and she had thrown away Sydney. Her heart felt like it had been chewed up and left on the cold sidewalk at Sydney's feet, a bloody, palpitating mess. And what's worse, she only had herself to blame. Brooke, she was ready to live without. Living without Sydney, however, was something she would have to learn to do.

Several bags containing all of her belongings from Brooke's condo were already loaded into her car, and while she would prefer to slink away, she knew she needed to face Brooke and gain whatever closure she could.

The light was fading but she didn't bother to turn on a lamp. She sat on the sofa, engulfed in darkness and feeling strangely at peace with her decision. Occasionally, painful thoughts of Sydney came to her but mostly she thought about her time with Brooke, allowing herself to enjoy the happy moments they had shared and objectively consider her future that she now knew would not include her.

After eight p.m., she finally heard Brooke's key in the lock. She turned on the light next to her on the dimmest setting so she wouldn't startle her by speaking out of the darkness. Brooke entered, dropping her bag by the door before registering the light and Birdy's presence. She noticeably stiffened briefly and then regained her composure, plastering a bright smile on her face.

"Hi, baby. I didn't realize you were waiting on me. I'm glad you're here. I've missed you." Brooke sat on the couch next to her and tried to kiss her cheek.

Birdy pulled away. "Brooke, we need to talk." She thought about all of the times she had walked on eggshells with Brooke, stroking her ego and smoothing her feathers. Always playing it safe, trying to keep Brooke on an even keel, but not now. She was done playing it safe. She was ready to risk it all for herself and, hopefully, for Sydney.

Twisting off her engagement ring gave her the most satisfying feeling she'd felt in months. She held it out to Brooke. "I can't marry you." When it became clear Brooke wouldn't even look at her, much less take the ring, she laid it softly on the coffee table.

"Leave," Brooke said icily. Birdy recognized the defense mechanism. Brooke's pride was now in the driver's seat.

"We need to talk about this."

"Why? You want me to beg you to stay?" Brooke finally looked at her and spat, "I don't beg."

"I'm past the point where begging would matter, but we need closure. We've never even discussed the fact that you cheated on me." The emotion was rising in Birdy and for once she didn't check it. So what if Brooke's temper was flaring? This time she didn't mind if she added her own anger to the fire.

"Is that why you're walking out? Because I had *sex* with someone else." Brooke acted as if that was the most ridiculous thing she had ever heard.

"No." Birdy clamped down on her nerves, determined to say what she needed to say. "I'm leaving because there was someone else in *my* life."

Brooke stiffened, obviously taken aback. "Who?"

"It doesn't matter. This is about us, not her."

"That fucking bitch. I knew she was a deceitful cunt. She couldn't have me so she came on to you, huh?" At Birdy's confused expression, Brooke supplied, "Sydney. She wanted to fuck me that night at the bar and when I said no, you were her consolation prize, huh?"

Birdy flashed back to that night, remembering Sydney's accusations. She knew better than to believe Brooke when her ego was wounded. This was about taking Birdy down into the darkness with her.

"Brooke, I'm sorry I've hurt you."

Barking out an aggressive laugh that lacked any humor, Brooke spat, "You think you can hurt me?"

Getting through to Brooke when her defenses were up was next to impossible, but she had to try. She fell back on the only real weapon she had—her honesty. "It hurts me that you had sex with someone else."

She laughed at Birdy again. The pain she was so desperately trying to hide behind a mask of viciousness was clearly visible. Her eyes gleamed with a metallic glint and she went in for the kill. "Do you think it was just the one time? How stupid can you be, Birdy? As if one person…as if *you* could ever be enough for me."

She had never known Brooke to be so cruel, so nasty. Though Brooke was just trying to protect herself with walls of anger and meanness, Birdy didn't doubt the truth in her words. She had been prepared to end her relationship tonight, but not for the ugliness of how it would unravel. Tears welled in her eyes. Brooke would see it as weakness, but she was no longer afraid to show her pain.

Birdy held the doorknob, ready to leave this vindictive woman she felt she hardly knew anymore. When she turned back, though, she caught the pain in Brooke's face, pain that all of her bravado couldn't hide and she recognized the woman she had once loved.

"You made me fly, Brooke, and I'm thankful for that. The problem was that I kept crashing. Over and over again, I kept tumbling from the sky. I thought if I tried harder, watched what I said and did, I could make our love work. I thought I was the reason for the fall but I was wrong. It was you. And I thought you were the reason I could fly, but I was wrong about that too. I've learned how to fly without you Brooke. I hope you can learn how to stay grounded without me. Goodbye, Brooke."

She closed the door firmly and left the dull, beige high-rise for good. As she rode the elevator down to the parking garage her relief was quickly overtaken by sorrow. She barely managed to keep her sobs in, nearly running to her car before bursting into tears. Brooke was gone.

But so was Sydney.

CHAPTER TWENTY-SIX

The wedding calendar had Birdy on a party bus visiting Willamette Valley wineries with Brooke's bridesmaids. Obviously, that had been canceled. Instead, she found herself at a downtown bar with her two best friends on New Year's Eve.

In the two weeks that had passed since ending her engagement, the peaceful resignation that had washed over her in the waning light of Brooke's apartment had returned. Breaking off the engagement had been the right decision. There also was a sadness that had taken up permanent residence in her chest, but not because she missed Brooke. It was the knowledge that she had let the best thing in her life get away—Sydney Ramos. Her days now consisted of work, which only served as a constant reminder of Sydney, and time spent on her boat, usually curled up in bed with Hoots. Her miserable depression left her feeling utterly hopeless, but she was bitterly resolved to start over alone.

Tonight was the first step.

She had strapped on her handy lifejacket of Avoidance and Denial and did her best to compartmentalize, a skill she was getting rather good at. Tonight she would focus on her friends, her escape from Brooke and the wedding, and celebrating the New Year, as fucking miserable as it might be.

And to dance, which is what she was doing now with exuberance.

She flung herself around the dance floor with Saul and Mare, screaming with the rest of the sweaty revelers to a remix of Kelly Clarkson's "Since You've Been Gone." Screeching the lyrics and not caring that she could never hit the high notes, she felt like she really was breathing for the first time. Maybe there was something to this compartmentalizing business.

As the song faded and some undanceable dubstep track took its place, Birdy slowed her pace and giggled at Saul, who was flailing his limbs like a possessed *Peanuts* character. "I'm really feeling this one, guys. Come on, dance with me!"

Birdy and Mare cracked identical grins and joined him. They laughed like maniacs as they thrashed, flapped and whirled into each other. She hadn't felt this good in a long time. Sydney was gone but maybe there was still hope. Somehow she would find happiness. Somehow she would heal. And tonight she let her new found optimism wash over her. She could be miserable again tomorrow.

Saul made Vs with his fingers and floated them across his eyes like a disco phenomenon. With a sincerity that belied his ridiculous gestures, he said, "I've missed you, Birdy. I've missed seeing you happy."

Her throat tightened from the sentiment. "I missed it too. Thank you for being patient with me."

"I knew you'd come to your senses about Brooke eventually," and then he held his nose and pretended to be diving down into the ocean. Mare joined in and Birdy couldn't help her glee. She started doing the sprinkler, spraying her diving friends with imaginary water.

"Speaking of coming to your senses," Saul continued, "what are you going to do about Sydney?"

Before Birdy could answer, Mare interrupted mid-dive. "I invited her tonight."

Saul and Birdy both straightened up, their silliness forgotten. Mare switched into a goofy grocery shopping dance, rhythmically plucking imaginary items off a shelf and putting them in her cart, completely oblivious to the fact that her dancing partners stood frozen on the dance floor. "You did what?" Saul asked incredulously.

"I invited her to come out with us." Finally picking up on the tension she shrugged and asked, "What?"

"I thought she was still out of town," Birdy said.

"That's what I thought too but I guess she got back early or something. Oh, actually, there she is right over there."

Birdy paled and turned to the door, her surprise mirrored on Sydney's face.

* * *

Sydney entered the dark, crowded bar searching for Mare and Saul. She found them on the dance floor twirling like idiots but her laughter died on her lips when her gaze slid to Birdy. When she had made plans with Mare for New Year's Eve a week ago, she assumed Birdy would be out with Brooke's friends. Mare had mentioned something about a party bus that she and Saul hadn't been invited on.

Unable to move, she watched them with an intense pain in her heart. Birdy seemed happy, so much happier than she had seen her in a long while. There was unchecked joy in Birdy's movements, no doubt excitement for their wedding that was… *God, less than a week away.*

The music changed as Sydney struggled with indecision. That night when her drunken confessions had ruined everything… she *had* been pathetic, playing right into Brooke's game. Her actions had been unforgivable, and she still hated herself for going against her better judgment. She had ruined any chance to be with Birdy, however miniscule it might have been. Birdy probably wouldn't even accept her friendship. Seeing her happy and dancing tonight was a vicious reminder of all she had lost.

Though longing to be next to Birdy, to talk to her, nothing good could come of it. It was time to let go and move on. She had come back to Portland early because she was miserable at home. Even her family couldn't cheer her up. She rationalized needing to spend the week following up on the applications she had submitted. She loved it at PDX Ink and liked working for Mare, but couldn't stand the torture of being in the same space as Birdy, knowing she meant nothing to her.

Having had just made up her mind to turn and leave, she saw Mare wave to her. Then, all the air rushed out the door, the bar went dim and the cacophony was muted when Birdy slowly turned around and their eyes met.

Each step across the bar was ripping out a stitch she had roughly hewn into her heart but she was helpless to stop. She barely noticed Saul tugging Mare away as she neared Birdy. Twenty feet to go and her stomach lurched with longing. Fifteen feet and her eyes glistened, threatening to spill over. Ten feet and she could almost swear she saw a flash of need in Birdy's eyes. Five feet and she forgot how to breathe. They were chest to chest in the middle of the dance floor. The crowd swarmed around them, enclosing them in their shared space.

Sydney had no idea what to do. No words came to her. She was simply giving herself this moment to be with Birdy, to fall inside her and to get lost in her. When Birdy's chin tipped upward and her lips parted, Sydney fell over the cliff. The heartache or painful consequences didn't matter. Birdy's hands came up to cradle her face and unblinkingly, Birdy closed the gap between them, bringing their lips together in the sweetest kiss she had ever experienced. They stayed like that for several moments, barely moving, allowing themselves to be lost in the moment.

Reality flooded back in as the crowd all chanted, "Ten! Nine! Eight!"

Sydney pulled back and blinked, more confused than she could ever remember. They were doing it again—going all the way to the water's edge and then rushing back to shore, never to know the thrill of the waves catching their feet. She exhaled deeply and when she breathed in again, the air in her lungs was replaced with loss.

"Seven! Six!"

Defeated, she said, "You look so happy tonight."

"I am," Birdy said, smiling.

"Five! Four!"

"I...I wish I could have given you that."

"Three! Two!"

Birdy's smile faded away and Sydney resigned herself to her heartbreak. She nodded once and turned away.

"One! Happy New Year!"

* * *

Sydney was gone.

Birdy stood on the dance floor with streamers and confetti drifting around her. She blinked, unsure of what had just happened. The moment had been so fast and fleeting but the feelings intensely acute. She touched her lips. The taste of Sydney was the only thing telling her it had been real. The music started up again and the crowd passed around bottles of cheap champagne as they celebrated.

Mare and Saul grabbed her, hugging her and wishing her a Happy New Year.

"Where did Sydney go?" Saul asked.

"Birdy," Mare said, "I am so sorry I invited Sydney tonight. Saul told me everything. I had no idea you liked her."

Birdy stared at the door. "I don't just like her. I'm in love with her. I just hadn't let myself admit it before."

With that realization, she sprang into action, rushing out the door and tightening her jacket against the cold. The sidewalk was packed with the huddled throngs of people streaming out of the bars, but Sydney was nowhere to be found. Walking several blocks in one direction in search of the face that filled her dreams, she circled around a parallel street to head in the other direction.

Everything about tonight had been so unexpected. She hadn't expected to have fun, to find a thread of happiness in her tattered life, and she sure as hell hadn't expected to see Sydney. Or to kiss her.

Considering the way they had left things, she had assumed she would be greeted with a wall of hostility. Instead tonight she saw only openness, buoying her hope, emboldening her. As soon as their eyes met, her heart leapt in her chest and finally she was able to feel for Sydney without restraint. And, God, did she feel.

So why then had Sydney walked away?

Birdy desperately needed to find her and explain what had happened since she'd left Portland, and how much had changed. How she had changed for Sydney and how she wished she could take back the hurtful words.

She pulled out her cell phone and scrolled anxiously for Sydney's number. After several rings the voice mail picked up and Birdy ended the call, frantically considering her options. Her first thought was to hail a cab, to chase Sydney down or wait her out on her front steps if necessary. But looking up, she noticed the huge stone and brick building across from her—the library. Golden light hugged the shelves of books and then spilled out from the glass doors and windows.

After crossing the street, she walked alongside the stately building, letting the peacefulness of it wash over her. She was nervous but filled with hope as she rounded the corner and approached the grand entrance. Bathed in soft light, Sydney was hunched halfway up the steps, her face buried in her arms. Birdy slowly climbed the steps until she was standing at her feet.

Sydney looked up, her face tear-streaked.

"Can I sit?" Getting only a shrug in response, Birdy sat next to her, wanting so badly to wrap her in her arms and make the pain go away. The only thing that stopped her was the uncertainty over whether or not Sydney would allow it. Taking a moment to gather her thoughts, she wasn't completely sure how to put her feelings into words.

Sydney beat her to it, apparently desperate to vent. "I don't know what you want from me, Birdy. I tried to be your friend but I couldn't. I just wanted so much more." She sniffled. "I want you so badly. To touch you and kiss you. To hold you. It's killing me." Her eyes begged for answers. "What do you want from me?"

Birdy looked at her and then up at the stars, thinking about the last time they had been here. The feel of the rain on her face, of Sydney's lips against her own.

"Everything," she answered simply, still gazing at the constellations above. She heard Sydney's breath hitch and she smiled. "I want everything from you, Syd. I want tonight and tomorrow morning. Next week and next year." She took Sydney's hand, wrapping it in both of hers.

Sydney showed no resistance to her touch. That didn't mean she wanted it though. Undeterred, Birdy held tight. Feeling how cold Sydney's hand was, she brought it to her lips and kissed the knuckles, then blew into her hands to warm the skin. The intimacy felt only natural here where they had shared their first kiss. Birdy could almost picture the scene—the two of them, linked closely together at the foot of the stone steps, the rain doing nothing to quell their desire. And she thought of Sydney's declaration. Her unwavering dedication to Birdy and her willingness to fight for her. It was time she fight for Sydney.

"I want you to love me again, Syd, because I'll die if you don't. I know I don't deserve it," she rushed on. "I know I've been weak and stupid and a total shit. I'm so sorry for hurting you." Tears welled in her eyes and she felt the weight of her love for this woman and of the need to be a part of her. "Please love me again," she repeated softly. Their eyes held for a long moment and the stricken expression on Sydney's face nearly killed her.

Finally, quietly, Sydney replied, "I never stopped."

"Oh, thank God," she murmured as the sincerity of Sydney's words sank in. Sudden tears fell as relief washed over her. She held Sydney's face as she pulled her close, kissing her deeply.

Eventually she pulled their lips apart and rested her forehead against Sydney's. Sydney's cold nose against her cheek almost made her laugh, she was so overcome with joy. Still holding her face close she said, "I love you so much, Sydney Ramos. I am so in love with you."

She heard Sydney's soft gasp and could feel her smile. This time it was Sydney who drew her in for a kiss, even more passionate than the one before.

Then with a moan, Sydney retreated, her smile replaced by a look of doubt. "I don't understand. Brooke…you're getting married in five days." With the dismal pronouncement, pain marred her beautiful face.

Birdy kissed her forehead trying to ease her worries. "No, I'm not," she mumbled into her hair, "It's you, Syd. It's only you. I'm not marrying anyone else."

A spark of relief flashed in Sydney's eyes, but her brow was still furrowed in doubt. "What happened? I thought…"

She silenced her by placing her thumb over her lips. "Let's just say I finally realized it's high time I started fighting for you. I've been a coward and I'm so sorry I was weak and hurt you so badly." She was rewarded with a smile and a kiss against her thumb. So much forgiveness in that small act. "Now, how about I take you home and tell you all about it?"

* * *

By the time dawn broke Sydney and Birdy were tangled together under a wool camp blanket on the small love seat built into the cabin of Birdy's boat. Sydney looked ridiculously adorable in Birdy's sweatpants and hoodie. Something about seeing the woman she loved in her college sweatshirt sent a delicious shiver of happiness through her. A shiver that was only being intensified now by the feel of Sydney's hand pushing her own sweatshirt up and drawing her nails lightly across her stomach. She was lying between Sydney's legs, her back against her chest. A warm, comfortable silence fell for the first time in hours. They had talked continuously since arriving at the boat. Everything from Brooke's drunken admission to their breakup had been unpacked. Birdy's third cup of coffee sat on the floor cold, but the attention Sydney's hand was giving her was making her feel anything but.

Sydney continued stroking Birdy's stomach. Her circles went lower until she dipped just under the waistband. She lightly dragged her fingernails the length of Birdy's torso and stopped under her breast. Birdy moaned loudly and pushed herself back into Sydney, urging her hand to continue its path.

Rocking back again, Birdy tipped her head against Sydney's shoulder as she whimpered with pleasure.

Kissing her hard and wrapping both arms around her, Sydney cupped Birdy's breasts, running her thumbs over the fabric of her bra.

Birdy rocked against her, desperately trying to apply pressure between Sydney's legs. They both moaned into a long kiss. "I need to touch you, Syd."

Birdy stood, pulling Sydney up with her. A sharp stab of lust shot through her at the feeling of Sydney's hands against her stomach, lifting her shirt over her head. Her mind reeled as Sydney pulled her tightly against her and she flashed back to the day in the river, only her lacy bra separating them, and how she had wished Sydney would rip it away, greedily taking her into her mouth. She had been able to imagine the sex, need and passion, the lace-ripping lust, but she hadn't imagined the tenderness with which Sydney now touched her. The steadiness of her hands along her back, the softness of her lips and tongue along her collarbone. This tenderness left her even more aching and inflamed than she could have imagined.

Sydney's tongue traced the straining muscle in her neck and continued along her jawline until she kissed the tip of her chin. "Do you love me?" Her breath warmed Birdy's ear.

"Yes," she said, finding Sydney's mouth with her own. "I love you so much."

The kiss blazed a path through her body, until every inch of her skin and soul felt touched by Sydney.

Birdy pulled forcefully on the hem of Sydney's shirt, needing to feel her skin. She regretted that she was forced to break the kiss as the sweatshirt passed over Sydney's face, but she immediately reclaimed her lips, this time finding no fabric to impede her searching hands as she roamed over Sydney's stomach and back. Impatiently, she made quick work of Sydney's bra clasp and felt her own give way just after. They parted briefly, studying each other and Birdy wished she could forever burn this image of Sydney in her mind. How many times had she imagined this? How many times had she imagined the feel of Sydney's skin under her palms? Imagined the taste of her?

Dipping her head, Sydney resumed her earlier path along Birdy's collarbone, but this time continued even lower. She took Birdy's nipple into her mouth and they both moaned loudly at the sensation of flesh against flesh, one wetting the other as Sydney's tongue slid against her hardened skin.

Taking control, Sydney wrapped her arms around Birdy's waist, pulling her breast more firmly to her, and slid her hands under the waistband of the sweatpants. They fell easily, leaving her in only her underwear. Her equilibrium was dangerously impaired when Sydney pushed her own sweatpants to the floor as well. Sydney grasped Birdy's hips firmly, guiding her down the three steps to the stateroom and then turning her around until her calves were against the bed frame. Then, Sydney gently nudged her and Birdy fell back, desire burning in her stomach and between her legs.

Birdy let her knees fall apart, showing Sydney the wetness that soaked her silk underwear. There was no hiding how badly she wanted her. Thankfully, Sydney came to her immediately, filling the space that Birdy had made for her.

She was pretty sure she couldn't survive this. As Sydney ground her hips into her center, Birdy was sure she would implode. Or melt. At this point she wasn't sure if she was fire or water. The burning lust could scorch her, or the slippery desire might wash her away. Either way, it felt like there was no way she could come out of this alive. She had never needed someone inside of her as badly as she did now.

Digging her heel into the bed, she gained the leverage to roll herself on top, straddling Sydney. For the first time, she tasted her breast, tugging her nipple into her mouth, feeling it become impossibly hard against her tongue. She kissed her way to the other nipple, inhaling the scent of Sydney's skin. Her perfume had a spiciness she couldn't identify but she adored it. She allowed her hands to roam the length of Sydney's body, pausing often to slip a finger under the waistband of her bikini briefs. Just enough to earn a desperate moan from Sydney. With each touch, she was rewarded too because Sydney's hips bucked against her forcefully until finally she couldn't take it anymore.

She released Sydney's breast and threw her head back, grinding the fabric of her underwear as hard as she could against Sydney.

"Fuck, Birdy. You're so beautiful." Sydney reached up, holding one of Birdy's bouncing breasts in her hand.

Birdy gave one last hard thrust. She needed more. Much more.

Standing, she bent over Sydney's supine body and kissed her stomach. With both hands she grasped Sydney's hips hard before hooking her fingers onto the elastic there. Slowly she pulled the fabric down and Sydney squirmed in desperation to be touched. It excited her to see how openly Sydney was willing to show her desire, so she teased her some more before finally slipping the sweatpants over her legs and tossing them away.

Every part of the woman she loved was finally exposed to her. She took in the gorgeous sight and breathed deeply, the certainty of her love calming her.

Sydney sat up on her elbows. "I want to see you too."

Standing between Sydney's knees, she thrust her hips forward to invite her touch. Sydney first ran her fingers under the last layer that separated them until they brushed along Birdy's mound, and then back along the hip and around until she firmly grabbed Birdy's ass in both her hands. Then she followed the path her hand had just taken, this time with her mouth, kissing the silk, letting her tongue slip under and run along her hip.

The sensuousness unhinged Birdy and she trembled, feeling more supported by Sydney's firm grasp than her own legs.

Now using her fingers to trace her hips again, Sydney then gently pulled the panties down until they were a puddle on the floor, which is exactly what Birdy was about to be as Sydney's tongue traveled along her underwear line, this time without the fabric getting in the way. Birdy held on to Sydney's head for support when she found her center, her tongue tasting her for the first time.

Sydney seemed to sense that Birdy could no longer stand and guided her back to the bed before once again finding the same spot with her tongue.

Birdy moaned loudly, unable to hear herself over the tidal wave of passion that roared in her ears. The flat of Sydney's tongue was against her now, tasting her fully and desperately. The slowness, the gentleness of before was abandoned and her hips rose violently when Sydney reached up and pinched her nipple.

With the other hand, Sydney entered her, sending Birdy's lust skyrocketing. They moved against each other wildly, the intense rhythm too much for Birdy to bear. She cried out, her hands grasping Sydney's hair, the bedsheets, her own breasts until she crested, her back arching off the bed. Her hips surged forward as she came forcefully while calling out Sydney's name between moans of ecstasy. The ache she had felt for Sydney finally subsided, being replaced by a pulsating warmth.

Gasping for breath and needing an anchor, she blindly reached down, groping for Sydney, needing to be held. Her hips still churned rhythmically, remembering Sydney's stroke, and her body jittered with adrenaline.

Sydney lay on top of her, holding her molecules together.

"I love you, Syd," Birdy was finally able to get out, no thanks to a pleasant numbness that had settled in her body.

"I love you too, Bird." Sydney stroked her hair and kissed her forehead gently. She rolled off and gathered Birdy in her arms. "Do you want to go to sleep?"

"No way," Birdy said, forcing control over her heavy limbs and rolling Sydney onto her back again. Straddling her, she rubbed her hands along Sydney's ribcage and then higher. "The only thing I want is you."

* * *

After a long while, with the morning light filtering into every corner of the room, Birdy was deeply satisfied. She could smell Sydney on her hands and taste her on her lips. With Sydney pressed against her back, she felt as warm and heavy as the blanket draped over their bodies.

She groaned with tired pleasure as Sydney lightly bit her shoulder before tightening her hold and kissing the small mark her teeth had made.

Birdy had been battling exhaustion from their long, emotional night but now she gave into it, feeling safe and loved in Sydney's arms as sleep fell thickly over her.

Just before drifting away, Birdy felt Sydney's arms tighten around her. "Goodnight, my little bird."

She smiled contentedly and fell asleep in her lover's arms, dreaming of a birdhouse that Sydney had made. Her home.

Bella Books, Inc.

Women. Books. Even Better Together.

P.O. Box 10543
Tallahassee, FL 32302

Phone: 800-729-4992
www.bellabooks.com